WAKING UP
WITH A
RAKE

CONNIE
MASON
AND MIA MARLOWE

sourcebooks
casablanca

Published by Sourcebooks Casablanca, an imprint of Sourcebooks, Inc.
P.O. Box 4410, Naperville, Illinois 60567-4410
(630) 961-3900
Fax: (630) 961-2168
www.sourcebooks.com

Printed and bound in Canada.
WC 10 9 8 7 6 5 4 3 2 1

To you, dear reader. Without you and your imagination to give life to our story, it's all just ink on a page.

Chapter 1

January 1818
London

FOR THE FIRST TIME IN HIS LIFE, LORD RHYS Warrington wondered if he was too foxed to properly bed a woman.

"Nothing ventured," he murmured as he latched the door behind him and stared at the courtesan lounging on the bed. Light from a dozen candles kissed the curve of her bare shoulder. The boudoir was awash in scent, expensive jasmine and attar of roses, with a sensual undertone of muskiness.

She smiled, letting the satiny sheet drop enough to reveal the swell of her breasts. The lady knew how to tease. Miranda Doublefield had been Lord Tottenham's mistress for the better part of last Season and had lasted through the turn of the New Year. She might have been petite, but there was nothing the least small about her allure. Her eyelids half closed, she gave him a sultry look.

Despite having consumed enough spirits to drop a horse, Rhys roused to her silent invitation. He was relieved by his body's dependability. A woman like Miranda would trumpet a man's bedroom failures if she thought the tale would amuse and titillate others. Rhys wasn't her protector and wasn't likely ever to be. She'd have no need to guard his dignity.

Rhys wasn't interested in acquiring a mistress. Or in any encounter that lasted beyond the moment, for that matter.

With good reason.

Even among the demimonde crowd, he was alone.

Besides, there was much to commend a bedding that was purely carnal with no bothersome emotions to cloud matters. He'd made a concerted effort to feel nothing since he returned from the Continent, and the result was a hollowness in his chest. He considered it a fair trade for continuing to breathe.

His heart might be dead, but that didn't stop another part of his anatomy from demonstrating with regularity that it was fully alive. He ached to wallow in Miranda and feel the only dregs of emotion he'd allow himself.

"I fear you may think yourself ill-used," Rhys said, his words slurring only slightly as he weaved toward her. There'd been entirely too much rum in his evening's activities, but at least he was still upright. "Just because your protector was foolish enough to wager a night with you, do not feel yourself bound to honor his gambling debt."

"Ill-used?" She giggled musically. "Nonsense. My fingers were crossed that Totty wouldn't take that final trick. I look forward to being used by you, my lord. Just don't be surprised if I use you right back."

Miranda raised herself to her knees and let the sheet

fall completely. As she settled between the plump pillows, she teased him with a glimpse at the shadowy heaven between her legs.

The house party at the St. James love nest where Lord Tottenham kept Miranda had degenerated into a bacchanalia within hours of its beginning. Then it stretched into a sennight of drinking, gambling, and indecent games. Rhys's bedding of Tottenham's mistress under his own roof was probably the least scandalous coupling that would transpire this night.

Rhys wondered absently if Tottenham had bored peepholes into the room to keep an eye on Miranda. If the earl was watching now, Rhys couldn't be bothered to care. Serve the fool right to be cuckolded before his very eyes.

Rhys plopped down on the side of the bed, hoping the room would stop spinning, and tried to tug off his Hessians. He really ought to have passed on that last round of Jamaican rum. He'd probably been drunk enough already not to have to worry about troubling dreams later.

Tottenham's mistress wrapped her arms around him, pressing herself against his back. She lavished kisses on his neck and then latched onto his earlobe, sucking hard.

Sinking into Miranda Doublefield's lush softness would be oblivion that trumped an alcoholic haze all to pieces. In the heat and friction of mindless rutting, Rhys could forget.

Or at least pretend he had forgotten, if only for a little while.

He turned and pinned Miranda to the mattress.

"Boots be damned," he declared. If Tottenham

didn't mind Rhys despoiling his mistress, he wasn't likely to fuss over ruined sheets. Rhys would take his time with the lady later, but since she seemed more than ready, the first time would be hard and fast.

He lost himself in her mouth, in the abandon of suckling tongues and shared breath. Her hands rippled over his body, teasing and stroking. She moaned into his mouth.

Real passion or feigned? It was hard to tell with an accomplished courtesan like Miranda. Perhaps it didn't matter, Rhys decided.

Perhaps nothing did.

Laughter and shouting from the rest of the party floated up to his ear, a faint summons from another world. He shoved it aside to focus on Miranda's silky skin, the soft fuzz of tiny blond hairs on her forearms, the tight, responsive nub on each pert breast.

Steps pounded down the hallway outside the door, but Rhys figured they had nothing to do with him. His only problem was how to unfasten the stubborn flap of his trousers. The confounded button seemed too large to fit through the hole, despite the fact that he was almost certain it had slipped through there with ease when he put the blasted trousers on.

Where was his valet when he needed him?

"Here, let me." Miranda bent to take the button between her white teeth. He ached at the nearness of her lips, but the thread wouldn't give.

"Damned French tailor," Rhys muttered. "Too much thread." *Damn the French altogether.*

A familiar red haze descended on his vision, and for an instant, he was back on the plain near Maubeuge again.

Too much blood. Too many arms and legs. Too many cannonballs. Where's that relief column? I sent an urgent summons over an hour ago. His horse was dying, screaming its agony as only a dumb creature can. Or a man who knows his immortal soul is about to flee his all-too-mortal body. *Have to put him down. Only one shot left…*

"Damn the French," Rhys growled aloud this time, closing the invisible portal in his mind that led back to that cursed battlefield.

Then Miranda's real door shattered behind him and the pounding footsteps grew louder, tramping inside his head. The courtesan shrieked and pulled up the sheets to cover herself as the footsteps surrounded the bed.

Rhys turned, but too slowly. Something solid and unyielding caught him on the temple. A black curtain descended on his mind, and he went dark as a Drury Lane stage after the last ovation.

Chapter 2

SMELLS PENETRATED THE BLACKNESS FIRST. MELLOW pipe tobacco tickled his nose, making him inhale sharply. Too late, he realized the pleasing scent was mixed with the pungent odor of large dog. A hissing and popping blaze in a nearby fireplace blended in an odd note of sweetness.

Apple wood fire, Rhys thought disjointedly.

Male voices pricked his ear. He couldn't make out any of the words. A china teacup clinked on a saucer. Leather creaked as someone settled into a chair close by. Something wet touched his hand.

Rhys forced open his eyes to find a boarhound nudging its broad muzzle under his palm. He patted the huge head and was rewarded with a slurping lick on his thumb.

"Good lad, then," he muttered, hoping the dog wasn't tasting him to see if a further sampling was warranted. He gave the dog a scratch behind its ear. Since the beast seemed disposed to be friendly, it was best to keep it that way.

"Ah, Lord Rhys, how good of you to join us."

Careful not to move his head lest it tumble off his shoulders, Rhys slid his gaze toward the source of the smarmy voice. "Did you give me a choice, Alcock?"

"Not really, no." Mr. Fortescue Alcock chuckled. It was not a pleasant sound, a rude cross between a snort and a belch. Alcock was a powerful Member of Parliament and the political enemy of King George III's current Prime Minister, Lord Liverpool. His adversaries in Parliament could have told Rhys that Alcock's laughter never boded the hearer any good. Alcock signaled for his footman to shoo the boarhound away. Then the servant pressed a cup of something hot and dark into Rhys's hands.

He sipped tentatively. The tea was laced with several lumps of sugar. While it didn't completely expunge the alcoholic fog in his head, it sweetened his palate considerably.

"If it's any consolation to you, Warrington, we were given the same rough invitation."

Rhys hadn't heard that voice in three years, but he recognized the cultured tone of cynical boredom in an instant. He turned his head slowly toward the voice that belonged to his oldest friend in the world, Nathaniel Colton. Lord Nate was seated on a divan, his weight balanced forward so he could rise in a blink, ready for action. In a ballroom or on a battlefield, Nathaniel had few equals for grace in motion. The only sign that he'd been on the losing end of a scuffle was the ripped seam at the shoulder of his elegantly tailored jacket.

Rhys's second oldest friend, Sir Jonah Sharp, occupied the other wing chair flanking the fireplace. A purpling bruise on his left eye declared that Jonah had fared somewhat worse than Nathaniel had with the thugs who delivered his invitation to join Alcock's party.

But then Jonah had always been one to try to talk his way out of trouble first. Once he drew his blade, his considerable talent as a swordsman meant an uneven fight, and Jonah was a stickler for good form above all else. Alcock's men evidently hadn't been of a mind to parley and weren't fair-minded enough to give Sir Jonah time to arm himself. Jonah's eye was nearly swollen shut.

Rhys fingered the goose egg at his own temple. He hadn't acquitted himself with much distinction this night either.

He'd first met Colton and Sharp at school, long before any of their voices had dropped or they'd sprouted the first hairs on their balls. As second sons, they shared the common fate of being wellborn with no expectation of future elevation. Once they graduated from university, their respective fathers bought commissions for them and they gallivanted off to war together with the same esprit de corps with which they'd plotted schoolboyish mayhem. The last place Rhys had seen either of them was on the smoky battlefield at Maubeuge, France.

Now Nathaniel and Jonah eyed him with distrust.

Rhys returned the favor.

"I must apologize for the zeal of my agents," their host said, slicking back his thinning hair with a bony hand. "My men were ordered to invite you gentlemen here, not to abduct you. However, once you've heard what I offer, I trust you'll be disposed to forgive their…exuberance."

Rhys met his friends' unblinking gazes for a moment.

There'd been a time when they could finish each other's sentences and guess each other's thoughts. Now, Nathaniel and Jonah were blank slates or, worse, covered with some sort of scribbling in a language in which he was not fluent. Their suspicious glares were undecipherable, but potent with dark meaning.

"Very well, I'll ask," Rhys said to Alcock. "To what do we owe this dubious honor?"

"Maubeuge."

Rhys's gut clenched.

"Each of you were there at that horrendous defeat. Each of you survived when most of the men under your respective commands died," Alcock said, his tone as dry and dispassionate as if he were debating a new system of drains for a poor London neighborhood whose streets still doubled as sewers. "Only the fact that your fathers are all well-respected peers kept you from courts-martial and total ruin. Even so, it should come as no surprise that the whiff of scandal is still attached to your names."

"If this is going to be a recitation of what we already know, you can save your breath," Rhys said, rising to his feet. "I have someplace to be."

"But no place to go. At every turn, your life is hemmed about by your questionable past. It's the same for each of you," Alcock said. "I could catalogue the wasteland of your existence since that day in May, the way you hover just this side of 'beyond the pale,' but since you insist upon brevity, I will jump to the meat of our conversation. You see, I do know something you don't know, Lord Rhys. The outcome of that battle might as well have been etched in stone ahead of time.

Gentlemen, your regiments were betrayed before a single cannon shot was fired."

"Betrayed by whom? If you know the traitor, name the dog," Nathaniel demanded, his low tone laced with menace.

"Oh, I know who it was. And I can prove it, never fear," Alcock said, "but I'll keep that little secret for the time being. You see, I had to ask myself just what this sort of information might be worth to the three of you."

Jonah bared his teeth in an expression the unwary might interpret as a smile. Rhys recognized it as more akin to a wolf displaying its fangs.

"Well, you've just proved my long-held suspicion that politicians and prostitutes are alike," Jonah said. "But the main difference between them is that politicians charge more for their services and deliver less."

"Careful, Sir Jonah," Alcock said with a ferocious scowl. "You don't know yet whether my information further implicates one of you three sitting in this room."

"Does it?" Rhys said, voicing the thought he was sure his former friends shared. Any one of them might be the turncoat so far as the others knew.

"The guilty party remains to be seen. However, if you are innocent, your honor might be restored. Consider for a moment what full exoneration would do for you." Alcock drew deeply on his pipe and then loosed a perfect smoke ring into the center of the room. "And for your families."

Rhys hadn't thought anything could restore his honor, so he'd spent the last three years living down to his reputation. And while he'd drunk deeply of every hedonistic pleasure known to man, he'd missed out on some of the more homey ones.

His dear sisters had married while he was in self-imposed exile. He hadn't been barred from the ceremonies, but he detected a collective sigh of relief when he sent his regrets. Now he had nearly half a dozen nieces and nephews whom he'd never seen.

Could never see, lest his proximity taint them in the eyes of Polite Society.

Rhys had avoided his father, the Marquis of Warrington, even when they were both in Town, because he couldn't bear the censure on the old man's granite-jawed face. Last winter at the marquisate's countryseat, his father had taken to his bed with a lingering fever. Odds at White's pegged him for the Grim Reaper before Christmas.

No one sent word asking Rhys to come home.

But the marquis was tougher than the wags at White's had credited him. By spring, his father was on the mend and well enough to terrorize the House of Lords once again.

However, the cut to Rhys's spirit went deep. Even languishing on what was rumored to be his deathbed, Lord Warrington hadn't asked for his second son.

Rhys was almost certain his mother would have written. The only explanation was that she had been forbidden to do so. The rebuke couldn't be stronger. Nothing would restore him in his father's estimation.

Unless Mr. Alcock really could clear him of the scandal.

"Suppose we are interested in your information," Rhys said, settling back into the wing chair. "What do you expect from us in return?"

Mr. Alcock stopped puffing on his pipe and smiled. Drawing his skin tight across his face, it was not a pleasant expression.

"In the years since your disastrous defeat at Maubeuge, the three of you have developed a talent of singular note. As it turns out, I have need of such men for missions of vital importance."

"What is it you need us to do?" A frown cut a deep cleft between Nathaniel's sandy brows.

Espionage or fighting, whatever it was, it would be better than the wastrel life Rhys had been living.

"In due time, my lord. First, you must appreciate the situation which drove me to my…unorthodox plan. You see, the people are weary of our mad king and his unlikeable son. We hoped for better things from Prinny's daughter and the child she carried." Mr. Alcock's mouth turned down in a grim line. "Surely even dedicated rakes such as yourselves noted that the princess passed away after the birth of her stillborn son in late autumn."

"It was hard to miss." Rhys drained the rest of his tea. Even the coffeehouses and clubs had closed down for two weeks last November after Princess Charlotte died. "The whole country donned crepe."

"All except Princess Charlotte's uncles, the royal dukes," Jonah said.

The unmarried sons of King George saw a chance to put themselves, or at least their progeny, on the throne if they could produce a legitimate heir. Unfortunately, His Majesty's sons were more inclined to mistresses than marriage. Only the Prince Regent had presented King George with a grandchild who didn't bear the stain of bastardy.

And now Princess Charlotte was dead.

"The 'Hymen Race Terrific' is engaged in earnest. The sons of 'Farmer George' are hot to wed, bed, and breed," Alcock said. "Three of the royal dukes have gone a-courting with the Crown as the ultimate prize, but I intend to see that their plans are thwarted."

"Are you suggesting that not everyone wants to see the House of Hanover continue on the throne?" Rhys guessed.

"Did I say so? Certainly not," Mr. Alcock said. The mere thought bordered on treason. "But for the sake of argument, suppose someone did want to see the Crown devolve to another ruling line. If one could confound these marriage-minded dukes, the task would be half accomplished."

Nathaniel laughed mirthlessly. "You'll need more luck than you deserve. What woman wouldn't jump at the chance to wed a royal duke and perhaps wear a tiara of her own if she manages to pop out a royal heir?"

"No doubt, the dazzle of a possible crown does tend to outweigh the general distastefulness of the sons of King George," Alcock said, his lip curling. "But since it would be impolitic to publicly point out their many deficiencies, I intend to marshal my forces in another direction."

"How so?" Rhys asked.

"Only the young, fertile, and *chaste* need apply for the position of royal duchess, you understand. I merely need to make sure the ladies in question are disqualified from consideration on account of impurity," Alcock explained. "I ask you, who better to make sure the dukes' intended brides don't remain virgins than three determined rakes?" He skewered them each with a pointed look.

"You mistake me, Alcock." Rhys rose and strode toward the door. The last wisp of rum-soaked fog lifted and his mind was suddenly clearer than it had been in weeks. "Thus far the depth of my depravity does not stoop to debauching virgins. Pray, do not include me in your machinations."

"Or me," Nathaniel said, falling into step behind him.

"Too bloody right." Jonah brought up the rear.

For a moment, Rhys's chest swelled with an unfamiliar sensation. *Satisfaction.* His old friends had backed him. Not that refusing to deflower a green girl was all that praiseworthy. In good conscience, what gentleman wouldn't? But at least Rhys and his friends had found common ground at the bottom of the pit into which they'd sunk. It felt good to have Nate and Jonah on his side again.

"So you care nothing for your honor?" Alcock said.

"Honor bought at such a price can hardly be worth the name," Rhys said, stopping with his hand on the parlor door.

In all his sexual adventures, Rhys had never seduced a virgin. A green girl was sacrosanct. Rhys had always been fond beyond the common of his younger sisters. If some rake had preyed on them, used them, and tossed them aside, nothing would have stayed him from demanding satisfaction and killing the bastard.

Now Fortescue Alcock wanted him and his friends to do the same despicable thing to someone else's sisters. Rhys balled his fingers into fists. The urge to throttle Alcock to within an inch of his miserable life was almost more temptation than he could resist.

"I wouldn't be so hasty to be noble were I you," Alcock warned. "You see, aside from information about the true traitor of Maubeuge, I can amass enough evidence to damn each of you as well."

"You lie." Rhys narrowed his eyes at Alcock.

"Perhaps," the man said with a deceptively affable smile. "It may well be that my informant is untrustworthy. But people are ever willing to believe the worst, whether it's true or not. Should I choose to launch an investigation—and rest assured, if you fail to comply with my wishes, I will do so—you will each be brought before Parliament to answer for your crimes. And this time, no amount of influence from your families will save you from the full weight of the law."

Rhys's throat constricted. If convicted, they'd be fortunate to escape with transportation. More likely, they'd be made examples of in a public execution. But worse than that, Rhys dreaded further shame to his family.

Alcock seemed to sense his dread.

"Sir Jonah, your brother's grasp has exceeded his reach in courting the daughter of an earl, and according to my information, the lady seems willing. But what do you think a public trial will do to his hope of wedding Lady Penelope?" Alcock asked.

Jonah's shoulders slumped a fraction of an inch. Rhys knew his friend was caught.

"And you, Lord Nathaniel," Alcock went on, hooking his thumbs under his lapels as if preparing to launch a filibuster. "I believe your younger sister is coming out next Season, isn't she? How would a convicted traitor in the family affect her chance of making a good match?"

A muscle in Nathaniel's cheek ticked, but he said nothing. Like Rhys, Nathaniel was devoted to his sisters.

"And you, Lord Rhys, of all people, should wish to avoid further disgrace. Your father may try to hide it, but word about town is that the marquis is not as hale and hearty as he tries to appear," Alcock droned on. "Imagine what it would do to Lord Warrington to see his son in the well of the House of Lords. In shackles."

The familiar red haze that was a precursor to visions from his past threatened to descend again, but Rhys shook it off. He had to keep his wits about him. Sometimes when the dark spells overtook him, he lost track of where he was. Wandering in the past, he sometimes feared he'd never find his way back. He couldn't afford flashes of Maubeuge intruding into his present reality. So he forced one foot in front of the other and returned to the chair by the fire.

One at a time, his friends followed suit.

"Very wise, gentlemen," Mr. Alcock said. "Why be my enemies when you can be my friends?"

Moving with speed that surprised even him, Rhys leaped up, grasped Alcock by the collar and lifted him off his shiny-booted feet. The man's eyes bulged as his hands clawed at Rhys's grip, but he couldn't wiggle free.

"You will never be our friend, Alcock," Rhys said, giving him a quick shake, like a terrier would a rat. "Answer one question and you won't see us again until we come to collect what you owe us."

"What's that?" he croaked.

Rhys glanced at his friends. When they both nodded grimly, he lowered Alcock until his toes brushed the ground.

"Who are we to seduce?"

Chapter 3

"FOR HEAVEN'S SAKE, POPPET, THE DUKE'S NEW EMISSARY is waiting," her mother said, hastily tucking a fichu into the neckline of Olivia Symon's drab bombazine day gown. When Princess Charlotte died, the Symon household had donned full mourning. Black was not Olivia's best color, and adding more of it so close to her face only served to wash her out completely. "Hurry up, child."

"I'm not a child." Olivia pulled out the fichu and let it drop to the floor. The gown was perfectly acceptable without it, especially since she had no bosom of which to speak. Her breasts were the size of carnation blossoms, and rather small carnations at that. It was bad enough she'd been yanked from the hothouse she loved before she'd had time to finish repotting her orchids. Having her mother try to dress her as if she were a china doll was an indignity that danced on her last nerve. "I'm not your poppet either. And I will not hurry just because the Duke of Clarence has sent another of his hounds."

"Hush." Her mother put two fingers to Olivia's lips. "Hounds, indeed. Must you be so vulgar?"

"Well, what would you call it?" A lock of hair had escaped her lacy snood. Olivia tucked it behind her ear to forestall her mother reaching for it. "The duke is using the poor fellow exactly like a hunting dog to flush the quarry from the brush."

Her mother made a tsking noise. "Your father never should have taught you to shoot."

"He shouldn't have taught me to do lots of things." *Like think for myself*, Olivia added silently as she headed down the corridor toward the house's grand main staircase.

"I trust you'll keep those unladylike accomplishments to yourself." Beatrice Symon almost had to trot to keep up with Olivia's strides.

Not that Olivia was in a hurry to meet with the duke's man. She simply knew she'd have no peace until the interview was over, so she might as well have done with it.

"Don't fret," she told her mother. "It doesn't matter a fig what I say to the man. I could be as dotty as a March hare, and it wouldn't change a thing. The Duke of Clarence isn't nearly as interested in me as he is in the forty thousand pounds Papa is settling on me."

"Don't be silly. He's a royal duke. What does he need with money?"

"Maybe to pay his debts?" Olivia read every copy of the *London Times* her father brought home, and according to all reports, the Duke of Clarence—all the royal family, in fact—had amassed mountains of debt. "Perhaps Clarence is merely tired of trying to wrangle funds from Parliament and considers me a tidy little personal bank."

"It's gauche to speak of such things."

Wonder if she'd rather I mention that I do, in fact, possess a virgin womb, which I know is the duke's other main interest. The Duke of Clarence had managed to sire ten children on his mistresses, all of whom were received in Society and were granted the surname Fitzclarence. He'd proven his potency. Olivia was the eldest of six daughters, and large families ran on both sides of her pedigree, facts not lost on the royal duke's advisors, she was sure. Her chances of being fertile were as high as her father's pockets were deep.

"Now promise me you won't mention money to the nice gentleman," her mother demanded as they descended the grand curving staircase together.

Olivia rolled her eyes. "How do you know he's nice?" Most gentlemen she'd met hadn't been at all nice once one scratched beneath the surface of their courtly manners. She didn't believe, as her mother apparently did, that "blood will out."

Olivia's family boasted no blue blood, but her father, Horatio Symon, had returned from India with wealth to rival the most decadent maharajah. Despite being rich enough to buy all the trappings of the Upper Ten Thousand—the expansive country estate, a well-situated Mayfair townhouse, and the latest fashions and buckets of jewels for Olivia, her mother, and sisters—the Symons still weren't considered "good ton" by the elite.

But in some circles, well-moneyed trumped well-born. More than one heiress had bought herself a title when a land-rich, cash-poor peer decided he'd over-look his bride's pedigree in favor of her father's purse.

A royal duke was the largest of all possible noble prizes for a wealthy common girl to bag in the "title hunt." Her mother would have been horrified to hear her daughter put it that way, but to Olivia's mind, her dowry was merely the bloody bait. His Highness, the Duke of Clarence, was sniffing about it, trying to decide whether to risk a bite.

If the royal dukes could admit they were on a hymen hunt, why should she not admit what having such an exalted title in the family would do for her siblings?

And of course as a royal duke's consort, I'd be far too lofty a person for Mother to nag, Olivia thought with a wry grin.

"Promise me," her mother repeated. "Let your father handle any discussion of money."

Olivia sighed. "Very well, Mother, I won't mention my most obvious charm."

"Nonsense, child." Beatrice Symon turned to give her a quick assessing gaze. "You have plenty of charms. You're perfectly…well, you're entirely…oh, hang it all, you're attractive enough for ordinary purposes."

Ordinary. Olivia bit her lower lip. Unlike her curvier younger sisters, she was all knees and elbows, too thin for fashion, but she never could seem to add any weight. Her mother complained it was because she spent too much time riding or puttering in the garden like a common servant. But aside from the freedom of being in the saddle, there was nothing Olivia loved more than burying her fingers in rich loamy soil and helping green things grow.

Olivia knew she was no beauty. It was part of how she'd managed to stay unmarried despite her status as a great heiress.

But would it hurt her mother to pretend once in a while that it was possible for a gentleman to become interested in her for her instead of her father's fortune? Olivia refused to believe she was destined merely to be some man's bottomless purse.

Somehow, some way, she'd know love, she decided. If not, she'd just as soon die alone.

Her mother stopped at the parlor threshold.

"You're not coming?" Olivia asked.

"No, his lordship asked to speak with you in private, and since he's here on behalf of the duke, I decided it would be perfectly appropriate," her mother said.

"No doubt if he wants to examine my teeth and check my limbs for soundness, that will be appropriate too," Olivia muttered.

Her mother puffed up like a guinea on the nest. "Honestly, Olivia, where you get such outlandish notions I'll never collect. Don't fret, dear. I'll be nearby should you need me."

"Listening at the keyhole, no doubt."

"Hush, chi—I mean, oh, never mind." Her mother gave her a little pat on the shoulder. "Remember your sisters are counting on you and, well—" Her mother's fingers fluttered in a helpless gesture. "Just do your best, dear."

Olivia stifled a groan. Trust her mother to remind her once again that her sisters' expectations would catapult skyward if she managed to capture the Duke of Clarence.

And plummet to perdition should she muff this chance of a lifetime.

She pushed through the double doors and swept into the meticulously appointed room. Despite the fact that the Symons were nouveau riche, and her mother had questionable ideas when it came to appropriate situations with strange men, Beatrice Symon did possess excellent taste in home furnishings. The country estate sparkled with elegant understatement rarely found, even among the bon ton.

The man on the settee rose to greet her, and Olivia dipped in the requisite curtsey.

"Good afternoon, my—" She raised her gaze to the man's face and her tongue cleaved to the roof of her mouth. The last emissary the Duke of Clarence sent had been a loathsome little toad of a fellow who snickered when he spoke, finishing his sentences with an upward lilt and a nervous giggle.

But this man was…magnificent.

It was more than merely flawless features. It was the balance of the individual parts that created such an arresting whole. His strong jaw matched his firm lips and fine straight nose. The high cheekbones of a man of action were tempered with the broad forehead of a poet.

And his snapping brown eyes. They were dark wells of intelligence and…did she detect a hint of amusement glinting in their depths?

Well, of course she did. The man was looking at her, wasn't he?

It was rare to see a human face with this kind of symmetry and pleasing proportions. Usually a nose would be outsized for the rest of the features or a person's eyes would be too wide set. Olivia ordinarily found this sort of perfection in flora, not fauna.

The only bit of him that seemed out of place was a streak of silver marring his seal-brown hair at one temple. Judging from the lack of lines around the man's eyes and mouth, he was young to have that shock of gray. But even what should have been an impediment to his arresting appearance instead lent him an air of mystery.

"It is my honor to meet you, Miss Symon. Lord Rhys Warrington, your servant," the man said with a correct bow from the neck. His ramrod straight back proclaimed him no one's servant, but he followed proper conventions to the last jot and tittle. "Allow me to present this letter of introduction."

His voice was resonant and deep, with a slightly ragged edge that sanded away at the sharp angles of Olivia's soul. The sound shivered over her like liquid seduction. She took the gilded envelope from him and broke the wax bearing the Duke of Clarence's ornate seal. She ran her gaze over the flowery script but found it difficult to focus on the words.

Every time she glanced up, the man was *looking* at her.

Granted, the other emissary had given her an unhurried perusal upon their first meeting as well, taking in her slight frame. His lips had pursed in a disdainful expression that declared her unremarkable in the extreme.

But this man's gaze was focused on her face, not her

figure. A faint smile played about his lips that invited her to smile back at him.

Against her better judgment, the corners of her mouth turned up. He bared a set of dazzling teeth in return.

Olivia's belly fluttered as if she'd swallowed a bee. She'd never been so undone by the mere sight and sound of a man before.

This is ridiculous, she told herself crossly. She refolded the letter and tried to stuff it back into the envelope. No matter what she did, the foolscap wouldn't cooperate despite the fact that it had all fit neatly in there only a few moments before. She finally tossed the whole thing on the tea table in exasperation.

"Please have a seat, my lord, and I'll ring for refreshments." Olivia's hand shook a bit when she gestured toward the settee, so she rang the bell for tea louder than required. She perched opposite him on the blue damask seat of one of the Hepplewhite chairs, folding her hands in her lap to still them.

"That's not necessary," Lord Rhys said. "I'm not here to be entertained."

"It's no trouble. No doubt you'll need a spot of tea to revive you once you begin regaling me with the excellencies of His Royal Highness, the Duke of Clarence," she said, feeling more sure of herself once a maid brought in the tea things and she had something to do with her hands. Olivia was ready for the conversation, and thus the battle was to be enjoined. There was little chance she'd be allowed to say no to the duke's suit should an actual offer be forthcoming, but she didn't intend to make things easy for his representative. "Your predecessor waxed long and often over the duke's…virtues. I feel as if I already know his character well."

One of his dark brows arched, indicating he caught her hesitation and the unspoken disdain beneath her words. "Extolling His Highness's…virtues is not my purpose."

"Oh?" She raised the sterling creamer to offer him milk for his tea, but he shook his head. "But the letter of introduction…"

"While it's true that I'm here on behalf of the duke's suit, I'm not here to sing his praises. In truth, that would be a rather short song."

Olivia nearly dropped the creamer in surprise.

"And as you say," he went on, "someone else has already done that. No, I'm here to become acquainted with you in the duke's stead, Miss Symon."

"Oh." The other emissary hadn't asked a single question about her. It was assumed she should be overjoyed with His Royal Highness's attention and not miss being courted in the usual sense. "Isn't that something the duke should do for himself?"

"One would think so, wouldn't one?" Lord Rhys chuckled pleasantly. "However, as I understand it, a royal courtship is almost always accomplished by proxy. I come before you today to stand in his royal shoes, as it were. Thanks to the duke's previous representative, you know a good deal about him. But I'd wager he knows very little of you."

Except that I'm an attractive-enough-for-ordinary-purposes virgin who just happens to be worth forty thousand pounds per annum danced on her tongue. Remembering her mother crouched at the keyhole, Olivia bit back the words.

"It's wicked to wager," she said primly and wished she hadn't. *For heaven's sake, I sound like a Puritan, at war with every conceivable pleasure.*

His smile was more potent than a pilfered jigger of whisky. "Gambling is the least of my sins, I assure you."

She added a dollop of cream to her tea, set down the creamer, and stirred furiously. His frank admission shocked her to her toes. And sent a strange little thrill coursing through her belly. To be wicked and willing to admit it. Now, that was an accomplishment. She burned to ask about his greater failings, but her eavesdropping mother would want her to stick to the main topic of conversation.

"What sort of things would the duke like to know about me?"

"To be honest, I'm not sure," Lord Rhys said. "It's hard to say what such lofty persons might find of interest. You see, like you, I am technically a commoner. The 'Lord' affixed to my name is merely a courtesy. My older brother will inherit my father's marquisate, and I'm left to make my way in the world however I may."

His openness was surprisingly refreshing. "Such as serving as the duke's proxy."

"Exactly."

"Have you always been part of the Royal Court?" She knew the Prince Regent liked to surround himself with pretty women, but she doubted he'd suffer such a remarkable male specimen in his entourage.

"Lord, no. That's for much more exalted folk than I."

Just when Olivia thought he couldn't be more appealing, a devastating dimple appeared on his left cheek. But even more than his charming appearance, she liked his self-deprecating directness. A commoner, he'd said.

Just like her.

"Let me hazard a guess then," she said, surprised to find she'd relaxed enough to enjoy this interview. "As a second son, your options are somewhat limited. You don't seem the sort to go for the church."

"One lump, if you please," he said, though she'd quite forgotten about the tea. "Why do you say that?"

Olivia wished she'd stuffed her handkerchief into her mouth before she allowed such a foolish thing to spill out. She couldn't very well admit he'd lead his female parishioners into sinful thoughts during each Sunday sermon simply by virtue of his handsome face and deep, whisky-tinged voice.

"You don't seem the scholarly sort," she said, grasping at any reason but the real one as she dropped a brown lump into his teacup using her mother's elegantly filigreed tongs.

"Surprisingly enough, I did graduate top of my class, but you're right about me and the Church," he admitted. "I have no calling to become a country parson. When all else fails, too many gentlemen in my situation turn to that living without the requisite passion for it, and I would not be one of them."

Just hearing him say the word "passion" brought a rush of heat to her cheeks. She added two more lumps of sugar before she remembered he'd only asked for one.

"A man of action, then," she guessed, handing the cup and saucer to him and hoping he wouldn't notice the additional sweetness. She wasn't usually so addlepated.

What on earth was wrong with her? "You've borne arms for the sake of our king, I'll wager."

A shadow seemed to pass behind his eyes, but it was gone so quickly Olivia decided she'd imagined it. He leaned forward, elbows balanced on his knees. "I thought you said it was wicked to gamble."

Olivia knotted her fingers together. "A figure of speech. I didn't mean anything by it. There is no true wager unless stakes are agreed upon."

"An important distinction." He nodded. "I'll bear that in mind. But you're right. I was a captain in His Majesty's forces but have since resigned my commission."

"Now that we have settled matters with the French, I suppose there was little to keep you thus engaged," she said, liking him even better for his military service. "And now you meet prospective brides for royal dukes for a living."

"For the moment, though it should please you to know that I am not being compensated for my service. I…volunteered," he said. "I don't wish to shock you, Miss Symon, but I believe honesty is the best foundation for a friendship. Given your abhorrence for gambling, you may despise me for this, but I must admit that I usually do support myself by being lucky at cards."

Her mother would have had to whip out her smelling salts at such an admission, but Olivia was more struck by his suggestion that they might become friends.

Was it possible that a man and woman could form such an unusual bond? She'd never heard of the like. Men befriended men at their clubs. Women exchanged social visits in their homes. The sexes rarely interacted except for courtship, and then once the wedding took place, it was an extraordinary marriage that could also count itself friendly. Even her mother and father addressed each other as Mr. or Mrs. Symon instead of by their Christian names.

"I've heard plenty of cautionary tales about people who've squandered their living at cards, but never of anyone who kept body and soul together with it," she said, anxious to keep this unusual conversation going. "Surely gambling isn't your sole occupation?"

"Not at all. I also drink and carouse and engage in any number of questionable pursuits," he said with a crooked grin. Then he took a sip of his over-sweetened tea and the grin became a grimace. "I am, in fact, an incurable rake. A dedicated libertine. You may ask anyone."

"Since you've been so forthright, there's no need for me to ask, is there?" She ought to have been scandalized, but instead, she was intrigued by his confession. "It's one thing to be wicked. Another to be unabashedly so. I shall consider myself duly warned of you, sir."

"Good. You should be." Something flashed in the depths of his dark eyes that she couldn't decipher, then it dissolved when another winning smile made the corners of his eyes crinkle. "Now it's my turn to guess about you."

"Very well, though I warn you there's nothing in my life remotely as interesting as being an incurable rake and dedicated libertine."

As soon as the words were out, she clamped a hand over her mouth. They were unladylike in the extreme. She expected to hear a dull thump on the other side of the door at any moment. If her mother truly was listening at the keyhole, she'd undoubtedly faint dead away.

Lord Rhys merely laughed. "You've made my task too easy. I perceive that you, Miss Symon, are a woman of strong opinions and do not hesitate to express them."

"Guilty as charged." She buried her nose in her teacup.

"You also have a consuming interest in something that takes you outdoors, even on blustery January days."

"How could you know that?"

"A charming smattering of freckles on your cheeks," he said. "Plus, there's a smudge of dirt on your right sleeve near the elbow. Potting soil?"

"Yes." She set down her teacup and rubbed vigorously at the offending smudge. So he had looked at more of her than her face, though she hadn't caught him at it.

"An excellent gardener then," he said, leaning back and cocking his head at her quizzically. "But I sense your interest runs even deeper than most."

Did this man have a way to tap into her private thoughts? "Again, you are correct. I love green growing things, but I also study them. I'm fascinated by the way they flourish and by the multitudinous variety of them."

"What are your favorite types?"

"Orchids," she said quickly.

"Aren't they parasitic? You don't strike me as the type who'd champion an organism that survives by taking from others."

"While it's true some orchids thrive anchored to the bark of trees, most merely cling to their host without taking nourishment from it. Rather like a sparrow alighting on a twig, actually," she said. "There are a few species that are parasitic, but they grow below ground. And I've read that they smell like something rotten. Not at all the type I'd choose to cultivate."

His mouth twitched, and the smile she'd found so engaging no longer reached his eyes. "Very wise of you not to cultivate types who prey on others."

Olivia had heard that conversations at court were often laced with double meaning, but she couldn't imagine what cryptic message he might be trying to send with this one.

"Nevertheless, I find raising orchids most agreeable," she said, taking up her cup and saucer again. It was a very small shield, but she sheltered behind the fine Limoges. Until she figured this man out, it seemed safer.

"I'd imagine so, all that pollinating and germinating and whatnot. And I find it most agreeable that a young lady such as yourself isn't put off by such close acquaintance with reproduction." A hint of sin returned to his smile. "Is it true that orchids take their name from the Greek word for a certain part of male anatomy?"

Olivia choked on her surprise.

And her tea.

Lord Rhys was on his feet in a trice, thumping her back and lifting her arms over her head. She sputtered for a good half-minute, then finally caught her breath. Olivia pulled her hands away from him and bent to retrieve the cup and saucer that had landed in a damp puddle on her mother's Aubusson carpet.

"Thank you, my lord." Her cheeks flamed with embarrassment. "I'm quite recovered."

"I can see I've shocked you," he said as he returned to the settee. "Forgive me. I naturally assumed your familiarity with plants and their procreation would cause you to take a liberal view of what constitutes acceptable topics to be discussed between friends."

"That presupposes that we are friends."

"Do you think we're not?" he said, leaning back and hooking an ankle over his knee, clearly at ease. He spread his arms across the back of the settee, filling the space and the room so completely Olivia had difficulty drawing breath. And not just from choking on the tea. "I'd hate for that to be true. I can't tell you the last time I enjoyed a conversation with a young lady quite so much. Do you find me irksome?"

Despite his inappropriate comments, she couldn't find him so. She almost wished she did. In addition to the fluttering in her chest, the hair on the back of her neck prickled. If she'd been a wild creature, she didn't know whether she'd be drawn to him like a moth to flame or run like a hind that catches wind of hunting dogs.

"No, my lord," she said. "I doubt any lady of your acquaintance finds you irksome."

"I'm gratified to hear it. In that case, would you do me a favor?"

"If I can."

"Oh, you can. The question is whether or not you will."

She shifted on her seat, wishing she could rise, but then he'd have to stand as well. He dominated the room while merely sitting. How much more commanding would he be if she had to crane her neck to peer up at his handsome face? "You've made this favor sound rather wicked, my lord."

"Not at all. It's just that when you call me 'my lord' it seems so stuffy, especially since I don't truly deserve it," he said. "I was wondering if you'd consider calling me Rhys instead."

Olivia couldn't remain seated after that. She rose and wandered toward the window to put a bit more distance between them. "That's a rather unusual request."

The sharp clack of his boots on marble announced that he had followed her. She plopped down in the center of the window seat, trying to claim all the space.

"And here I thought you were a rather unusual girl." His knowing look dared her to flout convention.

Agreeing to such familiarity was the sort of thing that would turn her mother's complexion an unhealthy shade of puce.

Of course, that only made the notion harder to resist.

"We would have to make a pact. It could only be when we are alone, you understand," she said, considering the idea so seriously she wasn't immediately aware of when he sat down beside her. "And I suppose to be fair I would have to give you leave to call me Olivia as well. But there could be no slips in public."

"Perhaps we should wager on it in order to insure that we keep the pact," Lord Rhys said. He wasn't touching her at all. There was a good inch separating them, but his heat radiated toward her, sending a tingle up her thigh. "The one who uses a Christian name in public owes the other…what?"

"Not money," she said, forgetting for the moment that she held wagers of any kind to be morally wrong. Besides, she wasn't likely to call him Rhys unless she was absolutely certain no one was about. If she couldn't lose, surely it wasn't really gambling. "My family has buckets of it, and you support yourself by the turn of a card, so wagering money doesn't seem particularly fair."

"Very well, let us leave it that the offending party

would owe one as yet undetermined favor, which we would be honor-bound to fulfill, whatever it is." He cocked his head slightly. "Do we have an accord?"

"We do." She nodded, wondering what an undetermined favor from a confessed libertine and incurable rake might entail. If the roiling in her belly was any indication, it promised to be wildly diverting and probably more than a little sinful.

A secret part of her burned with curiosity.

"Well, this has been most enjoyable, *Olivia*," he said, caressing her name with his silky baritone. Then he consulted his pocket watch. "I fear I've monopolized far too much of your time this afternoon, and a friend shouldn't impose. I must be going now, but I wonder if I might return on the morrow to continue our discussion." He closed the pocket watch face with a snap and stowed it away. "Perhaps at that time you might show me your orchids."

Unlike the duke's previous representative, this man had made Olivia sorry to see him go, even if he had made her choke on her tea and was sitting too close for her comfort. "Of course, my lo—I mean, Rhys. But my plants aren't much to see at present, it being wintertime. My work now amounts to merely laying the groundwork for blossoms in the spring."

"I understand. I'm undertaking a project of a similar nature. One that requires careful planning and strategy so the going may seem slow at first. But one must walk before one runs." He stood. "Then perhaps instead you might show me over the grounds. The estate here at Barrowdell has many lovely features, I'm told. Do you ride?"

Olivia nodded and rose to her feet. She felt far more at home on the back of a horse than in a parlor exchanging niceties. Especially slightly wicked niceties with a man who didn't realize the window seat should have only accommodated one.

"Good," he said. "We can get some fresh air, some exercise, and it will give me a chance to call you by your Christian name without fear of slipping in public."

"You don't want to lose the wager."

"No, I'm counting on you to do that," he said with a laugh. "Let's make it early, shall we? Say, eight o'clock?"

"Good. I'm a bit of a lark. An early ride suits me." She extended a hand to him, palm correctly down. She hadn't done so at their meeting, but it seemed right now. After all, they were going to be friends. "It would be my honor to show you over Barrowdell."

"No, the honor is mine." Rhys Warrington took her hand and instead of bowing over it, he brought it to his lips. He planted a soft kiss at the juncture between her fore and middle fingers. A little thrill zinged up her arm and warmed her belly. His breath feathered over the back of her bare hand, setting every nerve dancing.

It had been a huge mistake not letting her mother dress her after all, she realized. Beatrice Symon never would have forgotten to make sure she donned a pair of gloves. Then she wouldn't have found herself teetering on a precipice, about to tumble into a pair of brown eyes.

Lord Rhys looked down at Olivia over her knuckles.

"There's one more thing I'd like to guess about you, if I may," he said, his voice a rumbling purr.

"What's that?" she whispered, grateful her voice even worked. A strange warmth pooled between her legs.

"You have no idea how lovely you really are." He kissed her hand once more and held her with an intense gaze. "Until tomorrow then, my dear Olivia."

Chapter 4

RHYS STRODE OUT THE MASSIVE DOUBLE DOORS OF Barrowdell Manor and into the frosty air. He narrowly resisted the urge to swear as he mounted the deep-chested bay while his servant, Mr. Clyde, held the horse's head for him.

"I'm going to Hell," he muttered.

"Assuredly, my lord," Clyde said agreeably as he hauled his wiry frame up onto his piebald cob and fell into a jolting trot beside Rhys. "If I may make so bold as to ask, why are you bound for perdition this time?"

"I warned her," Rhys said with frustration. Why did she have to smell like alyssums? His mother lined every walkway in her garden with the sweet-smelling flower. The scent always took him home. The home that was now closed as tightly against him as the gates of Heaven. "I told the chit straight out what I was—gambler, drinker, rake, libertine—and she didn't turn a hair."

"Perhaps the lady is…well, less ladylike than the duke's advisors believe."

"No, she's the genuine article," Rhys said. "No one can feign a blush. Olivia Symon turned pink as a dandy's waistcoat pretty damned convincingly several times. She's exactly what she seems—a total innocent."

I'm the one who's a fraud. He'd thought he despised himself when he woke in a brothel one day with no recollection of the previous fortnight. His self-loathing then was nothing compared to the weight of guilt pressing on him now.

She'd melted when he kissed her hand, like frost sizzling away in sunshine. If he'd pressed the issue, he could have kissed her rosebud of a mouth as well. Judging from the tremble he detected in her fingers, she was ripe for it. Rhys had an almost sixth sense when it came to feminine arousal. When the time came, he doubted Olivia Symon would put up much of a protest.

"If it not be impertinent to ask, milord, why did the Duke of Clarence choose you to court the lady for him?"

"His Highness is badly advised, that's why." How Mr. Alcock had arranged for Rhys to assume the role of Clarence's representative was a mystery shrouded in the steaming pile of excrement called politics. Undoubtedly, Alcock knew a few juicy royal secrets no one wanted brought to light in order to pull off this coup and procure the royal letter of introduction Rhys had presented to Olivia.

Rhys glanced at his servant, who had wisely clamped his lips together on the subject of ill-advised princes. Actually Rhys thought of Clyde more as a friend than servant. After Rhys saved him on the field of battle, Clyde insisted on becoming his valet-cum-butler-cum-general-factotum and man of all work. Even when Rhys's pockets were light on occasion and he couldn't pay what was owed for a few weeks, Clyde refused to leave him for a more lucrative position.

"I'll stick with you like you stuck with me, your lordship, leastwise until I clear my debt to you," was all Clyde would ever say on the matter.

As a result, Rhys confided in Clyde far more than most wellborn gentlemen did with their valets. He knew exactly what Rhys was tasked to accomplish at the Symon household.

And exactly how high were the stakes.

"I've no difficulty seducing a woman, Clyde, but this will be like shooting fish in a barrel."

"Perhaps that's why you warned the lady, milord," Clyde said. "You don't really want to succeed."

"Don't be an ass. Of course I do." Rhys reined his mount to a sedate walk. Mr. Clyde breathed a heavy sigh of relief as they slowed. His servant had always been an indifferent horseman.

"I know you want what Mr. Alcock's promised you," Mr. Clyde said. "But I have to wonder if you warned Miss Symon away because being with her reminds you of who you really are."

Rhys snorted. "Devil if I know what you mean."

"This Symon girl, she's a lady, you say. Not like the randy widows and wayward wives you usually favor, if you'll pardon my saying so. Miss Symon sort of taps you on the shoulder and calls to mind that you're still the son of a gentleman in your heart of hearts."

"You've been with me long enough to know better than that." Rhys had lost count of the number of times Clyde had held his mount in the alley behind a house, ready for a mad dash should the lady's husband arrive home unexpectedly. "Only a fool doubts the evidence of his own eyes."

"My ol' pater used to say it's a fool who sees *only* with his eyes." Mr. Clyde's father had been vicar of a small parish, so Clyde waxed philosophical more often than Rhys liked. "You may have chosen to act the rake, but that's not who you are. I'll lay my teeth on it."

"In that case, you'd best get used to eating porridge. You forget yourself, Clyde. I do not need your moralizing. Save your country sermons for someone who'll listen. I intend to rut Miss Symon senseless and in record time."

Rhys laid a crop across his horse's flank and leaped into a canter, leaving Clyde to bump along behind him.

"I'll succeed," he muttered to himself. "Miss Symon is as good as ruined."

Like the cavalry officer he was, Rhys had reconnoitered the situation before he turned up in the Symon's parlor. He'd known all about Olivia Symon's penchant for orchids and had been prepared to converse intelligently about them. He'd discovered her tendency toward outspokenness before he set foot on her father's vast estate and knew she sat a horse better than most young ladies of her station. He'd also learned that the heiress was the wealthiest wallflower in England, shy in social situations despite her strongly held opinions.

She needed a friend.

So Rhys pretended to become one. As Olivia toiled in her winter garden in order to gather buds in May, so he too was laying the groundwork for the time when he'd pluck her maidenhead as neatly as clipping a daisy. She'd relaxed visibly once he leveled the class distinction between them by insisting he was a commoner like her. He'd known just how to flatter her intellect, to build up her trust. Telling her the truth about himself had been a calculated risk, but it had paid off. She was intrigued rather than repelled by his admitted status as a rake.

Seducing this virgin was going to be far too easy to be sporting. If she weren't so earnest about everything, he could almost despise her for being such a naïve little twit.

As Rhys bolted down the rutted road toward the sleepy little hamlet where he'd bespoken rooms at the inn, he decided he could be earnest as well. He would never lie to Olivia. He'd consider it his handicap in this game. When he managed to seduce her, he'd be fully exonerated for what happened at Maubeuge. He'd have his life back.

If he kept this one promise to himself—not to lie to Olivia Symon—perhaps he'd actually be able to bear living it.

Chapter 5

THE LONGCASE CLOCK IN THE HALL BELOW CHIMED three-quarters of the hour. Olivia adjusted her jaunty little riding hat, pinned it firmly in place, and studied the effect in her vanity mirror. The rest of her ensemble was mourning black, but the hat was a cheerful shade of lilac trimmed in dove gray. The colors lent a soft rosiness to her complexion that unrelieved black had robbed from her. She gave her reflection a nod.

Could Lord Rhys be right? Was she lovelier than she knew?

"Oh, don't be a ninny," she chided herself. "The man was only being polite."

Then she teased a lock of hair loose so it seemed as if she'd only just plopped the hat on her head. She'd been ready for her ride with Rhys Warrington since the clock chimed seven, but she didn't want him to know it.

A soft rap sounded on her door.

"Come," she called softly. Her lady's maid, Babette, slipped into the room.

"Pardon, Mademoiselle Olivia. Your gentleman caller, *alors*! He is here."

"Lord Rhys is early," Olivia said, the strange flutter in her chest starting afresh. She strode toward the door determined not to show how the mere mention of the man sent her pulse racing.

"Oh, mademoiselle," her maid said, raising a hand to halt Olivia's progress, "if I may make to suggest…"

"What is it, Babette?"

"You see, my last mistress always said—and she had a way with the gentlemen, *bien sur*—she always said a man's sense of appreciation for a lady, it is improved by a teensy bit of a wait."

"Oh, really?"

"*Oui*, really."

"And who was your last mistress that I should take her advice about men?" Olivia's mother had hired all their servants and considered Babette an excellent find since everyone knew French lady's maids were the best sort. Babette was assigned as Olivia's abigail without consulting her as soon as the Duke of Clarence began to show interest in her. "What was your previous employer's name?"

One of Babette's pale brows twitched. "*La Belle Perdu.*"

The Beautiful Lost One. Olivia had heard of the famous French courtesan. The mystery surrounding her was greatly enhanced by the fact that she always wore a half-mask. Even her many lovers claimed never to have seen her whole face. Her life and exploits were emblazoned across the tabloids her mother read, and occasionally the fashionable highflyer even caught a mention in her father's *Times*.

La Belle Perdu had moved in the most rarified of circles, privy to the secrets of the high and mighty in both London and Paris. Her death was as spectacular as her life. She died in a desperate leap from the London Bridge into the murky water of the Thames rather than be arrested as a French spy.

"La Belle Perdu. A way with the gentlemen indeed," Olivia said. "So you think she'd advise me to wait until eight o'clock to meet with Lord Rhys?"

"Oh, *non*." Babette shook her head. "She would say a lady must make to wait until a quarter *after* the hour before she puts her oh-so-dainty foot on the stairs."

"Well, my feet are not oh-so-dainty, and there's no lady before my name," Olivia said. "I feel like riding now, so now is when I'm going."

She pushed past her servant, feeling a bit surer of herself. Olivia tried to push away her mother's unending advice as well, but that critical voice was too deeply engrained in her head.

Don't talk too much. Don't move too quickly. If this man recommends you to His Royal Highness, you'll be a princess. Act like one.

How should Olivia know how a princess behaved? She could only act like herself. If Lord Rhys didn't like what he saw, he could look the other way.

When she rounded the bend in the grand staircase, he came into view, pacing with his hat in his hands in the marble foyer. His garrick caped over his shoulders. If Olivia half-closed her eyes, it seemed the dark coat draped about him like leathery wings, trailing as he paced. He looked even more delicious—and dangerous—than he had yesterday in the parlor, but now a frown marred his brow, and his mouth was set in a tight line.

What vexes him so?

She took another few steps and he must have heard her soft tread, for he looked up at her. The frown faded as he swept her with his gaze. A frank glow of masculine approval emanated from him.

"Miss Symon, you're so radiant the sun will surely refuse to shine from pure jealousy."

"Thank you, milord, but as near as we are to Scotland, the sun rarely puts in an appearance in any case. I fear you're trying to shine me on with such extravagant praise."

"Never think it." He bowed over her offered hand. This time she'd been careful to wear gloves, but his penetrating gaze made her insides dance as drunkenly as his kiss on her hand had yesterday. "I'll never lie to you…" and since no one was about, he added almost shyly, "Olivia."

She smiled. It was a game, this little secret familiarity of theirs. Even the wager with its hidden stakes added a fizz of excitement. "If you won't lie, then tell me. Why were you frowning…Rhys?"

"Was I?" He helped her don her spencer, then led her out the doors with her hand tucked securely into the crook of his elbow. Rhys might not lie, but the sun in the eastern sky did. It promised heat but lent no warmth to the crisp, cold day. Frost crunched underfoot as they strolled around the manor toward the stables.

"When I was coming down the stairs, you were a veritable storm cloud," Olivia said, her breath puffing into the air. "What troubles you?"

"Oh, it's nothing. Just that project of mine I mentioned yesterday."

"The one you likened to my gardening?"

He nodded, his smile hardening a bit. "Toiling now to gather blossoms later."

"It's not going well?"

"No, on the contrary, it's going quite well," he said. "The problem is that my valet thinks I'm not sure I want it to."

He was being cryptic enough she didn't feel their fledgling friendship permitted further prying. "Now you have me completely confused."

"That makes two of us."

When they arrived at the stable, Rhys's mount was waiting for him where he'd left it, with a blanket draped across its withers against the cold. After the ride from town, the horse was already warmed up. The bay gelding stood sixteen hands high with a deep chest and such knowing brown eyes Olivia felt it must surely possess a soul.

"Oh, what a lovely fellow!" She held out her palm and let him sniff it before she stroked his soft nose.

"Duncan's a good lad." Rhys patted the beast's strong neck. "I'd say he has the manners of a prince, but I've known too many princes and wouldn't want to insult him."

"Is that your way of trying to put me off the Duke of Clarence?"

"Not at all. Just an observation about princes in general," he said.

Olivia really didn't want to talk about princes, in general or otherwise. The Duke of Clarence was a dissolute stranger in his early fifties. Everything she'd heard about him made her less anxious to learn more. Horses seemed a safe topic.

"I've read that the cavalry favors Thoroughbreds. Did Duncan go to war with you?"

"No, I took his brother, Dougal."

"And now I suppose he's retired from the military too."

A shadow passed over Rhys's face and his jaw tightened. "I left him on a battlefield in France."

Olivia bit her lower lip. She should have stuck with princes. After so many English lads bled to see Napoleon defeated, did one offer condolences for a fallen horse?

Rhys's strained expression made her wish she could.

The head groom, Mr. Thatcher, came to her rescue, leading her dapple gray mare out of the stall. Molly was already saddled and ready to go, but with a dainty sidesaddle instead of the sturdy regular one Olivia preferred.

"Mr. Thatcher, where is my other saddle?" she whispered while Lord Rhys was occupied with checking Duncan's hooves for stones.

The groom grimaced in apology as he bent his back and offered his laced fingers, inviting her to step into them to mount. "Mrs. Symon sent word that you were to use this one today."

Olivia fumed in silence. It wasn't as if she were going to be trotting down London's Rotten Row to see and be seen. Granted, she was an accomplished rider no matter which style of saddle she used, but she always rode astride on her father's land.

And it always irked her mother. Beatrice Symon thought riding astride mannish and unrefined, but her father was amused by it and encouraged Olivia whenever he was in residence. When he was not, it was a small point of rebellion for Olivia to do it in any case. However, to insist on a change of saddle now would only make her appear hoydenish before Rhys Warrington.

Drat Mother and her interfering ways. It would almost be worth marrying an aging royal duke in order to get out from under her domineering thumb.

Olivia slipped her foot into Mr. Thatcher's waiting palms and allowed him to heft her up. Then she hooked her right thigh over the horn and settled her left foot into the single slipper stirrup.

"Thank you, Mr. Thatcher." It wasn't the groom's fault that her mother thought she needed to be hemmed about at every turn. "That'll do."

"Beggin' your pardon, but I'll be accompanying you and the gentleman this morning as well," he said softly. "Your mother's orders."

"As you will, Mr. Thatcher," she said as she tucked her riding crop under her arm. "But I trust you won't fall afoul of Mother."

"Why would I be doing that, miss?"

"Her order presumes you can catch us!"

Chapter 6

OLIVIA SYMON WHEELED HER MARE AROUND AND dug her heel into the horse's side. With a surprisingly loud "hi-up!" she bolted past Rhys and clattered out of the stable yard, making for the open, frost-kissed meadow beyond.

Rhys mounted his gelding in a smooth motion and streaked after her, wondering how on earth she managed to keep her seat riding aside at that breakneck pace. She was slight enough; he hadn't expected she'd have that much strength in her legs. But what Miss Symon lacked in body weight, she made up for in balance.

As he gained on her, she leaned forward and crooned urgent endearments to her mare. Her words brought out more speed than the well-laid smack of a crop. Olivia's body rocked with the mare's gait in perfect rhythm. They took the hill that rose before them as if the going were straight and level. When they reached the top of the rise, she drew back on the reins and the mare danced in tight circles, still aching to run but willing to obey the superb horsewoman on her back.

Olivia's color was high, her eyes bright. Her unabashed pleasure in the ride lent her a sensual glow. There was an appealing flush on her skin, and she panted slightly from exertion. She was fairly quivering with excitement and the rush of risk-taking.

That's how she'll look after a good hard swive, Rhys thought, warming to his goal, his guilt over it be damned. *If the rest of the ton could see her now, she'd never be a wallflower again.*

"You've a marvelous seat," he said, smiling and remembering how her neat little bum had bounced along. "If you were riding astride, you'd be the equal of any male equestrian."

She laughed, not the affected twitter of so many debutants but the full-throated sound of a thoroughly pleased woman. Why had he ever thought her the least girlish?

"Even aside, we beat the two of you up this hill, didn't we, Molly?"

She leaned forward to stroke the mare's neck and gave Rhys a quick inadvertent peek down the front of her riding habit. Her breasts were small but perfect. At every step, Olivia was a surprise to him. He was usually drawn to more buxom women, but his body quickened readily enough to her slender figure.

The mare whickered softly in response to Olivia's praise and bobbed its head as if in agreement with Rhys's unspoken assessment of its mistress.

"You did have a head start," he pointed out.

Her gaze flicked back toward the estate's manor. The groom was only just now trotting out of the stable yard. If Thatcher intended to join them on their ride to act as a chaperone of sorts, at least he seemed intent on giving them a sense of privacy.

"Are you going to quibble over details, Rhys, or are you game for a jump or two?" she asked, her pixyish face alight with mischief.

Rhys swallowed back his surprise. He'd only heard of a handful of equestriennes who jumped while riding aside. "You don't need to attempt it to impress me."

She laughed again. "There's no attempting about it. Molly and I can clear yonder hedgerow as easily as breathing. Or is jumping too unladylike an activity for the Duke of Clarence's liking?"

"If I said it was, would it dissuade you?"

"Not in the slightest." She flashed an impish grin and spurred the mare into a spirited canter toward the waist-high hedge.

"This girl doesn't need me to ruin her," Rhys muttered. None of his carefully gathered intelligence about Olivia Symon had revealed this daredevil side of her personality. "She's determined to do it herself."

Olivia and Molly hurtled toward the hedgerow, gathering speed. At the last possible moment, the mare launched herself skyward, and horse and rider vaulted over the obstacle, clearing it with plenty of room to spare.

But when they landed on the other side, the horse reared suddenly, whinnying in pain. Head down, she struck out her hind hooves.

Rhys watched in helpless horror as the saddle slid to one side. Most riders would have been unhorsed on the spot, but Olivia kicked her foot free of the slipper stirrup as the saddle crashed to the ground. The mare trampled it, adding the final touch to her panic. Then she bolted with Olivia clinging to her back, skirts and reins flying, her fingers digging into Molly's mane.

"Hold on!" Rhys shouted, his heart pounding in his throat.

He spurred Duncan into a gallop across the frost-crisped meadow. They cleared the hedgerow without breaking rhythm, gaining on the runaway mare with each pounding stride.

Olivia clung to the mare's back, tight as a tick, and though she couldn't check Molly's headlong flight, she seemed determined not to tumble off. Since the meadow was dotted with stones that worked their way up through the soil each spring, a fall at this speed was likely to result in broken bones at the very least. Eventually, Molly would tire if Olivia could just hold on.

But when Rhys looked ahead, he saw something to which the mare seemed oblivious. Olivia was unlikely to be able to see it either since her cheek was plastered against the horse's neck. A steep ravine opened before them.

Rhys's gut churned. He laid his crop on Duncan's flanks, and the horse poured on more speed. Yard by yard, the distance between Rhys and Olivia shortened until he was close enough to hear her pleading with the mare to stop.

She must have known the ravine was there, yawning its scree-strewn mouth. There was no time for Rhys to snatch Molly's trailing reins. In order to free his hands, he was forced to drop his as well.

Guiding the gelding with his knees and will alone, Rhys leaned over. He grabbed Olivia around the waist and hauled her off the bolting mare's back. She wrapped her arms around his neck and held on. Leaning in his saddle to counterbalance the extra weight, he barely managed to turn Duncan from the ravine's edge.

But Molly tumbled over the lip, screaming and thrashing, to the boulder-strewn bottom twenty feet below.

"Are you hurt?" he asked as he brought his gelding to a shuddering stop.

"No." Olivia clung to him, burying her face in the crook of his neck. "Oh, no. Molly!"

Wiggling out of his arms, she slid off Duncan's back. Olivia lifted her skirts and ran back toward the edge of the ravine. Rhys dismounted, quickly hobbled the gelding, and followed in close pursuit.

Molly was still alive, but she was lying on her side at the bottom of the ravine. She thrashed and emitted a shrill cry of distress. When Olivia called out to her, she tried to rise, but one of her forelegs collapsed under her weight. Molly whinnied and Olivia put a hand to her own chest, as if she could feel the mare's agony.

"Step away," Rhys said quietly as he reached into the pocket of his garrick and pulled out his horse pistol. He always kept it with him, even though he hadn't used it for anything since Maubeuge. Memories of the last time it had thundered and smoked in his hand raced through him.

A strident cry rose up from the recesses of his brain. It resounded in his ears, the screams from another dying animal pricking the edges of his consciousness. And from a dying man.

"Finish me, damn you!" Rhys schooled himself not to react to the flashes of vision beyond the tick in his

cheek he couldn't control. The remembered boom of cannon made the air shudder around him. The acrid stench of gunpowder burned his nostrils. He was the only one who could hear the cacophony of the battle-field exploding in his head, but knowing it wasn't real didn't make it feel any less so. His past threatened to burst into his present.

A small hand touched his forearm, and Rhys drew a deep breath. He firmly shut the door in his mind that led to Maubeuge.

"No, please," Olivia pleaded. "Don't shoot her."

"I don't want to." The last traces of the evil vision from his past dissipated, and he faced the crisis of the moment with clear-eyed decision. "But I may have to. If the animal is suffering and there's no help for it..."

"We don't know that yet. Not for certain." Olivia sat down on the edge of the ravine and scooted forward, attempting to climb down the steep incline. Rhys grasped her arm and yanked her back up beside him.

"No, you don't," he said gruffly. He didn't scare easily, but watching Olivia careen toward the ravine had sent his heart pounding. "Stay here. I mean it."

He scowled at her furiously, intending to impress upon her the foolhardiness of attempting to climb down the sheer face of the ravine, but her look of abject misery made him soften his expression. "I'll do what I can for her."

Even if that means a bullet.

She nodded, clearly unable to speak. He chose his way down the embankment with care, making use of rock outcroppings as finger and toe holds. The mare's cries were softer now and with more silence between each outburst.

"Easy, girl," Rhys said in a low tone. He needed the mare to remain calm. A downed animal might thrash and further injure itself if it perceived him to be a threat.

He continued to speak softly, letting the horse know he was approaching. When he laid a hand on her neck, she whickered and lifted her head, rolling her eyes at him in barely contained panic. Her breath snorted out in the cold air like dragon puffs. Blood streamed from several gashes on her glossy gray coat, but none of the wounds appeared life-threatening. He ran his hands over her haunches, and she kicked her hind legs.

Her spine was intact. That was a good sign.

Then he turned his attention to her forelegs. One fetlock was swollen and bleeding. If the leg was broken at that joint, she was doomed. Rhys cleared away some of the larger stones from near where she lay.

"Come, girl. Let's get you up," Rhys said, taking her reins in hand. He chirruped to her and she rolled, trying to gather her legs under her body. Whickering with effort, Molly finally struggled to her feet. Muscles quivered under her heavy winter coat and her head drooped. She wouldn't put any weight on the injured leg and shied when he tried to examine it.

But at least Molly was up and, with coaxing, she took a limping step.

Rhys glanced up at Olivia, who stood at the edge of the ravine, hands covering her mouth to keep from making any noise that might further upset the mare. Duncan stood at her side, his ears pricked forward as he watched what was happening to Molly with interest.

Though Olivia didn't say a word, Rhys read hope in her eyes.

For now, at least, he wouldn't have to dash it.

Molly had tumbled into the ravine at its deepest point. One hundred yards to Rhys's right, the narrow rift in the earth ended in a box with no outlet. To his left, the ravine widened and became less steep until better than a quarter mile in the distance it emptied into the sloping meadow. From that direction, another horseman approached, picking his way carefully along the ravine floor.

Mr. Thatcher, Rhys realized as he led Molly toward him with halting steps. The groom picked up his speed and met them before Molly had traveled twenty limping paces.

"See this mare back to her stall, if you please, Mr. Thatcher," Rhys ordered the groom. "I believe she'll make it if you take her slow and easy."

"Aye. Will you be needing my mount, my lord?"

Rhys tossed another look up at Olivia. After her brush with disaster, she might not feel up to handling another horse at the moment. If there was only one horse between them, she'd have to ride double with him on Duncan. She'd have to hug him to stay on.

Using this accident to advance Alcock's cause was beyond despicable.

That's why I have to do it.

"Thank you, no, Mr. Thatcher. We'll make do with my mount."

Rhys scrambled up the rocky face, ripping the knee of his trousers and scuffing his boots beyond saving. As he neared the lip of the ravine, he heard Olivia's soft sobs.

She stood, her hands covering her face, her slim shoulders quaking. Rhys put his arms around her and turned her so she couldn't look down into the ravine through her fingers. She didn't need to watch the mare's tortured journey along the bottom of the wash.

"Hush," he whispered into her hair. "What's done is done. Mr. Thatcher will see to her now."

There was still a good chance the mare would have to be destroyed, depending on the extent of the injury to her fetlock. But the way Olivia wept meant she knew that without him saying so.

She continued to sob as he stroked her head in an attempt to soothe her. Her little hat had flown off sometime during the helter-skelter dash. He'd have to look for it later, along with his own wide-brimmed one. It was a small matter, compared with a wounded horse and weeping woman. In the meantime, her hair had come unpinned and was trailing down her back in thick waves.

The long tresses smelled of alyssums. The scent made his chest constrict. *She must bathe in the stuff.* He pressed his lips to her temple. "Please don't cry."

It only made her sob more loudly.

"But it's my fault. If Molly has to be…" She couldn't bring herself to say the words. "I'll never forgive myself." Her tears fell in fresh torrents.

"There now. She may recover," he said with the same soft tone he'd used to gentle the mare. He kissed her cheek. She stopped crying and went completely still.

She seemed suddenly aware that he was holding her, a situation that made perfect sense given the shock she'd suffered due to the accident. But it was definitely beyond the bounds of propriety for an unrelated man and woman.

However, Olivia didn't pull away. Instead she tipped up her face to him. "You kissed me. Why?"

"Because you seemed to need it."

"After that climb and everything, perhaps…you need one too." She stretched up and tentatively touched her lips to his.

It was a chaste kiss, a virgin's kiss. The sort of weak gesture that he ought to have been able to brush off as if it were a kiss from one of his sisters.

Instead, the sweetness of it went straight to his heart in a sharp-edged rush.

Alarm bells jangled along his spine. He was here to seduce her, not the other way around. It was high time he remembered why he was there and acted accordingly.

He bent to claim her mouth in another type of kiss altogether.

Chapter 7

WHEN RHYS COVERED HER MOUTH WITH HIS, OLIVIA'S eyes flared wide with surprise. She'd meant her little kiss simply as a thank you, as innocent as the kiss he'd placed on her cheek. Clearly he thought it an invitation to more.

I ought to protest, she told herself.

Her eyelids fluttered closed despite her best intentions, the better to focus on the delicious sensation of his lips sealed on hers.

This is clearly inappropriate.

Her inner scold continued as his mouth slanted over hers. The tip of his tongue traced the seam of her lips, sending a flood of warmth coursing through her.

Well, that was wicked.

But for the life of her, she couldn't pull back. It would mean stopping the little flicks of pleasure dancing along each nerve. Inside her riding boots, her toes curled.

Her lips parted slightly and—

Oh, no, he wouldn't. He couldn't!

But surely he did. Rhys's tongue invaded her mouth,

turning her whole world wet and molten. In ladies' retiring rooms amid giggling confidences between the more popular debutants, she'd overheard rumors of such kisses, the ones labeled "French" for their bawdy decadence. The thought of a man's tongue in her mouth then had seemed more than a little repugnant.

The reality was a far cry from her imaginings. A curious heaviness settled between her legs, a downward pull she'd never felt before. Even though the sensation might be properly described as an ache, to her surprise, she didn't find it at all unpleasant.

He pulled her closer against the solid maleness of him—hard chest, hard thighs, hard—

Oh, good heavens!

She might not have much experience with men, but she'd been around horses enough to know what that hardness meant. Olivia pulled back and, slack-jawed, stared up at him.

He smiled down at her, wickedness sparkling in his dark eyes.

She pushed against his chest and he released her. The low ache inside her thumped in disappointment, but she tamped down her body's bewildering response.

"Yes, well, thank you very much for your assistance with Molly, my lord."

"Rhys," he corrected. "Now more than ever, you ought to call me that."

"Now more than ever, I ought not."

"Just because we shared a kiss?"

His tone implied it was a small thing. Perhaps for him it was, but for Olivia, the glory of his mouth on hers fairly stood the world on its head.

"If that kiss means so little to you, it should be easy for you to pretend it didn't happen," she said as she walked over to where Duncan had wandered head-down, munching on winter-brown grass.

"It's hard to unring a bell. We kissed. It happened," Rhys said. "And I didn't say it didn't mean anything. I simply meant in the grand scheme of things, a kiss is not of much moment. I won't report it to the Duke of Clarence, if that's what's troubling you."

The Duke of Clarence was the last thing on her mind.

"And in any case, if I did report it to the duke, he should be happy about it," he said. "That kiss confirms your untouched state."

She looked up sharply. "What's that supposed to mean?"

"Simply that you kiss like a virgin."

"And well I should because I am." Irritation scraped her spine. His kiss had been a revelation, a glimpse into an unexplored sensual world, dark with mystery and potent with promise. Her kiss evidently revealed how little she knew about that world.

"At least, thanks to you, I'm now a knowledgeable virgin." She tried to corral her hair into some semblance of order, but without the pins that had escaped during her wild ride, it was a hopeless gesture. "I can recognize the kiss of a rake when I receive one."

"I hope you'll try not to find yourself in situations that lend themselves to another rake's kiss. You can't trust those sorts, you know." He snorted as he mounted Duncan and leaned down to offer her his arm. "We should get you back to the house."

"Riding double?"

"Duncan can handle the weight," he assured her.

She didn't doubt that. She was more concerned about being so close to Rhys Warrington. Just the thought of it had her belly turning cartwheels.

"If Mr. Thatcher arrives before we do, no doubt your family will be worried."

Olivia sighed. Drat the man, he was right. Her mother would pitch a fit if she heard Molly had been returned to the stable injured and riderless before Olivia appeared. Beatrice Symon would never listen patiently to Mr. Thatcher's explanation. She'd be certain that Olivia was bleeding in a ditch somewhere and it all could have been avoided if only she'd listened to her mother.

Olivia's mother in hysterics was a sight to avoid at all costs.

She grasped Rhys's forearm, stepped on his foot in the stirrup, and let him heft her onto the scupper behind him, both her legs draped sedately on one side of the horse. Her skirt was wide enough to accommodate riding astride, but after the strange ache she'd experienced when he kissed her, she didn't think snuggling up to Lord Rhys's backside with her legs spread was a wise course.

Since she couldn't hug the horse with her knees, that meant she had to hug Rhys in order to stay on Duncan's back. Gingerly, she slipped one arm around his lean waist.

He claimed her hand with his.

"Hold on."

Rhys nudged his mount into a quick trot. Olivia was forced to wrap her other arm around him and cling tightly lest she be bounced off Duncan's rear. After a few yards, Rhys slowed his mount to a sedate walk, but she was obliged to continue hugging him in case he kicked Duncan into a canter without warning.

"Now then, this isn't completely unpleasant, is it?" he said.

Far from unpleasant. The faint sun had disappeared completely behind a growing cloud bank, but Rhys Warrington threw off as much heat as a roaring fire.

"You're wide enough through the shoulders to provide an admirable windbreak, I'll give you that," she said.

"One of my proudest accomplishments," he quipped. "I live to serve, milady."

"You know full well that I'm simply Miss Symon. I'm no lady."

"In all the ways that matter you are," he said, his voice rumbling through his broad back and into her ear that was pressed against it. "You may as well get used to a title, you know. You'll have to answer to Your Highness if you wed the royal duke."

With her cheek resting on Rhys's strong back and her arms around his waist, Olivia decided the prospect of an aging groom, royal or not, was more depressing than usual. When she kissed the Duke of Clarence for the first time, would he make her toes curl?

Somehow, she doubted it.

"Penny for your thoughts?" he said when they'd ridden in silence for several paces.

"They're worth far more than that." Embarrassment heated her cheeks. She couldn't admit she'd been thinking about his kiss so soon after trying to convince him to pretend it didn't happen.

When they reached the hedgerow, Rhys reined Duncan to a stop. He tossed a leg over the horse's head and slid off to retrieve Olivia's saddle from where it had been trampled into the wintry turf.

She took the opportunity to scoot forward and settle herself astride on Duncan's saddle. By the time Rhys turned back with the sidesaddle in hand, Olivia had adjusted her skirts to make certain her ankles were modestly covered.

"My turn to handle the reins," she said with deceptive sweetness. She suspected he disliked not being in control, but after her accident, the sooner she held the reins, the better. She'd be less likely to lose her nerve altogether.

His brows knit together. "Duncan can be a handful."

So can I danced on her tongue. After her abysmal showing as an equestrienne this morning, the boast died before it could pass her lips.

"Very well." She held the reins out to him. "But let's see how fast you go when you're on the scupper for a change."

He grinned, put a foot in the stirrup, and swung himself up behind her with her sidesaddle balanced on his left shoulder. He steadied it with his left hand and reached his right arm around her waist, cinching her close.

"Actually, with this saddle in tow, I'm rather short-handed. It appears you do need to keep the reins," he said, his breath warm in her ear. "But bear in mind, if I tumble off, I'm likely to take you with me, so no jumping this time."

"Being unhorsed once a day is more than enough."

Her voice caught, thinking of poor Molly. As soon as Olivia explained to her mother that there had been an accident, but that she was fine, she intended to spend the rest of the day seeing that Molly had hot mash and a gentle rubdown and all the care she required to mend.

They rode in silence, and after only a few paces, Olivia decided it hadn't been a very good idea to change places with Rhys after all. His chest expanded and contracted against her spine. His strong thighs were tight around her hips. And his arm at her waist felt strangely proprietary. Even on a dance floor, she'd never been so physically close to a man.

Every fiber of her body was on high alert. She was acutely aware of his deep breathing, even if his warm breath hadn't been washing over her nape. His splay-fingered hand touched the slightly ticklish spot at the base of her ribs, but she didn't feel at all like laughing. That odd fluttery feeling was back, threatening to swamp her chest.

A cold wind soughed over the rolling hills. The clouds that had been gathering began to spit rain at them, stinging needles of it with a hint of ice thrown in for good measure.

"I think we might chance a bit more speed," Rhys suggested. "Unless you prefer a drenching."

She squeezed the gelding with her thighs, and he answered with a brisk trot that quickly smoothed into an even, rocking canter.

Olivia loved to ride, loved the speed, the freedom, the thrill of power that controlling such a large animal gave her. Having a large man at her back only intensified the experience. She and Rhys moved as one, settling into the rolling rhythm of Duncan's gait.

The effect was decidedly…unvirginal.

She was relieved when they pulled into the stable just as the rain turned to snow. Rhys dismounted and then helped her down, holding her longer than necessary before allowing the tips of her boots to touch the hard-packed stable floor. She moved away from him quickly and stood at the open doorway.

"Poor Molly," she said, looking out at the gathering whiteness.

"You there, boy," Rhys called to the stable lad who was mucking out stalls. "Have you a cart that will hold Miss Symon's mare? She's been injured and needs to be brought in without having to walk through this weather."

"Right-o, guv."

He told the boy where he might find Mr. Thatcher and the two horses he was leading back. When Rhys promised him a crown if he managed to bring the mare back safely in less than half an hour, the lad fairly flew to the other part of the stable where the draft horses were kept.

"A crown?" It touched Olivia that Rhys seemed as concerned for Molly as she was. "For a man who lives by the turn of a card, you're liberal with your gratuities."

"I've been winning of late. Why not spread the good fortune around?"

"And what do you do when you lose, my lord?"

"I buck up and bear it." He propped one booted foot on a stall slat and looked out the stable door at the white flurries. "But I don't lose often. And what happened to calling me Rhys?"

"We're close enough to the house that it's time I stop addressing you so familiarly." Olivia hugged her arms around herself against the wet cold that drafted in the open door. "Count upon it. You'll lose our wager."

"That's yet to be seen."

"No, it's not. The wager hangs upon a willful act. I have purposed in my heart not to call you by your Christian name in public. Therefore, you'll lose," she said. "You're a sporting man. Lay odds on which of us has more self-control. The virgin or the rake?"

His dark-eyed gaze swept over her, sending a delicious tingle across her skin. "You might be surprised to learn how much self-control I'm exercising at this very moment."

"Oh really?" She knew it was dangerous to bait him like this, but the same reckless part of her that rode astride when she could and took jumps when she shouldn't plowed ahead. "That must be difficult for you. I can't imagine you have much practice with restraint."

"I don't, but my current quandary is your fault." He ran a hand over his dark hair, dusting away a few snowflakes, and Olivia's palm itched to do the same just to learn what those thick locks felt like. She'd never much thought about a man's hair before, but Lord Rhys had such a glorious head of it. "You see, I've been thinking about something you said earlier."

His words jerked her back from her musings over the man's hair. "What's that?"

One corner of his mouth turned up in a smile. "That our kiss had made you a knowledgeable virgin."

Olivia's chest tightened. Whether it was because of his words or the way his dark hair fell forward and obscured one eye, giving him the disreputable aspect of pirate king, she couldn't be certain. Either way, she didn't trust herself to speak.

"The idea that you're a knowledgeable virgin, that's not true, you know," he said. "Your sensual education is still woefully thin. We've only scratched the surface of what's possible between a man and a woman."

He came and stood next to her, close but not touching. Olivia felt pulled toward him like a daisy to the sun, but she didn't give in to the attraction. The snow fell heavier now, in large fluffy flakes that attached itself to the grass and trees and sucked up all sound in its heavy whiteness.

Then Rhys's seductive voice broke the silence. "What would you say if I were to tell you there is much more for you to discover?"

She swallowed hard. "Undoubtedly, there is. You're not telling me anything I don't already know. Innocence and ignorance don't always go hand in hand."

"Yet they are frequently seen in close company. Few virgins are well-versed in the sensual arts."

"That's to be expected."

"I would have thought you to be the sort who abhors any gap in her education," he said, his voice a rumbling purr. "I could teach you, you know. There's so much delight to be had. And through it all, it's possible for you to remain technically pure—"

"But not morally pure."

He shrugged. "Semantics."

"Reality," she countered, squaring her shoulders. "When two people share a part of themselves in the manner you're suggesting, it's impossible to get that part back. Or do you really believe we can so separate our bodies from our minds and hearts?"

He was silent for the space of several heartbeats. Then he turned and cupped her chin, forcing her to meet his gaze. Olivia hoped he thought the way she trembled was due to the cold, but it wasn't. Her insides were jumping about like a spring lamb loosed in the meadow for the first time.

"Tell me you haven't been thinking about that kiss, Olivia." His masculine scent, all saddle leather and spicy bergamot, crowded her senses. "Haven't you been wondering what comes next?"

He was a libertine. A rake. A cad. How many women had lost their resolve to this whisky-voiced, blindingly handsome man? Olivia gave herself a stern mental shake.

"Here's what comes next, Lord Rhys." She slapped his cheek in a stinging blow. Then she lifted her skirt and ran toward the main house, heedless of the falling snow.

Chapter 8

"ABSOLUTELY HARROWING, THAT'S WHAT IT WAS,"
Mrs. Symon was saying to the aging Baron Ramstead
at her right hand at the long dining table. Flickers from
the centrally placed candelabra bathed Olivia's mother
in the most flattering light. Rhys suspected Mrs. Symon
had been something of a village beauty when she was
a girl and hadn't ever gotten over not being the center
of attention.

Rhys occupied the place to her left "as a mark of
special favor" Mrs. Symon had declared before the party
settled into their chairs. After three courses of non-stop
histrionics from his hostess, Rhys didn't feel so favored.
The only bright spot was that Olivia was seated next to
the baron, kitty-corner across from him. She was close
enough he could send her looks that made her squirm
to his heart's content.

Rhys didn't regard that slap she'd given him as a
setback. In fact, it was proof positive he'd struck a
nerve with his offer to educate her. If her occasional
flush of color was any indication, he'd wager the entire
contents of his wallet that Olivia had thought about his

indecent proposal more than once since they sat down to dine.

Lord knew he had.

Mrs. Symon signaled for the footmen to clear the plates of poultry and bring on the beef. "I swear that girl scared a year off my life today."

"Mother, by the time you learned about the accident, I was standing right beside you," Olivia protested.

"But only think what might have been." Mrs. Symon put a hand to her breast, no doubt believing it an affecting gesture of motherly concern. "And in the presence of His Highness's representative too. Imagine how the Duke of Clarence would have taken the news if you'd tumbled into that horrid chasm. I told your father he ought to do something about that ravine. It's not safe to have such a dangerous natural feature on the place. If I told the man once, I've told him a thousand times."

Rhys didn't doubt that for a moment.

Mrs. Symon kept talking, but Rhys was adept at only seeming to listen. Instead he surreptitiously swept the dinner party with his gaze, wishing he could ferret out their secrets simply by looking at them.

After Olivia had stormed out of the stable and back to the house, he'd learned something that changed the nature of his business at Barrowdell completely.

Oh, he still intended to bed the girl. That was a given and not just to meet Mr. Alcock's requirements. Olivia Symon had done something no other woman had since he returned from Maubeuge.

She made him feel something beyond mere lust.

He had no name for it, but he thought bedding her

was the best way to learn what it might be. Olivia was fast becoming an itch he couldn't wait to scratch. But now he needed to protect her as well.

Her riding accident hadn't been so accidental.

While he'd waited for Mr. Thatcher to return with Molly, Rhys had examined the sidesaddle. The leather was thin where the girth attached. It was likely to fail if undue pressure was put on it. For instance, if the horse should happen to begin to buck and rear.

And a long thorn had worked its way into the padding under the saddle. If Rhys had found only one of those things, he'd merely have thought Mr. Thatcher was singularly unreliable. Together, the worn girth and the thorn suggested skullduggery. When Olivia took that jump over the hedgerow, as anyone who was familiar with her riding habits knew she would, the sharp spike would have jabbed the mare's back, triggering the saddle's failure.

It was cunningly done. Even if the thorn was discovered, there was no way to prove it hadn't gotten there by accident. And leather wore over time. If Olivia had ended up at the bottom of the ravine, it might have been days before someone became curious about the cause of the accident and thought to look. By then, the perpetrator could have covered up those two bits of evidence.

When Mr. Thatcher returned to the stable with Molly, Rhys had snatched him up by his collar and confronted him with his findings. The man's weathered face grew red with indignation over Rhys's accusations.

"I put that little miss on her first pony, your lord-ship," Thatcher had said with a glint of fury in his eye. "I'd sooner take a whipping than see her come to harm."

"At the very least you were negligent in saddling her horse," Rhys said, thrusting the man away in disgust. He heard truth in Thatcher's tone. The groom wasn't the culprit, but that didn't excuse incompetence. "Why didn't you check it?"

"Molly was already saddled when I come in this morning with a note affixed from Mrs. Symon ordering this saddle be used so her daughter would have to ride aside. Miss Olivia and her mother go round about that, you'll collect. In any case, I figured Davy had handled Molly's tack so's I wouldn't have to. We pick up slack for each other like that. I didn't think nothing about it at the time."

Rhys had demanded the note and tucked it into his pocket. He'd found a sample of Mrs. Symon's hand-writing later in the afternoon and compared it to the note on the saddle. Whoever forged the note was good, but there were enough differences in the script to make him doubt that Olivia's mother had sent it.

He and Mr. Thatcher both cornered the stable lad, but Davy denied having done anything but muck out stalls and pick the dray horse's hooves that morning. And since the big workhorse was housed in the far portion of the long stable and didn't generally cooperate when his hooves needed attention, Davy hadn't noticed anyone lurking about Molly's stall.

There was a chance the culprit was a servant who might have gone unremarked, but in his research on the Symons, Rhys had learned that they paid their people very well. The staff was given regular half-day liberties and alternate all day Sundays. The below stairs dining room was always generously set. It wouldn't make sense for one of the staff to turn on so open-handed an employer.

Rhys thought it more likely that whoever tampered with the sidesaddle was seated at the long dining table, breaking bread with Miss Symon.

So he studied his dinner companions with a jaundiced eye. There was the geriatric Baron Ramstead and his much younger baroness. The lady was seated to Rhys's right. It was a good thing she was attractive because she didn't seem to have the brains of a peewit.

Next to Olivia was a Mr. Winfield Stubbs, a portly fellow with a nose like a misshapen rutabaga and jowls to rival a bloodhound. Despite his unfortunate appearance, he was reputedly a great friend of Mr. Symon from his days in India. Mr. Stubbs was a dedicated trencherman and had remarked several times to no one in particular, "Splendid table, what? M'compliments to the chef."

Next to him, Lady Harrington, a distant relation of Mr. Symon, was seated. The dowager viscountess, still a handsome woman though she'd never see fifty again, was resplendent in dark silk and ropes of matched gray pearls.

"You see, Lord Rhys, we Symons are not without nobility in our lineage," Mrs. Symon had said as an aside when introductions were made before supper. "In fact, given the right circumstances, my own dear Mr. Symon might inherit the Harrington title one day."

"By right circumstances, she means the deaths of Lady Harrington's five strapping sons and all their twenty-six children," Olivia had mumbled under her breath when her mother and the viscountess moved on.

Across from Lady Harrington, a Lord Percy was flirting rather shamelessly with the young baroness and didn't even flinch when the lady's husband cast him a pointedly wicked glare.

Nothing to fear from a toothless lion, Rhys figured Percy had decided.

When the baroness began ignoring him, Percy turned his attention to Miss Amanda Pinkerton, who sat on his right side. With a few artful blandishments he had the dark-eyed beauty blushing in no time. Evidently, Lord Percy was a flirt of opportunity, not strategy.

"I say, Miss Pinkerton," he said, "I do hope you'll save a spot on your dance card for me when you arrive in London. You'll have the young bucks lining up, I shouldn't wonder."

"Amanda is being brought out by Lady Cowper and won't have much say in the composition of her dance cards." Doctor Nigel Pinkerton, Amanda's father, glowered at Percy from his position across the table on Lady Harrington's left.

Rhys decided there were no flies on Pinkerton. He respected men who protected their women. In short order, Pinkerton had sized up Percy and arrived at the correct number. The doctor had also befriended Horatio Symon when they were both in India. In fact, Amanda was born there and had only recently made the long cruise home with her father in order to have a proper London Season come spring. From what Rhys could gather from cryptic mentions, her mother, like many an English rose, had wilted and died in the East.

The last guest at the table was Colonel Billiter. He too had spent time on the Asian subcontinent, but served in the military instead of working to develop trade as Horatio Symon had done. If he'd heard of Rhys's less than distinguished service in France, the colonel gave no sign when Olivia's mother had introduced them.

The table was long enough to accommodate another twelve guests without crowding. The extra chairs were empty at present, as was the seat at the distant head of the table. With so many of his purported friends gathered round, Mr. Symon was conspicuous by his absence.

Mrs. Symon had assured Rhys that all the places would be filled by week's end. A much larger house party was planned as soon as the general mourning for Princess Charlotte was lifted.

"We'll have a sober little party of friends and family until then. Once it's decently possible, we'll shake off the winter doldrums with finer festivities," Mrs. Symon had told him grandly. "We don't want you to report back to the Duke of Clarence that we country mice are deadly dull."

But no matter who joined them in the days to come, Rhys marked the members of this "sober little party of friends and family." One of them, he was sure, had tried to harm the host's eldest daughter.

Why? Which of them stood to gain if Olivia didn't wed the Duke of Clarence?

Mrs. Symon was still worrying the topic of Olivia's "accident," picking at it as if she might unravel the horror of it like a knitter unravels a misshapen row of stitches. "I swear, I feel an attack of the vapors coming on every time I think about what might have happened to our dear Olivia."

"What about what *did* happen to poor Molly," Olivia said softly. Rhys heard guilt in her tone.

"She's still alive and, with any luck, will remain so," Rhys said. By the time he'd left the stable that morning, the head groom had rigged a tackle and sling so the mare's front half was lifted off the ground, giving the injured joint a chance to heal. "Mr. Thatcher is making every effort to save her."

He was rewarded by Olivia's small smile of gratitude for his understanding, but then she turned her gaze to her plate, refusing to look at him again.

Mrs. Symon recaptured the conversational ball. "Well, horse doctoring aside, thank heaven Lord Rhys was there to save the day."

"Hear, hear," Lord Percy said, taking the opportunity to clink his glass with the baroness's again.

"You know, Miss Symon." Mr. Stubbs nudged Olivia with his elbow between stuffing great bites of beef into his gaping maw. "In some cultures when a man saves a person's life, that person is bound to him from that time forth."

Olivia shot a glance at Rhys from under her sooty lashes. "I hardly think Lord Rhys is the sort who wishes to have a woman bound to him for any length of time. Certainly not from this time forth."

Mr. Stubbs laughed, a disgusting cross between a snuffle and a runaway case of hiccups. "Show me a man who does! The parson's mousetrap is the bane of the male race."

"I don't generally hold with what the heathen do, but the principle you describe, Mr. Stubbs, is a sound one," old Lord Ramstead said. "Here in Christian

England, we honor our debts. Surely we all owe Lord Rhys hearty thanks for snatching the dear girl from the jaws of death."

"Jaws of death," Mrs. Symon repeated, giving a little moan as her eyelids fluttered. She fanned herself rapidly, then stiffened as her eyes rolled back in her head. Finally she slumped gracefully in her chair, like a feather descending lightly to earth. It took Rhys a moment to realize she'd fainted. He leaped to his feet, patting her wrists and calling for smelling salts.

Olivia wasn't inclined to wait for salts. She rose from her place with her water glass in hand, dipped her fingers into the liquid, and then flicked them at her mother's face. Beatrice Symon sputtered and sat bolt upright, casting Olivia an irritated glare.

"Good thing you came to, Mother," she said tight-lipped. "I was just about to empty the whole glass on you."

Mrs. Symon's eyes flared for a moment as she dabbed away the droplets Olivia had showered on her. Then she schooled her face into a more pleasant expression before turning back to Rhys. "Thank you, Lord Rhys. I'm quite recovered. But mere thanks seem so paltry considering how you swooped in to save my darling daughter." The last two words were spoken through clenched teeth. She forced a smile. "I'm certain when dear Mr. Symon returns home, he will want to reward you. Tell me, Lord Rhys, how can we properly show our appreciation?"

"That's really not necessary." He suspected Olivia's mother kept beating this subject because it allowed her the most scope for theatrics. He was convinced now that the swoon had been feigned. If she hadn't married

Horatio Symon, she might have made a brilliant career on Drury Lane. She certainly knew how to capture center stage.

"Nonsense, dear boy." She patted his forearm affectionately. "What will you have? A continental tour? A townhouse? Name it and I shall see that it is yours."

A wicked idea took shape in his mind. "Actually, the reward I truly covet is something only Miss Symon can give."

A chorus of intrigued "oh's and "ah's" rose around the table. Olivia returned to her seat, eyeing him like a mouse who gives the sleeping tabby a wide berth.

He cast his most winning smile to his fellow guests. "I only wonder if she'll do me a simple favor."

All eyes turned to Olivia. She bit her lower lip and blushed a most becoming shade of cherry pink. "If I can, my lord," she finally choked out.

"In light of the small service I rendered this morning," he said, willing her to meet his gaze, "I think the time for formality between us is done. I'd count it an honor if you'd call me by my Christian name and give me leave to use yours henceforth."

"Well done, sir," Colonel Billiter said softly. "A modest request when offered the world shows a man's true measure."

However, Rhys knew the request was far from modest from Olivia's viewpoint. She'd name it a cheat on their bet, and she wouldn't be far wrong. When her face drained of all color, Rhys almost regretted putting her on the spot like this.

But he needed to win that wager. Now more than ever. This was no time to play fair.

"Well, Miss Symon?"

She swallowed hard.

"Olivia, answer the man," her mother said sharply.

There was silence so profound Rhys heard Olivia's swift intake of breath. "Yes," she said briskly, "you may use my Christian name…Rhys. And now, Mother, I beg to be excused. I fear I have the beginnings of a terrible headache. Good night to you all."

Without waiting for her mother's reply, Olivia stood and rushed from the dining room without a backward glance.

Rhys had won their wager, but he'd lost something even more important. Her trust.

He'd have the devil's own time trying to win it back.

Chapter 9

"Too much excitement, *non*?" Babette said as she brushed out Olivia's long hair before her looking glass. "*Naturellement*, you would have the headache after such a day."

"After such a man, you mean," Olivia said, forgetting for a moment that her mother wouldn't approve of her becoming too chatty with the help.

Babette could be relied upon to deliver sound advice about which shoes to wear with which gown and how to disguise the lack of a bosom with clever flounces, but Olivia wasn't sure she should take her maid's advice about men.

Especially not since Babette's previous employer had been La Belle Perdu. A courtesan specialized in saying "yes" to men, while Olivia categorically wanted to say "no" to this one.

"Lord Rhys might have asked for something harder than for you to call him familiar," Babette reminded her.

"Believe me. This is hard enough." How dare he force her hand like that? It proved beyond doubt that, despite his courtesy title, Lord Rhys Warrington was no gentleman.

She sighed at her reflection. He'd never claimed to be one. It served her right for entering into a wager with an admitted rake. Now she owed him another as yet unspecified favor.

What sort of favor would a rake want from her? Her toes curled inside her slippers.

"*Alors*, I will warm the bed for you and you will sleep like the babe, *non*?"

Babette took the copper tray filled with live coals from the fire and ran the warmer over the sheets. Then she wrapped a hot brick in several layers of flannel and tucked it into the foot of the bed.

"There you are, *chérie*. Snug as one could wish."

Olivia climbed into bed and allowed Babette to tuck the covers up to her chin.

"*Bonsoir*." The maid bobbed a quick curtsey. "Ring if the headache, she is not better, and I will make for you the hot chocolate."

Good as that sounded, hot chocolate was not what she needed. Olivia sat up. It might not be wise, but if she didn't ask, she'd stew all night. "Wait, Babette. I wonder if you might tell me your opinion on something."

"But of course. What is it you wish to know?"

"This is a case of pure supposition, you understand. An imaginary situation."

"*Je comprends*." Babette nodded sagely. Then she shook her head in self-reproof and answered again, in English this time. "I understand. Tell me your imaginary situation."

"Suppose a man could ask anything of a woman, and for one reason or another, she was honor bound *not* to turn him down. Whatever it is, she would have to say yes." Olivia drew up her knees and hugged them to her chest. "What do you think he would ask for?"

Babette pursed her lips into a smile that reminded Olivia of a cat warming itself in the sun. "Most people, they would think this imaginary man will ask to join this imaginary woman in her imaginary bed."

"I was afraid of that."

"But most people, they would be wrong," Babette hurried on to add. "You see, if a man could have anything from a woman, he would not ask for a bedding."

"No?" She'd never admit it to another soul, but something inside her wilted in disappointment.

"*Non*," Babette said with assurance. "That he can have anytime for the sake of a few fair words or the right amount of coins."

"What would he want then?"

"The same thing we all want, mademoiselle." This time, Olivia thought Babette's smile was tinged with wistfulness. "To be accepted. To be trusted. To be loved."

"Not all men, surely."

"All," Babette said emphatically. "And all women too. Oh, the men, they may not admit it, *bien sur*, but in their heart of hearts, it is what they truly want. What they need."

Babette hitched her hip on the side of the mattress and settled down on the bed. "Now, this imaginary man, he may ask for something else. Nothing is more likely. A man, imaginary or no, has no end of trouble making to speak what it is he really wants. But the imaginary woman, she would do well to realize what it is he is truly asking of her."

"To be accepted?"

"And to be trusted," Babette said. "And if he is oh so lucky, to be loved."

Olivia scrunched her toes under the sheets. Surely Babette's advice didn't apply to an admitted libertine like Rhys.

Then why did he tell her what he was if not to see whether or not she'd accept him and his continued presence? Even at their first meeting, he'd made it a point of honor to be sure she had every opportunity to think ill of him. Instead, she'd been intrigued.

And accepting.

Puzzling all this out was making her head start to pound in earnest.

"Thank you, Babette. That'll do," she said. "But if it's not too much trouble, I think maybe I will take some of that chocolate now."

"As you wish, mademoiselle." Babette rose immediately. The confiding friend transformed immediately back into the amiable servant. She stopped at the door and looked over her shoulder at Olivia. "I hope your imaginary woman, she is pleased by what her imaginary man demands of her."

"So do I," Olivia whispered after the door closed softly behind Babette. "So do I."

◈

After all that had happened, Mrs. Symon insisted Rhys stay at Barrowdell instead of returning to his room at the inn in the village.

"You may as well join the house party, my lord," Olivia's mother had said. "Do say you will. There'd be no cause for celebration without you. And besides, you'll be better situated to perform the duties His Highness has laid upon you if you bide under our humble roof."

She'd paused so he could protest that of course Barrowdell was far from humble. Rhys didn't disappoint her and said he'd be pleased to be a guest in such an opulent home. He sent Mr. Clyde back to the village inn to collect his belongings and took up residence in Olivia Symon's shadow.

If he'd been inclined to send progress reports to Mr. Alcock, the man would be pleasantly surprised by how quickly Rhys's project was moving forward.

When the time came for everyone to retire for the night, he'd met a handsome lady's maid in the hallway with a cup of hot chocolate in her hands and a delightful French lilt in her voice. Rhys charmed her into giving him a whispered tour of Barrowdell's upper stories. In hushed tones, she pointed out where each guest was housed. And most importantly, which room belonged to her mistress, Miss Symon.

Rhys waited in his chamber until the household was silent for better than half an hour. Then, moving stealthily as a sneak thief, he ventured from his room in the east wing to the family's section on the west side of the imposing manor.

When he reached Olivia's door, he scratched lightly on the oak and waited. Seconds crawled by. At any moment, another door along the corridor might open and someone might catch him hovering near Olivia's room. It was no skin off his nose if that happened, but if it did, she'd be even angrier than she probably already was over his trick at the dining table.

He was just about to reach for the crystal knob when the door opened a crack and Olivia peered out at him.

"What are you doing here?" she hissed.

"Standing in the hall where anyone might see me," he whispered.

The door swung wide and she yanked him into her chamber. Then she carefully closed the door behind him. The latch clicked with an almost imperceptible snick.

"You're far gentler with oak and hinges than you are my forearm," he said softly.

"The door hasn't done anything to irritate me," she whispered back. "Now what do you want?"

In the soft light of the banked fire, he gave her a swift assessing glance. Her correctly virginal nightrail was covered by an equally correct wrapper. Her long hair was plaited in a loose braid that draped heavily over one shoulder. Despite the fact that she was arguably the most "missish" woman he'd ever seen, his body was of the contrarian opinion that she was still entirely swiveable.

"What do I want?" he repeated. "Besides to come in, you mean."

"Yes, obviously, besides to come in. And for heaven's sake, keep your voice down." She crossed her arms beneath her breasts, unknowingly lifting them for his more careful perusal.

He forced his gaze away. No point in antagonizing her more.

"Keep my voice down, yes, of course." He put a finger to his lips to shush himself, walked over, and plopped down on the foot of her bed. "As to what I want, why, I think that should be self-evident. I want to stay the night."

"You most certainly"—her own voice had risen well above a whisper, but she caught herself and continued in a furious hiss—"will not."

He patted the mattress beside him, inviting her to sit. "What about our wager? May I remind you that you lost this evening?"

"I didn't lose." She remained standing, and as still as if she was carved of marble. "You cheated."

"I suppose I did from your point of view. Be that as it may, you still lost and therefore you owe me an unspecified favor." He waved away her objections. "We didn't set any ground rules that precluded trickery when we made our bet. Perhaps that's something you should consider the next time you decide to wager with me."

"There won't be a next time."

"So sure about so many things, aren't you?" The fact that he suspected she was in danger should have made this little interview deadly serious, but he was enjoying the view too much. Backlit by the fire, her otherwise chaste nightrail and wrapper were nearly transparent. The shadowy silhouettes of her legs were easy to make out. "And only this morning you were certain you'd never call me Rhys in public. Whether you like it or not, you owe me a favor."

"Not this one. You are not staying."

He stood and walked toward her. "Shall it be noised about that the daughter of Horatio Symon is a welcher?"

"Shall it be noised about that Lord Rhys Warrington is a cad? Oh, wait, it already is. I was simply foolish enough to give you the benefit of the doubt." She backtracked a few steps, then held her ground in a defensible position next to the pair of chintz-covered wing chairs by the fire. "Don't you care what people think of you?"

"Not particularly."

"Or what they think of me, evidently."

"Nonsense. Unless you insist on talking too loudly, no one will know I'm spending my nights here."

She made a disgruntled little sound in the back of her throat as she plopped into one of the chairs. "*I'll* know and—what do you mean by *nights*?"

"'When the plain sense makes sense, seek no other sense,' my old tutor used to say," Rhys said, settling his hands on the arms of her chair and leaning toward her. She pressed herself into the tufted back, but the way her breath hitched told him she was excited by his nearness. "I mean just what I said. *Nights* as in plural, as in more than one, as in for as long as I remain a guest here at Barrowdell. That's the favor you owe me and that's what I'll have. These chairs seem quite comfy. If you don't care to share the bed, we might push them together so you could sit in one and prop your feet on the other."

"No, I don't care to share my bed, and I will not sleep on a chair in my own room either." She pressed her palms against his chest and shoved. "Rhys, you're not staying. How can I convince you of that? I ought not to have allowed you through the door."

"Why did you then?" He straightened to his full height but wouldn't move away so she could escape him.

"Because someone…because you…because…oh, hang it all! I don't know." The way she rubbed her forehead made him think she hadn't been pretending when she pleaded a headache at supper. "You are, without doubt, the most infuriating person I've ever met."

"I shall take that as a compliment."

She shot him an evil glare. "It wasn't meant as one."

"Anytime one is designated 'the most *anything*,' it indicates a certain level of accomplishment beyond the common. That raises your comment to the ranks of a compliment, don't you think?"

The glare dissolved and was replaced by such a look of entreaty that his chest ached with guilt over the discomfort he was causing her.

"Oh, Rhys, please go away."

"I can't." He'd hoped to protect her without having to tell her that she needed protection. It was time to fall back on the truth. It was supposed to set one free, he'd heard. Rhys sat in the opposite chair and leaned forward. "Tell me. When you went back to the stable today, did Mr. Thatcher show you Molly's saddle?"

"No, he didn't," she said wearily. "He'd already sent it to the saddler to be repaired."

"Just my luck. You have a servant who's the soul of discretion."

"Why are you trying to change the subject?" She stood, determination radiating from her slight frame. "You're not staying, so we don't need to talk about Molly's saddle or the quality of our servants or anything else, because…you're not staying."

"You've said that once or twice already."

"Yes, well, I meant it every time."

"I can see that you do," he said. "And usually when a lady tells me no—and believe me, I can count on one hand the number of times that's happened—I don't argue. I bid the lady adieu and there's the end of it. But unfortunately, this time I can't take no for an answer."

"Do I need to scream to convince you I sincerely don't want you here?"

"That would certainly convince me of your sincerity, but you don't want to do that," he said. "Fair or not, if the two of us are found alone in your bedchamber, it would undoubtedly enhance my reputation. However, it would do no favors to *your* good name."

Her look of loathing made him cringe inside, but he was careful to give no outward sign of it.

"You are despicable," she said.

"More than you know," he admitted. "But I have good reason for my boorish behavior this time. You see, your accident today was no accident."

She sank back into the wing chair, wind spilling from her sails. "What do you mean?"

"I mean Molly's saddle was deliberately tampered with." He described what he'd discovered. She listened with far more calm than most debutants would if they'd been told someone meant them harm. Certainly more calm than he'd have been greeted with if he'd gone to her mother with the story.

"So, you see, until we learn why someone wishes you ill, I'll rest better if I know you're secure," he said. "If this person was bold enough to sneak into the stable and alter your saddle, they may be bold enough to slip into your chamber as well. That's why I want to spend my nights here. Let me stay to keep you safe."

She stood and paced before the fireplace, arms wrapped around herself. "It makes no sense. Why would anyone want to harm me?"

"You have captured the attention of the Duke of

Clarence," Rhys said. "Royal favor sometimes comes with unintended consequences."

Mr. Alcock might not be the only one who wanted to see the match between the duke and Miss Symon fail. Someone else may have decided the best way to go about it was to remove the potential bride for good. It was a bloodthirsty scenario, but the scheme of seducing her was at least as underhanded. In both cases, the results would be lasting.

Rhys stomped down his guilt. He was trying to protect her. That ought to count for something. For the moment, at least, he was on the side of the angels.

The guests in residence at Barrowdell didn't seem the sort to be swept up in political intrigue. But in the shadowy realm of royal machinations, that only made it more likely Rhys's supposition was right.

After all, who would guess the duke's emissary was also trying to sabotage the match?

Or was there another unrelated reason Olivia Symon had fallen afoul of someone who would go to great lengths to harm her?

"So you want to spend the nights with me simply to keep me safe." She cast him a wry smile. "That has to be a first for you."

He shrugged. "You have the right of it. My motives are pure for once. I am here to protect you."

She cocked her head at him, as if weighing his words for veracity. "You certainly kept me safe this morning. In the confusion and with Molly's injury and all, I'm not sure I even thanked you properly."

"Thank me now by letting me stay."

She sighed. "Very well. If I can't trust the man

who pulled me from the 'jaws of death'"—she crossed her eyes, stuck out her tongue, and gave a quick imitation of her mother's histrionics at the dinner table, collapsing back into her chair in a fake swoon—"whom can I trust?"

Rhys swallowed back a laugh but grinned so widely his cheeks hurt.

Then her expression sobered. "Thank you, Rhys. Truly."

"It was my pleasure."

"However, most people would not consider having a rake in my boudoir the least conducive to my safety."

She had him there. Perhaps he'd been wrong to be so honest with her. Then he noticed she bunched her wrapper tightly in her fists, the only outward sign of her inner turmoil. She'd just learned someone had tried to do her harm, yet she wasn't dissolving into a frantic puddle.

His respect for her ticked up several notches. Rhys reached across the space between them and took one of her hands between his. Despite the warmth emanating from the banked fire, her skin was icy.

"I give you my word, Olivia. Nothing will pass between us that you don't wish as well." He brought her hand to his lips and pressed a chaste kiss to it. He detected a slight tremble in her fingers. The softness of her skin made him ache to do more, but if he was going to win back her trust, he needed to be on his best behavior. "On my honor as a dissolute libertine, I so swear."

She laughed, covering her mouth with her other hand to muffle the sound.

"I like hearing you laugh." He rubbed the pad of

his thumb across the back of the hand that he still held. "You ought to do it more often."

"Not recommended when there's a man in my chambers, I expect." To his surprise, she smiled and actually squeezed his fingertips.

"Quite right. In this situation, there *are* better things to do."

"No doubt." She lifted a brow at him. "Those 'better things' are also not recommended for a young woman whose chief value is the possession of a maidenhead."

"No matter what else might happen this night," he said, lacing his fingers with hers; the tremble he'd noticed earlier ceased, "I promise you'll greet the dawn in the same state of purity you now enjoy. However, it's your choice whether or not you become a knowledgeable virgin."

Wide-eyed, she gazed at him, as if she were trying to penetrate to the last wrinkle of his misshapen soul.

She really ought to turn away.

His profligate life of the past three years rose up to taunt him. The last thing he deserved was this delicate creature treating him as if he weren't some sort of monster. She should raise the alarm, call out the peasants with pitchforks, and have him tossed off her father's estate for good.

Instead she did the last thing he expected.

"If I were to decide to let you educate me," she said with only a slight quaver in her voice, "what would the first lesson be?"

Chapter 10

HIS HOT GAZE SIZZLED OVER HER.

Dear God, please don't let the man ask me to repeat myself. I doubt my voice will work.

"Are you sure, Olivia?" he said, a hint of a smile playing around his firm lips. "Though knowledge is much to be desired, and believe me, this sort of learning is far more pleasurable than doing a row of sums, you can't un-know something once you've learned it. You must be certain this is what you want before we begin."

By seeming to take away his offer to open the door to sensuality, he only made her want it more.

"One lesson," she whispered. "One only."

There. She'd said it. Just as there was no way to undo the kiss he'd given her that morning, there was no way for her to unsay the words.

"Very well, if you're sure," he said. "Stand up and take off your wrapper."

She gasped. "My wrapper?"

"If you're going to repeat every directive before you do it, this will take a very long time." He leaned back in the chair and hooked an ankle over his knee, like a pasha contemplating his latest concubine. "Come to think of it, these things shouldn't be rushed. Whenever you're ready, then. Unless, of course, you've lost your courage."

Thought her a nervous Nellie, did he? She'd show him courage. She stood, unbelted her wrapper, and quickly began to yank it off.

"No, no, not as if you're killing snakes. Take your time. These things are meant to be savored." He stood and draped the garment back around her shoulders. "Close your eyes. Let it drift off one shoulder and down your arm. Just so. Now the other. Very good. Feel the texture of the fabric as it sloughs off."

"I can't," she said, her eyes scrunched tightly. "My nightrail has long sleeves. The wrapper isn't actually touching me."

"If you can't use your imagination, that's easily remedied. Take off the nightrail too."

"What?" Her eyes flew open.

"You wanted the first lesson. Here it is. Your body is beautiful and was designed to give you pleasure. You only need to focus, to revel in the sensations, and your body will do the rest."

She snorted. "In a pig's eye."

"You don't believe me?"

"I don't believe my body is beautiful, no."

"Then that is your first error and one we shall have to correct immediately. Come." He took her hand, led her toward the long looking glass in the corner, and positioned her so she could see herself. "The light isn't the best here, but it will serve. Now stand still."

Olivia watched his face in the mirror as he reached

around and untied the bow at the neckline of her prim nightrail. He was utterly intent on her. If the focused expression on his face was any indication, *he* believed her body was beautiful.

Or at least imagined it might be.

He unbuttoned the line of seed pearls that marched down the front of the garment. A piece of her came undone along with each button. Then he parted the fabric with deliberate slowness, drawing his fingertips along her collarbones as he exposed more of her skin to view. Pleasure sparked in the wake of his touch.

"You see? Smooth, silky, beautiful," he murmured into her hair.

Her breath ran shallow as he pushed the nightrail off one shoulder and let it slide down her arm. One breast was bared in the light of the fire, its tip a hardened nub. When she caught him looking at it in their shared reflection, her nipple actually throbbed.

She pressed a palm against it to still the strange ache.

"No, you don't," he said, gently moving her hand from her breast. "No hiding from yourself."

"But it...I..." She could find no words for what she was feeling. It had happened before when he kissed her, and now that dull throb between her legs returned. All he had to do was look at her and the low drumbeat started.

"It's all right," he said. "What you're feeling is perfectly natural."

"How could you know what I'm feeling?"

"Because I'm feeling the same sorts of things, only from a male perspective," he said, meeting her gaze in the mirror. "Every sensation is heightened, every touch potent with meaning." He ran his palm from her shoulder down her arm to engulf her hand in his. The sleeve of her nightrail fell away so her ribs and the indentation of her waist on one side were visible in the looking glass. He reached around and cupped her exposed breast.

Her breath hissed in over her teeth.

"I love holding you like this," he murmured and pressed a string of soft kisses to her nape. His hand was so warm, almost feverish on her skin. His thumb circled her nipple, making the ache even stronger.

She leaned back, reveling in the hard maleness of him. She'd always thought of herself as all angles and elbows, but in comparison to him, she felt soft. Feminine. Even her small breast seemed perfectly large enough, cradled as it was in his sheltering palm.

His kisses strayed to the side of her neck and up to her earlobe. He took the bit of flesh between his lips and sucked. All the air fled from her lungs in a whoosh. While he distracted her with that torrent of sensation, he pushed the nightrail off her other shoulder. The garment slid down and would have slipped past her hips to the floor if she hadn't caught it and clutched it to her waist.

"What are you doing?" she asked.

He straightened to his full height and eyed her reflection. The crown of her head fit neatly beneath his chin. "Showing you that you're beautiful. All of you. Don't you want to see that you are?"

All of her. Surely he didn't mean that.

"I've heard that even some husbands and wives might not ever see each other in the altogether," she said.

"Correct me if I'm wrong, but completely disrobing is not required in order to do the necessary, is it?"

"*Do the necessary*? Why on earth would you make something so pleasurable sound like a chore? From whom have you been taking sexual advice?"

Some of her information had come from giggled conversations with other girls who were likely as ignorant as she. Knowledge of the basic mechanics of the act came from her close association with horse breeding.

Then there was Mrs. Noddlingham's *Practical Advice for Young Ladies of Quality*, a book her mother had given her in lieu of actually talking to her about what passes between a man and a woman in the marriage bed. The book was light on specifics, but according to Mrs. Noddlingham, disrobing wasn't actually required for taking a bath either.

"*A chaste girl might do very well to bathe in her shift,*" Mrs. Noddlingham advised, "*in order to avoid seeing her own body and thereby entertaining any lewd thoughts that unwholesome sight might engender.*"

The sight of her bare body in the mirror didn't seem particularly unwholesome, and Olivia wouldn't class any of her thoughts as lewd. She was more bewildered than anything else. Olivia wished now that she'd asked Babette about it. Surely one who'd been a lady's maid for a courtesan would be a fount of sensual information.

"It might surprise you to learn that I do know something about the subject," she said, hoping to sound worldly while trying to ignore the way he continued to massage her breast. "Because, ah…" He gave her nipple a little flick and the shock of it resonated to her toes. "Er…you see, I've…I've read a bit about marital urges."

"Marital urges. Lord spare me. Something that could be called 'doing the necessary' with your clothes on is not my idea of how to satisfy any sort of urge, marital or otherwise." He cupped her other breast as well. "There's nothing about what you and I are doing that's 'necessary,' but you can't deny it's fun."

He was right. It was fun. Her skin was glowing. Her insides were a riot of excitement. She'd never felt more alive.

Or more guilty.

"It's also wicked."

He grinned at her. "That, my dear, is part of its charm." Then the grin faded. "But the truth is you are still as pure as when we began this lesson, are you not?"

"If you want to split hairs, I suppose—"

"A simple yes will suffice. In fact, 'yes' is all I want to hear from you for a while." Rhys smoothed his palms down her ribs, the calluses at the bases of his fingers nicking her skin with prickles of pleasure. He settled them on her hip bones where the nightrail neckline was still perched. "May I show you how beautiful you are all over?"

Yes, please. I know I'm not plump and pretty like Miss Amanda Pinkerton. I know my hips are too narrow and my legs too thin. I know my—

"Olivia?"

She swallowed hard. "Yes," she whispered. "Show me."

❧

Rhys drew a deep breath. Wanting had left him hard put to keep his voice from going ragged. As well as hard in another way. Now it would take all his self-control not to go too far with this first lesson. He'd meet Mr. Alcock's expectations eventually. There was no need to rush matters.

Olivia trusted him. He wasn't about to betray her tonight. Not when he needed her trust in order to keep her safe.

Gently, he eased her nightrail down, over her hips, past her lovely heart-shaped bum, and let it drop to the floor. He purposely didn't look in the mirror. He wanted her to watch him as he took in the exquisite lines of her back, her buttocks, and legs. He wanted her to see the glow of masculine approval in his face, because he was sure he was fairly lighting the room with it.

Rhys ran his fingertips across her shoulders and down her spine. He dallied at the small of her back and then traced the crease under each bum cheek.

"Oh!" she squeaked out.

"Like that, did you?"

"It was…enlightening."

"In what way?" He met her eyes in the mirror now. She dropped her gaze. "I'm learning that certain parts of my body seem to be linked to other parts in ways I'd hitherto not suspected."

He reached around and slipped a finger under her chin. "Look at me."

When she looked up at his reflection, the whites showed beneath her dark irises, making her eyes seem even larger than usual. Her mouth parted softly. She looked so vulnerable, as if she hung upon his next words.

"You are beautiful, Olivia," he said softly. "In every part." He let his gaze sweep down the mirror past her breasts, her slender waist, her tight little belly button, to the sleek triangle of light brown curls at the apex of her thighs. "Especially there."

He looked back up at her face and smiled.

She caught her bottom lip with her teeth for a moment, and then a smile stole over her, luminous enough to brighten the whole room. Rhys knew he should feel guilty over what he was doing with this innocent, but if he helped her believe in how lovely she really was, surely that wasn't a bad thing, was it?

Of course, he'd be the first to admit he was a bit fuzzy on the whole concept of good versus bad of late.

Once, his sense of "ought-ness" had been as well-honed as a preacher. One ought to do this. One ought not to do that. Even if his actions often placed him on the outside of the fence of propriety, at least he knew where the fence was.

Now he wasn't so sure.

He shook off his niggling conscience and pressed a kiss to her temple. "Do you feel beautiful?"

"When you look at me like that, I do."

"Then you should let me be your mirror all the time." He rested his hands on her shoulders and was pleased to find she was only trembling a little. She wasn't afraid of him.

Perhaps she should have been.

"You said parts of your body seem to be connected in unexpected ways. When I touch you here—" he circled her breasts with his hands, teasing her skin and reveling in the way her nipples responded to his touch, "where else do you feel it?"

Her eyelids fluttered closed for a moment, and a look

of pure ecstasy made her brows pull toward each other. When he rolled one of her nipples between his thumb and forefinger, her eyes popped open again.

"There, of course," she said. "But also in...well, it's rather like the zing of a bowstring inside me."

"And let me guess, the zing ends right here." He slid his hand over her flat belly and covered her sex.

Her ribs shuddered and her jaw dropped.

Don't scream, he thought furiously. *Please don't scream.*

Chapter 11

A SOFT "OH" ESCAPED HER LIPS. OLIVIA PULSED UNDER his hand, and it seemed for a moment as if all the heat in her body centered itself in that small triangle between her legs. To be held so tenderly. Especially to be held so tenderly *there* was a gift she'd never expected to receive.

He accepted her. He found her fair. Everywhere.

Her chest was full to bursting.

"Every touch is potent with meaning," she whispered, repeating what he'd said earlier. Now the words sang in her heart. More than her body stood naked before him. Her soul shivered in ecstasy over the way his hand cupped her. The tip of one of his fingers slipped into her intimate crevice and she nearly unraveled. "What meaning?"

"Hmm?" He didn't stop the string of kisses he was lavishing on her neck.

She covered his hand with hers, stilling his questing fingers. "What does this touch mean?" she said with more emphasis.

"It means I find you desirable. It means I want to give you pleasure."

"That's all?"

"Isn't that enough?" He brushed a sensitive spot between her legs and her breath hitched in gasps over the delight of his touch. "I don't want to take from you, Olivia. I want only to give."

It ought to have been enough, but it wasn't. Not for this level of soul nakedness. He ought to at least care for her a little as well.

Stop.

His fingers moved with tantalizing slowness, teasing that swollen spot. She sagged against him, unsure her legs would support her.

Hadn't she asked him to stop? She thought she had. Or maybe she only thought it. It was hard to tell. The way her body bloomed under Rhys's gentle caress crowded out impulses from her brain.

"Please, Rhys," she managed.

"Hush now. No need to plead. Just be patient. I promise every knot will be untied."

Knots. That was it exactly. How did he know how tangled up her insides felt?

Oh, that's right, she reminded herself. *The man's a rake, a libertine, a…*his fingers found that spot again and bliss washed over her…*a god in human form.*

He sucked the tender skin at the juncture of her neck and shoulder. One hand smoothed over her breasts, teasing and massaging her nipples.

And his other hand undid her completely.

Tightness gathered, her insides folding back on themselves like a Gordian knot. Then like Alexander in one clever stroke, Rhys loosed her and she came untied.

Her limbs shuddered and she would have collapsed,

but he scooped her up in his arms, holding her close while an ever-expanding circle of bliss radiated outward in concentric rings. She pressed her cheek against his chest, gratified to hear his heart galloping beneath her ear. If his rapid heartbeat was any indication, she wasn't the only one who felt as if she'd just run a marathon. And won.

Still carrying her, Rhys strode across the room and gently laid her down on her bed. Then he stretched out beside her as she tugged up the sheet and tucked it under her armpits. She might be naked under the linens, but as long as they were both in the bed, it felt marginally safer to have that thin shield of fabric between them.

Rhys propped himself up on an elbow, leaned down, and dropped a kiss on the tip of her nose. "How was that for a first lesson?"

"Illuminating," she said as her heart rate began to return to normal. And with it came the burning desire to know how the act they'd just performed changed matters between them. She willed her voice to sound even and measured. "Everything has a purpose, and we were discussing meaning before we were pulled off-topic. What we just did, I know what it meant to me. What did it mean to you, Rhys?"

❧

He frowned. "I don't understand the question. Why does it have to mean anything?"

"Because we are not beasts. Because what we do with our bodies also involves our higher selves."

"What if I don't have a higher self?" Surely one

who plotted to deflower a virgin in order to foil a royal succession must have very little soul left.

"Nonsense. Every human being, no matter how mean their station, is more than mere flesh." She looked at him so intently, he was forced to look away lest she see the duplicity in him. "So I ask again, what did that mean to you?"

Rhys shifted uncomfortably. Meaning, emotions, these were all things he'd avoided since returning from Maubeuge. He couldn't afford the luxury of feelings. If he gave in to one, he suspected a flood of them would burst over the carefully crafted dam in his soul and he'd be swamped beyond reckoning.

"It meant satisfaction for us both."

She arched a brow at him and chuckled. "I rather think I was the only one of us who was satisfied."

"On the contrary, it pleases me to give you pleasure," he said. Not as much as if the delectable pleasure was reciprocated, but that was another lesson altogether. "I hope by now I've convinced you that your body is beautiful."

She smiled shyly. "It seems you found me so."

"Any man would," he assured her.

"Perhaps it's enough that you do," she said, cupping his cheek in her palm. "It's not as if this is a theory I care to test with all and sundry."

"I should hope not." He covered her hand with his. A tightness formed in his chest. Surprisingly, he found the notion that some other man might see her in the glorious altogether unsettling. But if he kept in mind that once he'd ruined her she'd never have to submit to that old rogue, the Duke of Clarence, it might help him ease his conscience.

"And now what?" Olivia asked, her eyes enormous in the dim light. She moved her hand down and splayed her fingers over his chest, sliding a fingertip between two buttons to tease his skin through only his small clothes. "I suspect there is a good deal more you could teach me."

Hell's bells, yes. There was an ocean of sensual experiences he'd love to give this neophyte. In fact, if he decided he wanted to finish Mr. Alcock's commission and mount her this very night, he knew he could do it. All he'd have to do was kiss and tease and drive her to aching fury without release and she'd be begging him to take her.

But something checked within him.

It was the same subtle warning that told him to tread lightly on the hunt to keep from frightening away his quarry. It was the prickles on the back of his neck that advised him to take a different route through the backstreets of London to avoid cutthroats and thieves. It was the inner sense that he ought to hold back his company of cavalry until the opportune moment when their concentrated charge would win the day.

He'd always wondered why his sixth sense hadn't warned him at Maubeuge that the entire company was walking into a trap. He hoped that meant the real traitor wasn't someone close enough to him he ought to have sensed duplicity. But Alcock had said he had evidence to damn him and both his friends, so Rhys couldn't be sure Nathaniel or Jonah were guiltless.

Looking down at Olivia's freshly satisfied form, he knew he certainly wasn't. There was probably a special chamber in hell reserved for men like him who took without even letting their victims know they'd been robbed. A bit of Olivia's innocence was gone forever, but, for the moment at least, she didn't seem to miss it.

In fact, she was all but inviting him to continue educating her, but he'd never regretted listening to the small inner voice that urged him to reconsider a course of action. And now he had a bothersome sense that he'd done all he ought and more with Olivia Symon for one night.

His body fought against the restraint like a blooded hound tugging at the leash, but he forced himself not to bound forward. If he took her tonight, his commission would be done and he could report back to Alcock. There'd be no more chances to instruct her in wickedness. She seemed to have an aptitude for it. The longer he kept her virginal, the longer he could dally with her. It was a selfish reason not to despoil her completely, but it worked.

"There are many more lessons in the art of lovemaking," he said, rising from her side and tugging down the front of his waistcoat. Unfortunately, it was the cutaway sort and did nothing to disguise his aroused state. "That is enough for you to absorb now."

"You still see this as a lesson?" She sat up, bunching the sheet over her breasts. "But I thought…" The languid, satisfied expression she'd been wearing vanished. "Never mind. Turn around so I can put my nightrail back on."

He obeyed. "Not much point, you know. I've already seen you without a stitch."

"Yes, well, in that case, you've had enough to absorb, haven't you?" Her voice sounded tight and testy. She had forgotten her own injunction against raising her voice. "If you're still determined to stay the night, you'll have to sleep in a chair."

Before he could warn her against speaking too loudly, he heard the rustle of linen and knew she'd climbed back into bed. As he settled back into one of the wing chairs, he also knew he'd been thoroughly dismissed.

He listened to her soft breathing and realized there was something he *didn't* know—what their encounter had meant to her. He'd been so intent on avoiding her question, he'd neglected to ask any of his own.

Now the moment when he might have asked and learned was gone.

He tried to get comfortable in the chair, but it was built for someone much smaller than he. He scooted its mate close enough for him to prop up his feet, but even that didn't bring him any closer to slipping into sleep.

Once he succumbed to slumber, nightmares of Maubeuge often invaded his dreams. He usually relied upon consuming sufficient quantities of liquor to keep them at bay, but he couldn't be an efficient watchdog if he were foxed beyond thinking.

So now since he wasn't going to sleep and hadn't consumed enough alcohol to obscure his brain, his long dormant conscience reared its pointed little head. He didn't regret goading Olivia into removing her clothing and discovering her own loveliness. She was beautiful and it was high time someone convinced her of it.

And he didn't regret giving her the first sexual peak of her life. The way her brows had drawn together in need, the way her lips parted in a rictus of pleasurable agony, the way she glowed like a thousand candles when she came...no, he couldn't regret revealing that part of her to herself. And he rather liked the fact that he'd be indelibly linked in her mind with her first climax.

But he did regret that he'd touched her with an ulterior motive, with the threats and promises of Fortesque Alcock urging him on like a dark angel on his shoulder.

She wanted it to mean something. What it meant was Rhys Warrington was worse than a dog.

Chapter 12

"MADEMOISELLE," BABETTE'S CHEERY VOICE ROUSED Olivia from a sound sleep. "Are you well, *chérie*? If you do not make to rise soon, you will be missing the breakfast."

Babette drew back the heavy damask curtains to allow long shafts of sunlight to stream into the room.

Olivia pulled up the sheets over her head to shield her eyes. She didn't want to move. The linens were that perfect drowsy temperature they always assumed just before she had to leave them. She had sunken into the feather tick so deeply it curved around her in a warm embrace. And to make her bed even more enticing, her whole body still basked in an afterglow of the pleasure Rhys Warrington had introduced her to last—

Heart suddenly pounding, Olivia sat bolt upright in bed. There was no sign of Lord Rhys. Relief washed over her. He'd even reset the wing chairs over the indented spots on the carpet so no one would ever guess he'd passed the night in one of them. She suspected that awkward arrangement meant he didn't get much sleep. She, on the other hand, had slept so soundly, she'd not been aware of when he slipped out of her chamber and back to his own.

She supposed she ought to thank him for that. Clearly there was something about sensual release that allowed a body to sink into slumber so deep, it was near oblivion. And he'd guarded her reputation by taking care not be caught there. He'd been more careful than she.

Of the two of them, she'd been the wanton one. He'd remained fully clothed while she stripped bare as a peeled twig. She'd allowed him to look at her, touch her, all of her, for pity's sake! She'd let him take her to some dark, unfathomable place, a place that she never suspected existed inside her, and made her burst into glorious light.

How on earth had she outdone an admitted rake for scandalous behavior?

"And what shall mademoiselle wear this fine day?" Babette singsonged.

"I have my choice between black, black, or black," Olivia said. "I'm sad about Princess Charlotte and her son, of course, and the proprieties must be observed, but I'm mortally sick of nothing but black to wear. Some women look pale and interesting in mourning. Miss Pinkerton, for example, positively blooms in it."

"*Oui*, it is often the case with such dark hair and eyes," Babette said. "An exotic air, that one, and only more mysterious when she is draped in black."

Olivia would never be classed as mysterious. Her mourning clothes washed her complexion of all color and made her look as if she'd taken too many of her mother's liver pills.

She shook her head to clear away these unaccustomed thoughts. Since when did she care so much how she looked?

"But mademoiselle does not have to choose black this day," Babette said. "Only this morning, word has come from London that the mourning for your poor princess, it is lifted. *Alors*, you may choose whatever your heart desires."

"Whatever my heart desires…" Rhys Warrington's handsome face rose unbidden in her mind. He'd certainly introduced her to some new and bewildering desires. She glanced guiltily at the looking glass. Had she truly stood there, bare as an egg before it, while Rhys Warrington played his wicked games with her body?

The whole episode was tinged with a fuzzy echo of unreality. It smacked of the same ephemeral mistiness that dreams take on in the cold light of day. Surely it didn't actually happen.

The disconcerting flutter in her belly confirmed that it actually had.

"Mademoiselle, does something vex you?"

Not something. Someone.

Everyone should have a safe inviolate place within themselves where their secret self dwells. Someplace to think outrageous thoughts without censure, to imagine things as one wished them to be without worrying about how things might turn out if they actually happened. Olivia used to have just such solitary place tucked away in her mind, but now that private enclave seemed to have a permanent resident besides her own vibrant imagination.

Rhys Warrington had insinuated himself into her secret life so deeply she doubted she'd ever be free of him.

"Mademoiselle Olivia."

She startled and looked back at her maid. Babette was still waiting for her orders about a gown.

"The honey-gold wool, I think," she said. "And lay out the green pelisse. I'll go to the stables to see how Molly fares after I break my fast."

"Alas, that will not be possible." Babette's rosebud mouth tightened into a brief moue of apology. "Your mother, she craves a word with you, *tout de suite*. She waits for you in her apartments."

Mrs. Symon's suite of rooms sprawled over the entire third floor of the north wing. In addition to a sumptuous boudoir that would probably put Princess Charlotte's to shame, Beatrice Symon possessed a private bath with a large copper tub. A lumber room held all her trunks packed full to bursting with out-of-season clothing, hats, shoes, parasols, fans, and assorted frippery. There was also an elegant salon where Olivia's mother frequently held court with her "intimate friends." To be invited to Beatrice Symon's apartments meant glittering entertainment for a chosen few, patronage for an artist or poet, and a healthy commission for a modiste or milliner.

For Olivia, it usually meant a tongue-lashing.

❧

"Don't slouch so," her mother advised. "How shall Jean-Pierre fit you properly all slumped over like that?"

This time the tongue-lashing was accompanied by

fittings with the French designer her mother had taken under her wing as soon as he landed on English soil. Jean-Pierre du Barry was an acknowledged genius in all things haute couture. In order to ensure his designs were available exclusively to the women of the Symon household, Jean-Pierre was in permanent residence at Barrowdell Manor with a half-dozen seamstresses at his command to bring his creations to life. In the Symon's London townhouse, he had his own studio space, drawing and designing and ordering huge quantities of silks and lace to his heart's content.

Like all Beatrice Symon's fashion choices, this one was spot-on. Jean-Pierre du Barry was a terror with silk moiré. He produced miracles with a bit of lace, a little judicious ruching, and the occasional flounce. He was an engaging gossip, always knowledgeable about what transpired in every great house on both sides of the Channel. He also quietly rejoiced in his notorious lineage, claiming to be the grandson of the French king's favorite mistress.

"Your mother is right, Miss Symon," Jean-Pierre said, pronouncing her name as if it were "see-moan." His speech was only slightly garbled due to the handful of pins bristling from between his lips. "You spoil the line of the gown when you hunch your shoulders so."

"But the neckline is cut so low," she protested. Her small breasts rose like half-moons from the froth of scarlet lace that scarcely concealed her pink nipples.

"And that is why the gown has boning built into it. No need for stays, no need for a chemise. It is all-in-one," he said, removing the pins and securing a bit of extra fabric into another dart. "The fitting, it is oh-so-important. The gown should feel like a second skin. No one but you can wear it. And I doubt I need to warn you, ma'm'selle, but you must take care not to gain or lose any weight between now and the night of the ball," Jean-Pierre went on. "I cannot be held responsible for the consequences if you do."

"Ball? What ball?"

"Next month, when your father returns from London, we'll have a ball here at Barrowdell. Jean-Pierre has agreed to help me with the preparations," Mrs. Symon said, then turned her attention back to the designer. "Nothing too extravagant, now. Not more than one hundred people, you know. I want everything to be very high-in-the-instep. Very exclusive. It will be the event of the year. Of the decade, no, the century, I warrant."

Even given her mother's natural effusiveness, this seemed an excessive prediction, but Olivia knew better than to voice that opinion.

"After all," her mother said, waving her hand loftily, "how often does a royal duke announce his engagement?"

"The Duke of Clarence is coming here?" Olivia said.

"Why else would we be having a ball?"

"But...the agreement hasn't been formalized yet," she said, panic roiling her belly. "Has it?"

"No, not yet, but don't fret, darling. Your father's letters are very encouraging. And Lord Rhys is here to make sure all is well on this end. I'm sure the dear boy will send in glowing reports about you." Her artfully plucked brows drew together in a frown. "I do hope he neglects to mention your unfortunate equestrian accident, but one really can't blame him if he decides to take credit for saving the life of the future Queen of England."

Her mother clapped a hand over her mouth for a moment. Then she sighed and a satisfied smile spread over her features, turning up even the corners of her eyes in happiness.

"There. I actually said it. My little girl…the future queen!"

"Mother, that's not at all certain. Even if I wed the Duke of Clarence"—which seemed a more distasteful prospect each time she thought about it—"it does not signify that he will ascend to the throne. There's the small matter that his father still lives and his older brother…"

"The king's health is failing—God bless His Majesty, I'm sure—and as for the Prince Regent, he'll never get another legitimate heir. Clarence is next in line and his issue will assuredly wear the crown! Oh, that I may live long enough to see it."

Olivia sighed. "Mother, you might be a veritable Methuselah and never see that."

"Hush, child." She put two fingers to Olivia's lips. "Don't say such things. Don't even think them. Do you want to tempt the devil? The crown is ours—I mean, yours—to lose."

"She will never lose the chance for a crown in this gown." Jean-Pierre finished turning and pinning the hem and rose to his feet. Then he floated across the room in his gliding stride and returned, carrying a long mirror. "Voilà! I give you a royal duchess if ever there was one."

He held the looking glass up with a flourish before Olivia, inviting her to admire his handiwork. She stared at her reflection.

The gown played to her greatest strengths, emphasizing her slender lines, while subtly enhancing her meager curves. Even though Olivia had been accustomed to fine fabrics and embellishments since she was in leading strings, the lace and subtly inset jewel adornments on this gown were far more intricate and elegant than anything she'd ever worn before.

It was a gown fit for a princess.

Amazingly enough, she did credit to it. The warm red color made her exposed skin glow like alabaster. The design of the gown swept the eye upward and focused all attention on her face where her eyes, which were often a non-descript hazel, had taken on a decidedly moss green tint.

The girl in the mirror stared back at her, calm and regal. This reflection was so different from the one Rhys Warrington had shown her. Stripped bare, she'd been a sensual creature, passionate and adventurous.

The cool-eyed princess who looked back at her now was another being altogether. The young woman in this mirror would never let another see her secret soul, never bare her deepest longings in a wanton display.

Which one was the real Olivia?

Her mother expected her to be the elegant, unruffled young woman she seemed now, the one with a level head on her shoulders fit for a crown. The Duke of Clarence expected her to be his private bank and producer of royal children. And Rhys...

She didn't know what he expected. He said he'd come to her chamber in order to protect her, and yet their time together quickly degenerated into a lesson in lasciviousness. Her cheeks heated.

She was still a virgin, through no fault of her own. Rhys was the one who stopped matters. He'd had the opportunity to dally with her last night, and yet he'd halted the lesson before any lasting harm was done.

If the whole interlude was a test of character, she'd failed miserably. Tears gathered at the corner of her eyes, but she blinked them back.

"Oh, my dear, it's all right," her mother said, hugging her and laying a cool cheek alongside Olivia's hot one. "I'm so very happy too."

Chapter 13

RHYS CUT THE APPLE INTO NEAT SECTIONS WITH HIS pocketknife. Holding his palm flat beneath Molly's soft lips, he offered small wedges of it to the mare. She whickered her appreciation between bites and moved as close to Rhys as the suspended sling allowed. He patted her shaggy neck, heavy with her winter coat, and inhaled the homely smells of warm horseflesh and fresh straw.

Time spent with a horse was never time wasted. Rhys always found the quiet companionship gave a man a chance to think, and he had more than enough to think about. Who had tampered with Olivia's saddle? What sort of evidence did Alcock really have that might exonerate him for the disaster at Maubeuge? And how in hell had Olivia dropped off to sleep so quickly last night when he was up for hours willing his body to settle?

All these things and more tumbled in his head as he spoke softly to Molly and ran a currycomb over her shaggy coat. There was another reason for his trip to the stable besides having a solitary think.

He knew if he waited there long enough, Olivia would come to see to the welfare of her mare. Since she had avoided him by not coming down to breakfast, this was the best way to be sure he'd encounter her on the rambling Symon estate.

She'd looked so delectable when the first rays of sunlight filtered through the slit in her curtains. Her mouth softly parted in the relaxation of sleep, her breasts rising and falling beneath the linens; it was all he could do not to climb under the sheets and wake her properly. Instead he'd slipped out of the chamber before the household roused and Olivia's maid had a chance to catch him there.

Some rake I am, he thought ruefully.

While he waited for Olivia to come out to the stable, Mr. Thatcher came in to muck out the stalls and lay fresh straw for bedding.

"'Morning, your lordship," he said. "D'ye want me to saddle your mount?"

"No, thank you. I'm only here to check on Molly's progress."

"Aren't ye the kind one? She'll be off her front hooves for another couple weeks, but the old girl isn't off her feed," Mr. Thatcher said with a satisfied chuckle. "I take that as a sign that she'll mend, though I doubt she'll ever be sound enough to jump again."

Rhys ran a hand down her foreleg to examine the injured fetlock, glad he hadn't put her down in the ravine. The little mare seemed a sweet sort. "I daresay your employer is wealthy enough, he could afford to keep a horse as a pet, a sort of glorified dog, even if it wasn't sound enough to be ridden."

"Ye've the right of it there, I'd expect. If Miss Olivia asks him, there's not much Mr. Symon won't do for her," Mr. Thatcher said. "Fair dotes on all his girls, he does, but Miss Olivia, well, she's his favorite. Always says she reminds him of his dear departed mother, ye see. Same hair and eyes, Mr. Symon says. The rest of his brood takes after Mrs. Symon, ye understand."

"I haven't seen any of Miss Symon's sisters," Rhys said.

"And ye're not likely to. Still in the schoolroom, they all are, though Miss Calliope is fifteen and has been pestering her folks to let her come out this spring. O' course, once Miss Olivia's match with the royal duke is made, talk below stairs is that the sky's the limit for the younger ones."

Her sisters' futures were riding on Olivia's slim shoulders.

"For a doting father, Mr. Symon doesn't seem to spend much time with his daughters," Rhys said. "I've yet to meet him either."

Mr. Thatcher scratched his head. "And that's not like him, but something mightily important must be keeping him in London. Reckon it's to do with the royal duke and all. Mr. Symon didn't even make it home for Christmas."

Rhys made a mental note to send his valet Mr. Clyde on a mission to discover more about Mr. Symon's business and general whereabouts. If his business interests were at all dodgy, Olivia's father might have made an enemy who'd harm his favorite daughter as a way to hurt him.

"I suspect having all these houseguests has increased your workload," Rhys said, anxious to keep the information flowing since Mr. Thatcher seemed disposed to share it.

"Not as much as ye might think," Mr. Thatcher said. "Though all of Mrs. Symon's guests make use of the stables and ride a bit for form's sake."

"Any here more often than others?" Rhys wondered. Someone who frequented the stable might go unremarked while they altered Olivia's saddle.

"No, not so's you'd notice," Mr. Thatcher said. "Though Lord Percy is partial to taking out the gig for a run into the village tavern. And, present company bein' the exception, your lordship, none of the guests see to the care of their horses with any regularity." Mr. Thatcher gave him a gap-toothed grin and headed toward the stable door. "Well, that's all to the good though since that's my job, innit? Good day to ye, milord."

Rhys couldn't ask him the questions that burned his tongue most hotly. Which of the houseguests had reason to wish the match between the daughter of the house and the Duke of Clarence not to proceed? And who was willing to go to such bloody-minded lengths to see to it? Rhys was no closer to finding out who tampered with Olivia's saddle than when he first discovered the sabotage.

"Wish you could talk, old girl," he said to Molly.

"What would you expect her to say, Lord Rhys?"

His head jerked up sharply. He'd been so lost in thought he hadn't heard anyone's footsteps, but there was Miss Amanda Pinkerton, chin propped on the stall door, peeking over at him. She smiled, dimpling prettily.

"I expect she'd say, 'Thanks for the apple,'" he said with a shrug.

Molly snorted.

"She says she already thanked you," Miss Pinkerton

said, her dark eyes snapping with fun, "but you obviously didn't understand her."

"That's entirely possible. I frequently misunderstand what females are trying to tell me."

"Oh, I very much doubt that, my lord," Miss Pinkerton said, giving him the languid blink of an accomplished coquette.

The spot between Rhys's shoulder blades tingled. It wasn't unheard of for a young woman to insinuate herself into a compromising situation with a man of title or wealth in order to force a marriage. A chance moment of seclusion, an ill-considered kiss, or even the accusation that one had taken place and a fellow could be headed for the altar faster than a team of runaway horses if the lady's family was of a mind to force matters.

Perhaps Miss Pinkerton hadn't been in England long enough to know that Rhys's title was a mere courtesy and his financial situation was fluid at best. Still, his shoulder blades were never wrong and they seemed to be warning him this lovely miss was a parson's mouse-trap waiting to be sprung.

"Did you learn to ride in India?" he asked, hoping someone else would join them shortly. For the moment, the stall door separated them, but the stab of nerves reminded him why he'd always avoided virgins as if they carried the pox. God save him from debutants.

"Oh, yes, I rode every day as a child," she said. "Of course, riding a horse is easy after you've ridden an elephant. The fine fellow down two stalls is mine. An Arabian with a pedigree longer than most princes. Father bought him for me in Madagascar on the way Home. He's called Shaitan."

On hearing his name, the black gelding tossed his head and gave the slats in his stall door a vicious kick.

"It means devil," Miss Pinkerton said.

"No doubt he deserves it." Rhys gave Molly the last of the apple. "You must be quite accomplished to stay in the saddle of such a spirited beast."

Miss Pinkerton tilted her chin in a fetching manner. She'd turn heads once she reached London. A certain sporting class of fellow wanted his wife to be an ornament to his arm, and Miss Pinkerton was an embellishment to make any man proud. Even if her father could offer only a meager dowry, Rhys expected she'd not finish the Season without several offers of marriage.

Not that any would ever come from him. When Rhys ever thought about marriage, which wasn't often, the last thing he considered in a wife was a simpering China doll type. Marching through the decades with someone whose best asset was her appearance was bound to end in disappointment.

Time wounds all heels, my son. His father had been partial to mangling a few proverbs back in the days when he was still speaking to Rhys. *When you choose a wife, remember that a fashionable face now may sport three chins and a wart or two before death parts you. Look for a woman with something special inside her, and you'll spare yourself a lifetime of disappointment.*

Rhys shrugged off that remembered advice. He wasn't looking for a wife. Not ever.

"I'm frankly surprised that Miss Symon was thrown by this little mare. She looks too docile and too puny—the mare, I mean, of course." Miss Pinkerton laughed, a musical twitter of the sort that grated on

Rhys's ears. It didn't take much to imagine her with three chins and a wart.

"Miss Symon is a fine rider. Her equestrian skills are what truly kept her from harm," Rhys said sternly. "A lesser rider might have been killed."

"Oh, dear, I've upset you," she said. "That was never my intention, I assure you. I was just thinking how fortunate Miss Symon was that you were there to save the day. Only imagine. One moment, she's hurtling along toward certain destruction, and the next, she's safe in your arms." Miss Pinkerton gave a pudding-headed sigh. "It all sounds quite thrilling."

"Actually, it happened far too quickly to be thrilling," came a voice from the stable door. Rhys was more than a little relieved to find Olivia marching toward them. "The whole episode is a bit of a blur in my mind. And I was far too concerned for Molly at the time to even be aware of whose arms I was in. Besides, Lord Rhys comported himself like a perfect gentleman. I hope you didn't mean to imply the incident was something worthy of a scandal sheet, Miss Pinkerton."

"Oh, no, I didn't mean it like that," Miss Pinkerton sputtered. "I only thought it was romantic."

"Romantic? How can that be?" Olivia said. "Everyone knows Lord Rhys is only here on behalf of His Highness, the Duke of Clarence."

"Oh, but that only makes it more romantic, don't you see?" Miss Pinkerton said, her cheeks flushing rosily. "It's rather like the tale of Tristan and Isolde. You remember the one. He was supposed to deliver her to another suitor too, but he fell madly in love with her instead."

"If memory serves, that story ends rather badly for the lovers. They both end up dead. I assure you Miss Symon and I contemplate no such outcome," Rhys said with an indulgent smile. "I rather think you've read too many romances, Miss Pinkerton."

Olivia shot him a sharp look, then turned to Miss Pinkerton. "If you intend to ride, perhaps you should take Lord Rhys with you. That way if *you* feel the need to be swept from the back of a bolting horse, he'll be there to oblige."

"Very well," Miss Pinkerton said with a sniff. "Would you care to ride, my lord? I promise I sit a horse well enough *not* to need rescuing."

"Ordinarily, I would be honored to accompany you," Rhys said, "but unfortunately, I am expecting a message from the duke this morning and need to be available to send a reply immediately."

"Shall I ask Mr. Thatcher to show you over Barrowdell then?" Olivia suggested.

"No, that won't be necessary. I don't think I'll ride after all. I believe the weather may turn. Good day to you both." Miss Pinkerton gave Rhys a toothsome smile that tightened into a grimace when she looked at Olivia and then headed back to the manor.

Olivia ignored her, pushed open the stall door, and hurried to Molly's side.

"How's my brave girl this morning?"

"Full of apples," Rhys said. "Mr. Thatcher says she's eating well. It's a good sign."

Gently, Olivia ran a hand down the mare's injured leg. The muscles under Molly's thick coat shivered. "Still sore to the touch."

"So are you," he said, leaning against the side of the stall in order to stay out of Olivia's way as she smoothed her hands over Molly's withers and walked all the way around the mare to spread a blanket over her back and make sure it hung evenly on both sides. "You were rather sharp with your guest just now, you know."

"The Pinkertons are my mother's guests, not mine." Olivia dropped a handful of oats into a feedbag and settled it over Molly's nose. The mare's appreciative munching filled the air. "Amanda is a very silly girl who only wants to stir up trouble and—how was I sharp?"

"You delivered quite a set down. Miss Pinkerton meant no harm."

"Didn't she? All that foolishness about how thrilling the accident must have been. It was frankly terrifying. There was nothing thrilling about it." She picked up a currycomb and bent to give Molly's neck and chest several vigorous strokes. "You said yourself she'd been reading too many romances. And what about that nonsense about our situation being like Tristan and Isolde?"

"If she could see us wrangling now she'd entertain no such notions."

Her head popped up on the other side of the mare. "Quite right. You said it yourself. We contemplate no such outcome."

"I only meant we don't intend to end up dead as those lovers did." He stepped in front of her as she came around to brush Molly's other side so she had to stop. "If Miss Pinkerton had seen us last night in your chamber, she might feel completely vindicated."

Olivia shot him a glare that ought to have singed off his eyebrows. "Step aside."

"Not yet. I have a question for you first." He took a step toward her and she gave ground. "I took pains to make sure that no one saw me enter or leave your chamber. Our behavior in public has been beyond reproach. So why do you suppose Miss Pinkerton likens us to a pair of thwarted lovers?"

"That sounds like a question you should put to Miss Pinkerton." She ducked around Molly's broad rear and peered over the mare's back at him. "If you hurry, no doubt you can catch her."

"I'd rather catch you." He anticipated her dash for an escape and trapped her near the door between his arms and the side of the stall.

Olivia pressed her spine to the rough wood and held her arms tight to her sides lest he touch her. "Stop it, Rhys. You'll upset Molly."

At the sound of her name, the mare sidestepped and swiveled in her sling.

"No, I won't. I just gave her an apple. She's on my side, aren't you, girl?"

As if to encourage him, Molly nudged his back with her nose, pushing him closer to Olivia.

"You see? Molly trusts me."

"She doesn't know you like I do. Now let me pass."

"Not until you answer my question."

She crossed her arms over her chest. "How should I know why Miss Pinkerton has delusions of our romantic involvement?"

"I think she senses something you're trying to deny."

She studied the tips of his boots with absorption. "I don't know what you mean."

"Yes, you do." He cupped her chin and tilted her

head up so she had to meet his gaze. "There is a connection between us that's undeniable. Miss Pinkerton obviously caught wind of something hovering between you and me. I'm attracted to you. I'll not argue the point. And I'll wager you're not indifferent to me either."

"Not another wager." She clapped her hands over her ears. "The last one was responsible for last night."

He laughed. "No, no more wagers. But while we're on the subject of last night…you were adamant about knowing what being with you meant to me. But what did it mean to you?"

She dropped her gaze. "It meant that I am a rather easily led girl who let a rake fool her into an ill-considered adventure."

"So you thought it an adventure. Good. I like that. It was an adventure for me too."

She looked up sharply. "I find that hard to believe. An adventure implies something new, something previously unknown. You've been with countless silly women."

"I hadn't been with you before. And you're not silly." He palmed her cheek and traced her brow with his thumb. She trembled, but he knew it wasn't from cold. "You're brilliant and beautiful, Olivia. And passionate. And…you make me wish I hadn't been with any other women before you."

Her lips parted in surprise. "How can I believe that?"

He hadn't meant to say it. In fact, he'd trade a year in paradise to unsay it, but the words had just tumbled out. And blast it all, they were true. She'd said once that when two people share themselves they give away a piece of their heart they never get back. If that was so, he was missing a good many pieces of his. When he looked into her guileless eyes, he wished he was whole.

"You should believe me because I promised not to lie to you," he said.

"Oh, really? To whom did you make this promise?"

"To myself." He leaned toward her. The fresh scent of alyssums tickled his nostrils and made him ache to kiss her. "The first day I met you."

She peered up at him from under her lashes. If it had been any other girl but Olivia, he'd have called it a coquette's trick. "And do you lie so frequently, you have to make such promises to yourself often?"

"No, but perhaps you'll allow that sometimes a man is governed by expediencies that aren't conducive to full truthfulness."

He wanted to kiss her so badly, his soft palate arched as if from physical hunger. But she held herself so tight, so aloof; he didn't want to force her.

"So you're admitting you've not been fully truthful. Well, that's mysterious," she said. "You're here as the duke's agent. Is there something about His Royal Highness I should know?"

"I'm not at liberty to say."

Of course, he hadn't promised to tell her everything. And he couldn't very well tell her he'd come there to steal her maidenhead so she couldn't marry the Duke of Clarence. He'd only decided never to lie to her directly. It meant slicing his conscience thinly as a piece of paper, but it was the only way he felt he could continue his mission and not totally despise himself.

"When I tell you something," he said, "whether it's

about the duke or the price of tea in China or the way I find you absolutely irresistible, it will be the truth. You may believe me."

Her eyes widened.

Was not speaking the whole truth the same as lying?

Probably. But before he could puzzle out the moral conundrum, Olivia did something that surprised the question right out of his head.

She relaxed, letting herself melt against his body, wrapped her arms around his neck, and kissed him right on the mouth.

Chapter 14

SHE KNEW IT WAS THE WRONG THING TO DO. IF anyone caught them kissing in the stable, her mother's dreams of a crown for her would sizzle away like morning fog. But all sense of propriety fled from her mind. In its place, one truth sang in her heart.

Rhys Warrington found her irresistible.

Her. Irresistible.

How could she not kiss the man after a declaration like that?

Oh, he was delicious. And he smelled of saddle leather and warm horse. His mouth was sure and firm. When he slanted it over hers and his lips parted, she slipped her tongue in as he'd done to her.

It didn't matter whose tongue did the exploring. A French kiss was just as decadently wicked that way as the other. England had been at war with France on and off for more or less forever, certainly for the whole of Olivia's young life. But for the moment, she decided French culture had at least one thing to commend it.

Heartily.

Their kiss was a whole world. A circle of two.

A shared breath. Olivia felt certain their souls were mingling, all tangled up together, wandering from one body to the other, unsure which house of flesh they belonged in, but satisfied to share the space equally in both of them.

Rhys's kisses moved along her jaw and then down. Ripples of pleasure undulated in his wake.

"We ought to stop," she said, tipping her head to one side so he had full access to her neck. Propriety tried to rear its prim little head, but the heat gathering between her legs rendered her words breathy and unconvincing, even to her own ears. "We need to stop."

"Mm-hmm," he agreed between feather-light kisses, but he gave no sign he intended to stop.

"I mean it." She smoothed her palms over him, reveling in the solid expanse of his broad back, the warmth of him emanating through his wool jacket.

"I mean it too," he said as his fingers found the silver frogs that held her pelisse closed. Then suddenly his hands were on her breasts, kneading and caressing them through the sheer fabric of her column gown. Her nipples tightened, throbbing for him to touch and tease. His mouth dipped lower. For a moment, she wished she was wearing that new gown Jean-Pierre had designed for her with the built-in boning so she'd have two fewer layers separating them and a lower neckline that offered more of her décolletage.

"Rhys, please," she gasped when he rucked up her skirt and found the slit in her pantaloons. She was wet and swollen and aching for him. "Oh, please."

His questing fingers stopped, but he still held her. She pulsed into his palm, hot and needy. It wouldn't take long. She was almost there. She couldn't believe how quickly he'd driven her to that exquisite precipice, but there she was, teetering on the edge. He knew exactly what she liked, where her special spot was, and just how to stroke her. He could send her soul flying with another limb-bucking release. A flick or two of his talented fingers was all it would take.

"Please," she repeated.

"Please as in 'please stop' or 'please don't stop?'" he said in a hoarse whisper. It obviously cost him dear to halt long enough to ask.

Why had he given her a choice?

Please don't stop, she longed to say, but it wouldn't be fair. In a few minutes, she'd be sated and boneless as a cat and he'd still be…well, she could feel quite explicitly what he'd be since the full glorious length of his hardness was pressed against her hip.

How could she only take and never give? She loosed a shuddering sigh, trying to collect herself.

"Please stop," she whispered. "If anyone finds me like this, all mussed…"

His face went hard as winter oak, but he removed his hand and smoothed down her skirt.

Olivia bit her lip to keep from begging him not to. He refastened her pelisse, his gaze fixed on the silver frogs as he worked each fastener. His features were strained, his breathing ragged, but he won the struggle with the urges that drove them both.

"There," he said as he hooked the last frog. "You are now returned to an 'un-mussed' state."

Perhaps on the outside. Her insides were still definitely mussed.

She couldn't bring herself to meet his eyes. "If you'll excuse me, my lord—"

"Rhys. You agreed to call me Rhys," he said, grasping her arm so firmly she was sure it would leave a bruise. "Do not use my title to build a wall between us."

Didn't he realize she needed a wall? But she didn't want to argue with him. She was too weak. It was all she could do to keep the quaver out of her voice.

"Rhys, I need to spend some time in the hothouse with my orchids. Please let me pass."

His face was a war with itself for a few heartbeats, but finally he settled and released her arm. "I'll do better than that." He stepped back. "I'll walk with you."

"That's not necessary."

"Yes, it is." His tone was firm enough; it brooked no argument.

His hand resting lightly on her elbow was comforting. A complete separation would have been agony. When they left the stable, his hand shifted to the small of her back. Any place he touched felt as if it might burst into flames, but she didn't feel up to demanding they have no contact whatsoever. Especially when every inch of her skin wanted him to touch it with a fierceness that surprised her.

They walked in silence on the winter-hard path that led to the glass and iron structure housing her plants.

"I must have been mistaken," he finally said. "I thought you liked me a little."

"I do." The problem was she liked him rather too much. She'd never understood women who allowed themselves to be compromised by a man before. Had they no spine?

She was more sympathetic to the ruined girls now.

"Then if you do like me a bit, would you care to explain why you made me stop?"

She could protest that anyone might have stumbled upon them *in flagrante delicto*. She could argue that he was the Duke of Clarence's representative and she the said duke's possible royal fiancée and their outrageous behavior did neither of them any credit. She could point out that lust was one of the seven deadly sins.

But none of those would be the real reason.

"Because it didn't seem fair. I was doing all the taking," she said, darting a glance at him. "There was no way for me to give you pleasure."

He stopped walking, gave a little snort, and then a chuckle.

She kept going. "I fail to see the humor."

"I'm sorry. I shouldn't laugh when you're deadly serious," he said as he caught up with her. "There is pleasure aplenty in the giving of pleasure. This simply means you need another lesson tonight. Contrary to what you might think, you're still not a knowledgeable virgin."

Her belly quivered at the thought of more intimate education. "I don't think it's a good idea for you to come to my chamber."

Or for you to give me another lesson.

"The immediate reason for my being there—insuring your safety—has not changed. Until I discover who arranged for you and Molly to have an accident, you'll have my company by night." He waggled his brows at her. "Whatever else we may do once I'm there is, of course, your choice."

How could he make it all her responsibility? Why

was it her place to always say no? Society assumed a man could dally in any amount of sensual indulgence he wished so long as the woman didn't censure him. The world was indeed in error when it named females the weaker sex.

"You are impossible."

"Without doubt," he said agreeably.

They topped a small rise and the land surrounding the manor house of Barrowdell sprawled before them. In the distance toward the east, a conical hill of perfect symmetry rose from the meadow. No trees grew on its slopes, no hedge, only a thick stand of winter-brown grass.

"An ancient mound," Rhys said. "Hence the name Barrowdell, I gather."

Olivia nodded, grateful the subject had been changed. The thought of more sensual instruction from Rhys Warrington left her slightly light-headed.

"Papa has had scholars come from Oxford to look over the barrow. They found no way in. Some mounds do have an exposed entrance, I'm told, but this one is old enough that the wind and rain have covered it over with soil and Papa wouldn't give them leave to dig. But the scholars were of the opinion that it is a burial place of some sort. I think that's why Papa wouldn't allow them to excavate." A shrill wind whistled across the meadow, bending the winter grass before it in undulating waves. "He said the ghosts of Barrowdell have lain quiet all these years. No need to trouble their bones."

"A wise man, your father." A shadow passed over Rhys's face, and this time Olivia was sure she didn't imagine it. "Not all ghosts lie silent."

"Is there a ghost that vexes you?"

He looked down, his mouth drawn tight. A muscle worked in his cheek.

"I'm sorry," she said. "You don't have to answer. I shouldn't have asked."

"No, it's all right. Yes, I have ghosts. Every officer loses men under their command. It comes with rank," he said, tight-lipped. "It's never easy, and I suppose it shouldn't be."

Olivia walked on, deciding he'd say more or not as he chose. She wouldn't press him, but she was glad when he fell into step beside her.

"During the last battle of my command, things...went badly," he said. "I made a decision that day I've had to live with, but even now, I'm not sure it was the right one."

She remained silent but reached over to briefly squeeze his hand. If he was willing to speak of it, she was willing to listen. Whatever it was, she wondered if it was the cause of the premature streak of silver in his dark hair.

"My horse was wounded. Dying. Both forelegs shattered. My lieutenant, Morris Duffy, was also injured in a French volley. He took a round to the abdomen." Rhys cleared his throat before continuing. "The gelding was screaming and the French were overrunning our position. I had one shot left."

His Adam's apple bobbed in a hard swallow.

"No wound is a good one, but a gut shot is a particularly bad way to go. A man can linger a long while." His voice dropped to a whisper. "Duffy begged me to finish him."

Olivia's belly churned. "Did you?"

"No." He frowned at the distant barrow. From the faraway look in his eyes, she suspected he wasn't really seeing it. "I shot the horse, threw Duffy over my shoulder, and carried him behind the lines."

Olivia breathed a sigh of relief.

"The surgeons could do nothing for him. Duffy cursed me for three days, raving with fever before he finally died in bloated agony."

Rhys picked up his pace, and Olivia was forced to trot in order to keep up with him.

"You can't reproach yourself for this."

"Can't I? I gave a dumb animal more mercy than I showed Lieutenant Duffy."

"But you did the only thing you could do. Don't you think you'd carry even more guilt if you had shot him? I'm sure everyone you've spoken to about this says the same thing."

"I've never told this to anyone."

That stopped her in her tracks. Rhys trusted her with this horrible bruise on his soul. She would have to tread lightly lest she make it worse.

"And I don't know why I tell you now," he said, not slacking his pace for a moment. "Forget I said anything about it."

She'd never forget it. He trusted her.

"Contrary to what you may think, Rhys Warrington, you are not God." She stopped him with a hand to his forearm. "There was a chance, however slim, that the lieutenant might survive his wound. You couldn't take that chance from him. You did the right thing."

"I try to tell myself that, but I knew at the time there was no hope."

"There is always hope." She caught his hand between both of hers and held it tightly.

"I used to believe that." He smiled sadly at her. "I used to believe a lot of things."

"Like what?"

"That right would always triumph in the end. That a man's friends can be trusted to guard his back. That a merciful God looks down on us all with a loving eye."

She squeezed his hand. "You're right to believe those things because they are all true."

"No, they're not. I left them on a battlefield in France." He pulled away from her and walked on. "Next to my dead horse."

Chapter 15

RHYS TRUDGED ON, LENGTHENING HIS STRIDES. IT WAS beyond foolishness to tell her what had happened at Maubeuge. Did he imagine she could somehow offer him absolution?

There was no way she could understand, much less grant him peace over it. All she knew of life and death was what she'd been taught by her tutors and her vicar. She'd never looked into the face of a man who dreaded days of pain and putrefaction more than the great unknowable Dark. She hadn't heard Duffy's bleating pleas.

Or his virulent curses.

The stench of dying was on Rhys for days afterward. He'd stayed with Duffy to the end, leaving him only when the chaplain came. Rhys suffered with his lieutenant as Duffy lost his dignity and humanity by tortured degrees. A hundred times, Rhys wished he'd made a different choice and spared the man who'd been his trusted companion from that excruciating, demeaning death.

No one would have known it wasn't a French bullet

that carried Duffy off if Rhys had ended things for him on the battlefield.

But I'd know.

Men died in battle all the time, but this was different. This deliberate, willful taking of another life smacked of murder, however much Duffy begged for it.

Nevertheless, he was ashamed when Duffy suffered in hopeless agony. And when the lieutenant finally drew his last labored breath, Rhys was even more ashamed, because he was relieved to have it over.

Except that it wasn't over. He relived the whole thing countless times. The battle at Maubeuge was a miserable defeat in which all his actions were questioned. His decision about Duffy was just the final expletive-laced footnote to the dismal end of his military career.

He never should have brought it up to Olivia. Now, between one heartbeat and the next, the hated visions would crowd out his present reality and he'd be transported back to Maubeuge to experience those horrendous moments again.

It always started with a dull roar deep in his ears. The hellacious sulfur of spent cannons came next along with the coppery tang of blood. Then his head would fill with the distant bugle call of retreat, the clash of sabers, and shouts of men locked in mortal combat. And always there was Duffy's silent, accusing face, frozen in time, mouth drawn in a tight ring of despair as Rhys spent his last round into the thrashing gelding's head.

He steeled himself against the malevolent apparitions that were sure to come.

Ghosts that refuse to lie quiet indeed.

But to his surprise, no roaring rose up in his mind.

All he heard was the crunch of pea gravel under their feet, the rattle of bare limbs when the wind cut through the nearby woods, and Olivia's breathing as she labored to keep up with him.

He slowed his pace. When she slipped her hand into the crook of his arm, the tightness of unshed tears pressed against the backs of his eyes.

"You don't despise me?" he asked, tight-lipped.

"You vex me sorely sometimes, Rhys," she said softly, "but I could never despise you."

"Don't be too sure of that."

Once she learned his true reason for being at Barrowdell, she'd despise him with no effort at all. Ever since Maubeuge, it seemed he'd been faced with one winless choice after another. What to do with Olivia was only the latest in a long string of shite-covered crossroads.

He could destroy her or watch helplessly while Alcock used him to destroy his family. He thought he'd made the right decision, but now, with her slim hand tucked trustingly in his elbow, he wasn't so sure.

"Believe me, I know my own mind," she said, blithely unaware that she ought to run from him, shrieking all the way. "Though you may try to hide it, I think you're a good man."

For her sake, he almost wished he was.

The gravel path ended at the ornate wrought-iron door of the hothouse. He opened it and ushered her into the shelter, out of the blustery wind. Warm, moist air, rich with loam and earthy scents, washed over them. He helped Olivia out of her pelisse. Then he removed his garrick and hung both of them on pegs near the door. Another garment, a much patched but serviceable great coat, was already dangling from one of the pegs.

"Mr. Weinschmidt?" Olivia called out. When there was no answer, her brows drew together in a frown. "I'm so behind on the repotting, I sent him ahead to start on the *Dactylorhiza fuchsii*. He ought to be here. That's his coat."

If Mr. Weinschmidt was there, they should hear him puttering away with a trowel. The hair on the back of Rhys's neck prickled. The hothouse was too quiet.

"Mr. Weinschmidt? It's not like him to wander off." Olivia walked down the aisle between high benches laden with pots and seedlings. She tugged off her kidskin gloves as she went. Then she halted as if she'd run headfirst into an invisible wall. "Oh!"

Rhys hurried in front of her and saw what had stopped her so suddenly. A white-haired fellow was lying on his side on the hard-packed earth, his back curved like a question mark, his lips tinged with blue. His unseeing eyes were turned toward the iron girders overhead.

"Oh, Mr. Weinschmidt!" Olivia dropped to her knees beside him.

"Careful. Don't touch him." Rhys crouched beside her. "I'm no expert, but this death has the look of poison about it. Put your gloves back on."

To Rhys's relief, she obeyed him without question.

"Poison? But why would anyone want to hurt Mr. Weinschmidt?" A sob broke her voice. "He's been with the estate forever, a sweet old German who never harmed anyone or anything but aphids."

Olivia's chin quivered, but she didn't go to pieces or

keen hysterically like her mother would have if confronted with a dead body. Rhys could have kissed her.

He removed his gloves.

"If it's not safe for me to go gloveless, why—" Olivia began.

"Because I'll be careful and you might not be." He felt her stiffen beside him so he hurried to add, "Your concern for my safety is duly noted and appreciated."

He leaned over Mr. Weinschmidt and passed a hand over the old man's face to close his sightless eyes. Now, with the exception of the bluish tinge about his mouth and the general graying of his flesh, the little German looked as if he might have fallen into the light sleep of advanced age, albeit in a rather contorted position.

"His flesh is still warm," Rhys said. "He can't have been dead long."

A whiff of spirits wafted up from the body.

"He was a drinker," Rhys observed.

"I wouldn't say that. Oh, I know he hides a bottle of schnapps here in the hothouse behind the date palm. My mother has a firm policy against the help imbibing, but it was an open secret between us. Mr. Weinschmidt might tipple on occasion, but only if his rheumatism is plaguing him. You don't think the schnapps killed him?"

"No, but it may have made him less cautious than he should have been." Rhys studied the body, looking for a wound but found none. Poison still seemed the most likely cause of death. "Did he always work here in the hothouse?"

"For the last few years, yes. Mr. Weinschmidt was here even before Papa bought Barrowdell. He used to be the head gardener. He's the one who designed the maze." Her voice was flat and curiously impersonal, as if she were trying to push out as much information as she could without letting herself feel anything about it. "He wasn't strong enough for regular gardening anymore, but he didn't want to retire completely. He has no family, no place to go, so Papa kept him on to help me in the hothouse."

"What did you say he was repotting?"

"*Dactylorhiza fuchsii*. Common spotted orchids. We intend to plant them in a marshy bit of land this spring to see how quickly they colonize. Mr. Weinschmidt is really keen on the project and...I mean, he was keen on it." Her eyes filled with tears again, but she swiped them aside, obviously determined not to let her feelings stop her from answering his questions. "Lots of plants are poisonous if you ingest them, which I'm sure Mr. Weinschmidt knew. This species of orchid isn't poisonous to the touch."

"Then something else must have touched him."

Rhys carefully uncurled the man's balled fist and found an inch-long thorn imbedded in the fleshy part beneath his thumb. He draped his handkerchief over his fingers and pulled the thorn out. Then he stood and checked the potting soil on the nearest bench. Using his pocketknife, he stirred the dirt and found five more similar thorns mixed into the loamy soil. He spread out his handkerchief and lined them up, six miniature spikes on the white linen.

"This looks like the same sort of thorn that was worked into the padding of Molly's saddle," he said. "About the same length and shape."

"I never saw that one." She crowded close to peer down at the thorns. When she reached to touch one, he caught up her hand and held it fast.

"I think we have to assume whatever poison killed Mr. Weinschmidt is coated on those thorns."

"I'm wearing gloves," she said testily, but she lowered her hand. "They do seem a bit shiny. I have no idea how to determine what sort of poison it might be. However, I do know plants." She squinted at the thorns. "That's curious. We have hawthorns and several types of brambles here at Barrowdell, but these aren't from any of those. I've never seen their like here at all."

"So someone brought them on the property specifically for this purpose," Rhys said. "If we knew what sort of thorn they are, where they come from, it might give us a clue about the person to whom they belong."

"There's a book in Papa's library that might help. But I need to take at least one of the thorns with me so I can compare it to the illustrations in the text."

"We'll take them all." Rhys carefully folded the handkerchief so the thorns would be padded by the linen and put it in his outer jacket pocket. "And the small pot of soil they were mixed into, just in case we missed one. We don't want anyone else to be poisoned."

Olivia's slim shoulders quaked. "I don't think it really hit me before. Someone is trying to do harm to us here at Barrowdell."

Not *us*. Someone was trying to harm *her*. Whoever put the thorns in the potting soil wasn't after the little German gardener. At least she took the threat seriously now. He put his arms around her and she came willingly into his embrace.

A dedicated rake would have made the most of the situation. She was afraid. She was vulnerable. She was ripe for a panicked taking.

Instead, he held her until she stopped trembling, wondering what was wrong with him. Then he planted a soft kiss on the crown of her head.

"I think it best if we allow the rest of the folk here at Barrowdell to believe Mr. Weinschmidt died of natural causes." He stooped to arrange the body into a more relaxed position, as if the old gardener had fallen due to apoplexy or a stoppage of his heart instead of twisting in toxic agony.

"That way whoever did this will feel safe from discovery." She nodded in perfect understanding. "They won't see the need for caution."

"You, however, must be cautious."

"I'm spending time with you, aren't I?" She grimaced at him. He recognized it as an attempt to be flippant about the fact that someone had laced the soil she was going to work with poisoned thorns. "I'd be a fool to be other than cautious."

Olivia and Rhys trudged back to the manor house and reported Mr. Weinschmidt's demise to Mr. Falk, the estate steward. He concurred that the old gardener had gone to his reward suddenly while doing the work he loved.

"And what mortal can ask more than that?" Mr. Falk had said and efficiently made arrangements for the body to be transported to town for burial in the little churchyard.

Unlike the uproar caused by Olivia's accident, the solitary death of one of the servants made little difference to the residents in the guest chambers or the family wing. Only Olivia had had much to do with Mr. Weinschmidt, and her mother didn't want her bringing up such a morbid topic, especially now when more guests were arriving for the house party almost hourly.

Nearly all the places at the long dining table were filled, and conversation was lighthearted and full of plans for the coming days. Only Olivia noticed that the footmen wore unobtrusive black armbands in honor of Mr. Weinschmidt.

No, that's not right, she thought. *Rhys sees it too.*

His dark eyes didn't miss much. While he laughed and conversed with the diners around him, Olivia caught him quietly taking their dinner companions' measures. She could almost see the questions turning in that handsome head of his.

They'd spent most of the afternoon in the library together, huddled over Professor Hargrave's *Compendium of Noxious Plants*. A good bit of the text was given over to a treatise on the Genesis-based origin of weeds and thistles as punishment for the Fall of Man. Investigating a suspicious death certainly confirmed the professor's insistence on the existence of evil in the world, but the part of the book Olivia found most helpful was the hundreds of detailed illustrations.

On page three hundred and seventy, they discovered a picture that matched the type of thorn that had sent Molly into a frenzy and delivered the poison to Mr. Weinschmidt.

"The thorns are from *Euphorbia milii*, commonly

known as the crown of thorns plant," Olivia had said. "The long vines are pliable, but the thorns are certainly not, and they grow in excess of one inch long."

"Not native to England, I assume."

Rhys hovered over her shoulder, a comforting, solid presence. When he was near, she could pretend this was simply an intellectual exercise, not a deadly serious search for clues about the person who was trying to do her harm.

"Professor Hargrave says they are native to the island of Madagascar."

Rhys prowled the perimeter of the library like a wolf circling a small herd. "That narrows the field a bit. All your father's friends from India would likely have stopped at Madagascar on the trip Home. Mr. Stubbs, Colonel Billiter, and the Pinkertons have just moved to the front of the suspect list."

Her shoulders slumped. "Why would someone do this?"

"Attracting the attention of royalty also attracts other sorts of attention."

Olivia didn't know why any of the guests should object to her possible match with the Duke of Clarence. But she also had no idea why anyone would despise her so otherwise. Surely she hadn't lived long enough or unpleasantly enough to have created an enemy so vicious.

"So we are no closer to finding the murderer than when Molly first bolted."

Murderer. The word slipped out of her mouth and made her situation real.

But each time she thought the word *murderer*, it seemed more and more like nonsense syllables, a meaningless growling in her mind. She couldn't let the truth that she was the target sink in. If she did, she'd never be able to sit sedately at her mother's long table and make banal small talk with those around her.

And wonder about the gracious smiles and sparkling conversation at the long table. Which of her father's friends from India was duplicitous enough to hide their secret disappointment at seeing her alive and well?

Chapter 16

BABETTE HADN'T BEEN HER USUAL CHEERFUL SELF ALL evening. The maid was pensive and distracted. While she helped Olivia dress for dinner, requests had to be repeated several times before Babette leapt to do her bidding. Her maid usually wasn't the least clumsy, but she ham-handedly knocked over the bottle of expensive scent that had arrived earlier that day with a note declaring it came from the Duke of Clarence. The whole room smelled of spicy jasmine—a perfume Olivia thought too heavy for her to wear, in any case, so it was no great loss.

After supper, Babette was even more uncharacteristically quiet and fidgety as she brushed out Olivia's hair to prepare her for bed. Finally, Babette met her gaze in the vanity mirror.

"May I make to ask a question, mademoiselle?"

"Of course."

"Do you wait for—how you say?—the other shoe to drop?"

"What do you mean?"

"Disasters, they always come in threes, *non*? First,

your horse, it bolts and you are nearly killed. Then your helper in the hothouse, poor Monsieur Weinschmidt, he dies most unexpectedly." Babette started to do up Olivia's long tresses in a braid.

"No, leave it for now." Olivia pulled her hair away from Babette's clever fingers and turned to face her directly. "What are you trying to say?"

"I am saying the third evil thing, it is bound to come." Babette's pale brows nearly met in a frown over her fine straight nose. "What will happen next?"

"First of all, disasters do not come in threes. That's nothing but an old wives' tale," Olivia said, her tone testier than she would have liked, mostly because the thought had occurred to her as well. Having Babette say it only made the threat more real. "And second, your theory requires there be a connection between my mare bolting and Mr. Weinschmidt's death when there is none."

"There is you, mademoiselle. It was *your* horse. And the old gardener, he was doing *your* bidding, *non*?"

"If you're afraid to serve me, I'll have you reassigned first thing tomorrow—"

"*Non*, you must not think such a thing. It is my honor to be your abigail. Do not make to send me away. If I am afraid, it is not for myself." Babette crouched beside Olivia's chair so she could face her directly. "I fear for you, mistress."

Looking into Babette's wide eyes, Olivia was tempted to spill everything she and Rhys had discovered together, but he'd warned her to trust no one. So far, Rhys had focused on the houseguests, but he hadn't ruled out the possibility that the culprit had a willing ally below stairs. If Babette gossiped with even one of the other servants, news that the two tragic incidents were connected by some exotic thorns would circulate through the great house before Olivia snuffed out her lamp for the night.

And the guilty party might be warned.

"I'm not afraid," she lied. "Please ignore anyone who indulges in gossip or pointless speculation. You may leave me now."

"As you wish, mademoiselle," Babette said as she straightened the tortoise-shell comb and silver brush set on the vanity table before Olivia. She swanned across the room, imperturbable as always. But then she stopped at the door and turned back.

"If something makes a change and you do feel afraid, I wish you to know you may trust me."

"I know that, Babette." She hoped it was so.

"*Bien.*" She reached for the doorknob but stopped again. "Before I am come to this house, I have another… employment which required…certain other skills."

"Besides being a lady's maid, you mean."

"*Oui*, just so." She shot Olivia a pointed look. "Skills that will help keep you safe, mademoiselle."

Olivia swallowed back her surprise, wondering what Babette could possibly mean. La Belle Perdu, Babette's former employer, was rumored to have been a French spy. Had she taught her maid some of the craft? "Thank you. I'll remember that."

As Babette slipped out of the room, Olivia wondered about her abigail.

Not many lady's maids had…certain other skills.

If Babette was afraid for her, it meant the folk below

stairs had considered Olivia's riding accident and her assistant's sudden demise, put together the scraps of evidence, and arrived at the correct sum. None of the Symon's houseguests bothered to connect events.

Of course, Olivia and Rhys had taken pains to make sure they wouldn't. She could only imagine her mother's rants if Beatrice Symon suspected Olivia had been deliberately targeted both times.

For once, she considered that her mother truly did care for her, even if her means of showing it were overblown. Olivia turned down the lamp and wandered to the window. The frosty hills were bright under a three-quarter moon. But even with pinpricks of light sparkling on the skiff of snow, Barrowdell presented a stark vista in the dead of winter with its barren meadows and naked woods shivering in the wind.

She wished her father would come home.

The cavernous rooms and long corridors of Barrowdell never seemed as empty when his booming voice echoed in them. And Olivia's mother wasn't nearly as difficult to deal with when her "dear Mr. Symon" was in residence.

If her father was home, things would be different. When Horatio Symon was there, the children all had free run of the house. There was laughter in the halls. The entire family dined around the long dining table along with the guests, no matter who else might be visiting. No one worried that one of them might commit a breach of etiquette that could hamstring the family's entire future.

When her father came home this time, he'd have the Duke of Clarence with him. If the reason Olivia had been targeted was her impending betrothal to royalty, would the person who was determined to hurt her be even bolder then?

Her gut clenched in anxiety. She'd lied to Babette. She was afraid. Very afraid.

There was no true safety in her father's return, only the hazy illusion of it left over from her cosseted childhood. It was time she faced facts. Life would never go back to the way it used to be.

The snick of the door latch startled her, and her hand lurched involuntarily to her throat.

"Don't worry," came a deep, familiar voice. He spoke softly to keep from being heard beyond the confines of her chamber. "It's only me."

Relief flooded over her. She knew it shouldn't be so, but Rhys Warrington made her feel protected.

"I thought you'd never come."

She gave him a quick hug, but when she started to pull away, he caught her and tugged her closer. She didn't mean to, but she couldn't help melting into him. He was so solid and big and...safe.

"If I'd known being late would mean such a friendly welcome," he murmured into her ear, his warm breath spilling down her neck and teasing beneath her wrapper and nightrail, "I'd have stayed away longer."

She rolled her eyes at him. Her partner in this misadventure. Her protector. Her friend.

Was it workable for him to be all three?

Or even a fourth? What about...her lover?

The shocking possibility took root in her mind when he bent to kiss her. If she was destined for a loveless match with an aging roué like Clarence, shouldn't she have at least one shining moment when she shared herself with a man she truly liked and admired? Short of surrendering her maidenhead, why shouldn't she enjoy the lessons in lovemaking Rhys wanted to give her?

She'd never liked change, but that was all she saw in her future. Since someone had targeted her, her basic trust in others was shattered. It was yet another way her life would never be the same.

If and when she married the duke, it certainly never would be. And after Rhys Warrington, her life would never go back to the way it used to be either.

And of all the changes, only that last one had her thinking perhaps that would be no bad thing. She pulled his head down and deepened their kiss.

❧

Over the years, Rhys had been with some accomplished bed partners, but Olivia kissed him back with more fervor than any of them. She nipped his lower lip. She met his tongue and suckled it in welcome. She groaned softly into his mouth.

When he was with other women, he often thought their sighs and moans were merely play-acting to enhance his pleasure, as if pretending the encounter meant something would make it more enjoyable. He always made it clear at the outset of any new dalliance that nothing beyond their body parts would be involved. Any evidence of ardent feeling made him suspicious.

But there was no play-acting in Olivia. This kiss was all too real.

She wasn't experienced enough to feign passion.

This was unfiltered, uncensored lust in a newly awakened virgin. Her hitched breath, her shuddering sighs, the way she pressed herself against him went right to his heart.

She made him *feel* something, damn her. A hot, tight lump of something unnamable in his chest.

He didn't want to feel it. He couldn't afford to feel it. He was supposed to be here to ruin her, not fall in love with her.

Where the hell did that come from?

He shoved the unwelcome thought aside and concentrated instead on the soft give of her breasts beneath the thin muslin and the tautness of her lovely nipples, hard little buttons, against his chest.

He started to reach for them, but she surprised him by shoving his jacket off his shoulders without breaking their kiss. If she wanted him less clothed, who was he to protest? Then she tackled the buttons on his waistcoat with no gentleness at all. One popped off and rolled toward the fireplace.

"Mr. Clyde will be cross with you," he said as he kissed his way along her clavicle. He gave her soft skin a little nip and she shivered but didn't object. "A grumpy valet is a terrible thing to behold."

"Mr. Clyde doesn't frighten me."

She let him slide her wrapper and nightrail to the side to expose her shoulder to more kisses. Her skin smelled so sweet, so fresh compared to the cloying fragrance emanating from her vanity table, that he wanted to eat her up.

"I'll set my abigail after your Mr. Clyde," Olivia said, continuing to work the buttons on his waistcoat.

"Babette claims she has 'certain skills' that will keep me safe."

He caught both her hands and held them still so he could concentrate on what she'd just said. The way she seemed intent on undressing him threatened to shove other matters aside, but the prickle on his nape warned him this might be important. "What do you mean— certain skills?"

Olivia told him about the cryptic conversation with her maid. It bothered Rhys that the help had speculated so accurately what was really going on at Barrowdell.

"She's French, you say?" He stopped kissing her shoulder and straightened to his full height.

"Very."

That alone made him disposed to mistrust Babette. He longed to continue to kiss Olivia all over, but if he was going to keep her safe, he needed to know more about those who surrounded her daily.

"How long has Babette been with you?"

"A few months," she said. "Since her previous mistress drowned in the Thames."

He snorted. "That's not much of a commendation."

"No, you don't understand." She slid his waistcoat off and let it drop to the floor. "She had nothing to do with the drowning. She worked for La Belle Perdu."

"The French spy."

"That was the general consensus about her," Olivia conceded. "But Babette assures me her mistress was no such thing. The courtesan couldn't bear the thought of being arrested, so she leaped into the water in despondency."

"Someone who's willing to die rather than be

interrogated by the authorities generally has plenty to hide. Sounds like a spy to me," Rhys said. "I don't like the idea of this Babette being so near you."

"But you can't hold her accountable for her mistress's actions."

Olivia started to untie his cravat but tugged the wrong end of the starched fabric. It tightened around his neck instead.

"Allow me," he said, gentling her questing fingers away and quickly undoing the elegant waterfall of linen. "Before you garrote me with my own neckwear."

She pulled a face at him. "Pardon me for not understanding the intricacies of a gentleman's wardrobe."

"Before tonight, I would have said there is no wrong way to undress a man. Apparently there are a few," he said with a laugh. "But the ends justify the means, I suppose."

"Are you making fun of me?"

"I'd never do that," he assured her. "But I do want to have fun *with* you. If I teach you nothing else, I want you to know a man and woman should laugh together. But back to your Babette—"

"She's never given me reason not to trust her," she said as she unfastened his shirt, frowning at each button in concentration.

"Still, I don't like her being close to you."

She smiled up at him. Blast, if it wasn't as coquettish a smile as any courtesan's. Where on earth had she learned that? Since Eden, he supposed, women had been gifted with the means to distract a man. Olivia had come fully into her birthright as a daughter of Eve.

"Right now," she said, letting her fingertips slip inside his open shirt, "you're the only one close to me."

"And that's how I like it." He gathered her into his arms. "Not to complain, but it's not often a man is greeted by a beautiful woman who seems intent on undressing him."

"Surely, given your reputation, it must happen to you with regularity."

"Not as often as you might think." He smiled down at her. "And never as memorably as this time."

"Really? And what makes this so memorable?"

"Because you're doing it rather badly."

She huffed and pulled away from him. "What do you mean I'm doing it badly?"

"That's maybe not the best way to put it. If the goal is simply to see a man naked, you'll accomplish it, but you could reach the same end by asking me to strip. It would save time. And my wardrobe," he said with a grin. The topic had been officially changed, and he was in no mood to go back to the old one. "However, if your aim is to seduce a man beyond bearing, there are other ways to go about it besides ripping off his buttons." He cocked a brow at her. "Not that that can't be fun on occasion."

"I assumed the most direct route is best. What other ways are there?"

"So seduction is your aim?"

"To seduce you beyond bearing? You flatter yourself, sir," she said as she flounced into one of the wing chairs. "But last night you showed me something about me. Tonight, I want to learn about you." She tugged her sagging wrapper back up to cover her bare shoulder. "Or are you no longer interested in giving me lessons?"

Come here. Go away. Beg me to stay. Where had she learned those essential bits of the seductress's art?

"I'm interested." *Definitely.* His body was already primed and ready.

"Then how should I undress you?" she asked, innocently unaware that just those words dropping from her sweet mouth were blissful torture for him.

"You should undress a man in the same way you'd explore a pleasure garden. Slowly. Deliberately. Tarry to see the sights. Touch. Taste," he said. "Take all the time you need."

"All right." She stood and walked over to him. "Let's take it turn and turn about. I allowed you to disrobe me without interference last night. Will you trust me enough to stand perfectly still?"

"I'm at your command."

"Good," she said with a feline smile. "But I don't think you need to stand before a mirror. You already know what a fine-looking fellow you are. Let's see what you have hidden under your shirt."

Chapter 17

SHE FINISHED UNDOING THE ROW OF BUTTONS WITH agonizing slowness. Then she parted the front of his shirt and stepped back to view his bare chest.

After giving him a satisfied smile, she undid the button on one side of the flap front of his trousers. Olivia tugged at his shirttail. Then her breath hitched. The sound was slight, but it registered surprise. And, he hoped, delight.

"You're not wearing any smallclothes," she observed.

"I usually don't under formal wear, and your mother does require her guests to dress for dinner," he said. "Brummell always says they spoil the line of good trousers."

"Hmm. Not having them spoils my chance to help you out of them."

He smiled. She was determined to push this lesson to limits beyond his dreams.

"Sorry to disappoint you," he said.

"Oh, I'm not disappointed. I expect I'll find not unraveling the mysteries of masculine undergarments will fade compared to what else I'll learn tonight."

She touched the slight indentation at the base of

his throat and then slid her fingertips down his chest. She circled each brown nipple, and then ran her knuckle from his breastbone to the waist of his trousers. Anticipation tightened his gut.

He'd never been so undone by such a simple touch.

Then she tugged the rest of his shirttail out of his trousers, took hold of one side of the shirt, and walked around him, slipping the garment down one arm. It snagged at his wrist.

"Cufflinks," he said. She was so endearingly awkward. That strange lump in his chest glowed, but he tamped it down. He'd never complete his mission to upset her match with the duke if he allowed himself to have feelings for her. He had a job to do. He had to keep reminding himself of it.

"You might have warned me."

"I thought allowing you to discover the small details on your own would be more interesting."

She drew the shirt back up and removed the silver studs at his wrists. Then she circled him, sliding the shirt off his back and down the other arm before it joined his waistcoat on the floor. The glide of the fabric, the brush of her fingertips, the kiss of air on his bared skin made desire lance through him. This time her attempt to remove his shirt was much less awkward but no less endearing. Even though she was a novice in matters sensual, her efforts to seduce brought him to tingling need.

He'd been rock hard for a while, but now his erection throbbed, straining against the superfine trousers.

She stared at him in frank appraisal, a smile playing about her lips.

"Well?" he asked when she didn't seem disposed to move forward.

"Well, what? You told me to tarry to see the sights."

He bit the inside of his cheek. Why'd he have to be so blasted clever? He should have told her the right way to undress a man was to tear his clothes off like a wild woman, buttons be damned.

"Hold still now," she said as she reached out to smooth her palms over his shoulders and down his arms. "You told me to touch, you know."

"So I did," he murmured, his voice a throaty growl.

When her fingertips dipped lower, his ballocks drew up in a snug mound. Unfortunately, she didn't venture below the waist of his trousers. But his navel peeped above the superfine pants, and she teased the small hairs whorled around it mercilessly.

"Close your eyes," she said.

"I made you open yours," he countered.

"My night. My rules," she said. "Or are you trying to tell me this isn't at all the done thing and I'm hopeless at undressing a man so I may as well give up?"

"You are anything but hopeless." The way his cock bulged in his trousers would damn him for a liar if he tried to say anything else. He closed his eyes.

And felt the wonder of her mouth pressed squarely on the center of his chest in a soft kiss.

"You told me to taste," she whispered.

She nuzzled him with her lips and drew her soft cheeks across his chest.

"You smell wonderful, Rhys."

Her tongue circled his nipples, and when she strafed one with her teeth, an involuntary groan escaped his lips.

"Liked that, did you?" she asked.

"Lord, yes."

"Good. I've been thinking about it and I think I'd like it too. I mean, if you did that to me."

His eyes flew open and he reached for her.

She straight-armed him. "No, you warned me to be cautious, and the cautious virgin would make certain only one of us is naked at a time."

"Neither of us is naked," he pointed out.

"Something I intend to remedy."

"Not just yet," he said, mildly surprised at the words coming from his own mouth. He'd never stopped a woman from undressing him before, but it wasn't his favorite thing. He usually preferred to be in control of a sensual encounter. Amazingly enough, he more than enjoyed letting Olivia take the reins for a change, but he had to gentle them from her hands for a bit.

He'd been on the receiving end of her caresses, and he couldn't bear not returning the favor. He wanted to astound her. He wanted to give to her without thought of return.

"Let me," he said as he reached to tug the bow that held her nightrail neckline closed. "For only a moment. Then you can return to tormenting me."

Her brows scrunched together. "Is it really torment?"

"Only the best kind," he said with a smile as he slid her wrapper off and spread the neckline of her nightrail until it balanced on the tips of her shoulders. Her breasts were bared, but technically she was still clothed, since she was still wearing the thin muslin.

"You're so beautiful, Olivia. I hope I've convinced you of that by now," he said, "but looking isn't enough. I want to touch." He fondled her breasts, marveling at the perfect fit of the small orbs in his palms. "And taste."

He bent his head and kissed her nipple. Then he took it into his mouth and sucked.

She gasped and clutched his head to hold it there. She was so sweet between his lips, he was loath to stop, but he couldn't neglect the other taut berry. He moved to the other breast, and this time after a bit of suckling, he bit down on her softly.

"Oh!"

"Gets your attention, doesn't it?"

She made another indeterminate sound that might have been "quite" or "right." Either way, it seemed to mean "I won't let you stop without a fight." He'd given her a jolt of pleasure. It made him feel like a god.

Then he straightened and held her close so her bare skin was flush against his. She was like warm satin, all smooth and soft.

"Skin needs to be touched," he whispered. "It cries out for the warmth of another. Do you hear it?"

She nodded; then she put a hand to his chest and pushed away gently. "You're trying to distract me. Moreover, you're back to directing this lesson and I intend it to be an exploration at *my* leisure."

"I stand corrected." He took a slight step back. "What do you want to do now?"

"I want to touch you, Rhys." She tipped her head back so she could look up at him. "Everywhere. Will you let me?"

He swallowed hard. This would require all his

concentration if he wasn't going to spill his seed on her like a green boy. "I'll let you do whatever you like."

He ground his teeth together while she turned her attention to the last button that held his trousers up.

"No, that won't work."

"Why not?" She looked stricken. "What am I doing wrong now?"

"Nothing. You're doing everything right." If it was any more right, he'd have a fountain in his pants. "It's just that if you mean to drop my trousers, may I suggest you allow me to remove my boots first?"

"Oh, it's like the cufflinks," she said. "Very well."

He sat in one of the wing chairs and tugged at his Hessians.

Why was he talking so blasted much? He was here at Barrowdell for one purpose—to steal the maidenhead of the young woman before him. Why did he keep throwing up roadblocks between them? This whole business of lessons and wagers was a bunch of rot. He ought to swive her and be done with it.

That hard lump in his chest throbbed afresh.

The tight-fitting boots resisted his efforts for several more moments, but he finally toed them off.

"Goodness. That looked difficult," Olivia said. "Perhaps you ought to give your Mr. Clyde a raise in pay."

"No more complicated than your stays, I wager."

"That's a bet I'd win," she said with a smile. "Not that I'm inclined to enter into any more wagers with you."

He stood. "Why not? Paying off your last gambling debt to me has taken a very interesting turn."

"True," she said, sauntering over and renewing her efforts on his trouser button.

The nearness of her fingers fairly drove him wild. He worked cannon firing solutions in his head each time her hand grazed over his cock through the superfine. He mentally traced the route to Dover on the map he carried in his mind. When he made the mistake of casting a lingering gaze at the sweet hollow between her breasts, he was reduced to reciting the alphabet backward...in Latin. Anything to keep the pressure from clenching his balls and building in his shaft.

After what seemed like forever, she finally worked the button free and let the front flap drop.

"Oh, my," was all she said.

❧

It was all she could say.

Once when Olivia was a child, she and her sister Calliope had stumbled across some of the stable boys swimming naked in the pond. Their shriveled little male parts were hardly worth a giggle.

Rhys's was neither shriveled nor little. It rose like a grand tower, tipped slightly toward her.

Knowing where it was designed to go, she felt a bit of trepidation at the size and girth of him. Even so, that secret part of her throbbed at the sight.

A curiously pleasant throb.

She tugged at his trousers and they dropped to the floor. He stood still as a statue of Adonis.

"Um, aren't you going to step out of your trousers?"

"I could, but that would mean your role as leisurely explorer would be at an end. You wanted to be in control, remember."

"Very well." She crouched down before him,

achingly aware of the nearness of his male parts. She forced herself to concentrate on removing his pants from around his ankles. "Lift your right foot. Now the left."

She eased his trousers out from under his feet and then stood up.

"Aren't you forgetting the stockings?" he asked.

"A strategic forgetfulness," she countered. "So long as you leave your stockings on, you're not actually nude. Should anyone ask, I would be able to say with perfect truthfulness that I have not seen Lord Rhys Warrington naked."

"Flawlessly logical," he said with a smile. "If you'd been born a man, you'd have made a brilliant barrister. But do you really expect anyone to ask you such a question?"

"Well, no," she said.

"It helps you to tell yourself that I'm not completely naked, doesn't it?"

How could he know her that well?

"That's an exceedingly sharp blade you're slicing your conscience with." He cocked his head at her. "Are you sure it's necessary?"

"Well, now that you mention it, perhaps not," she admitted. "After all, I've seen any number of nude statues at the British museum."

"Indeed?"

"Yes, in the exhibit of classical Greek art."

"I'm surprised your mother allowed you to go."

"To be honest, she thought I was attending a lecture on Grecian pottery," Olivia said with a grin. "What my mother doesn't know won't hurt me."

"As I recall, there were more female nudes than males in that exhibit," Rhys said.

"Yes, drat it." And to make matters worse, more often than not, the male genitalia were hidden by strategically draped stolas or a well-placed fig leaf. Only one memorably unadorned male figure left nothing to the imagination—the statue of Dionysus.

The inebriated god was frozen in marble in the act of relieving his bladder. The Ladies' Society for the Advancement of Public Decency had staged a protest outside the museum over it. Olivia wasn't sure which offended them most—the god's publicly drunken state, his blatant nakedness, or the vulgar pose in which he was captured. But since the Society's objections only increased attendance at the exhibit, they stopped picketing immediately.

Still she'd thought the statue instructive. However, after seeing Rhys Warrington in the altogether, she had to conclude that the god's attributes came up woefully…short.

"At the risk of inflating your already ample ego, seeing you in the nude is rather like viewing art," she said. "You're quite wonderfully made."

He smiled at her. A perfectly wicked smile. "While flattering, there's only one thing wrong with that analogy." He took her hand and guided it to his shaft. "I'm not made of stone."

Chapter 18

HE WAS CERTAINLY HARD AS STONE, BUT STONE encased in warm male flesh. She wasn't sure which part of him fascinated her most—his hard shaft or the soft testicles beneath it.

She ran her fingertips over his length and then palmed his balls while she continued to stroke him. He moved toward her caresses, arching into her.

When she glanced up at Rhys's face, his eyes were closed and he was biting his bottom lip.

"Am I hurting you?"

His eyes popped open. "No, but if I stand still any longer, I'll burst."

"We can't have that. By all means, don't stand still."

He wrapped his arms around her and bent to kiss her, leaving enough space between them for her to continue to fondle him. He groaned into her mouth.

A thrill of feminine power coursed through her. She'd made him groan with need. She'd reduced him to bare lust. Her heart sang in wicked triumph as she continued to explore him.

His hands roamed over her as well, down her back, cupping her buttocks, lifting her against him in long languid strokes. She ached so deeply a groan escaped her lips before she could stop it.

Oh dear. Lust is contagious.

No, this was more than lust. There was such tenderness in his touch, such heart-stopping sweetness in his kisses, even the neediest of them. He cared enough to be concerned for her safety. Surely he cared for her in others ways as well.

She'd already admitted she liked Rhys. It was more than many marriage partners could say.

Certainly more than she could say for the Duke of Clarence. His reputation with women was such that she couldn't even console herself with fanciful imaginings of the royal duke's valiant and pure male soul. Any other man who'd sired ten bastards on two different mistresses and tried to force them on Polite Society would be met with only direct cuts. Without his royal standing, the duke was merely an aging libertine.

Of course, what was Rhys but a young libertine?

Nevertheless, she *liked* him. He was charming and clever and brave and...wounded. Her heart ached afresh for his pain over Lieutenant Duffy. There was a depth to Rhys Warrington most would overlook.

He wanted it overlooked, she realized. How much of his playing the rake was only to disguise his well-hidden pain?

Then Rhys deepened their kiss, and all coherent thought fled from her mind. She draped her arms around his neck as he scooped her into his arms and carried her to the waiting bed. Somewhere between the fireplace and the bedpost, her nightrail hitched up past her knees.

She didn't mind. She might not even have noticed if he hadn't run a hand over her leg from ankle to mid-thigh. She didn't stop kissing and touching him as he laid her down on the feather tick with care.

She didn't protest when he joined her there, settling with most of the weight of his upper body propped on his elbows while he kissed her to oblivion.

It was a little like heaven to feel the sheltering warmth of him. The thin muslin of her nightrail almost didn't exist. It was open to her waist so his chest covered hers, skin on skin. She'd never imagined a sensation so delicious.

His heart pounded against her breastbone. His breath filled her lungs. His scent, his taste, he crowded her whole world. If anyone had told her there was nothing else but this man, this moment, she'd have believed them.

Her thighs parted and his hips settled between them. That needy drumbeat between her legs was becoming habitual whenever he was near. Now it crescendoed into an entire percussion section. A low boom deep inside her, with pleasure sparking across her skin every place their bodies touched, her shin to his thigh, her thigh to his hips.

During the kissing and caressing, her nightrail hem somehow became entangled around her waist. She could feel *him*—all of him—rocking in a slow knock, now against her bare belly, now in the crease of her thigh. She gasped when the tip of him pressed against her opening. She turned her head to break off their kiss.

"Trust me, Olivia," he whispered. "Will you?"

She shouldn't. The man had a reputation. He freely admitted it. But she made the mistake of looking into his eyes.

She saw wanting there. Along with the desire to give. And there in the glinting depths of his dark eyes, wasn't that…hope?

He needed her to trust him. It was as Babette had said. All souls wanted to be accepted. Trusted. Loved. Even though he didn't voice it, his eyes said, "Please."

And she said yes.

⟿

That lump in his chest swelled and made it hard to breathe for a moment. Then Rhys kissed her once more, softly this time, holding back the surge of passion that threatened to break in him. Surely her lips would be bruised if he didn't bridle himself.

Then he moved his body off her and lay beside her.

Best to remove temptation for now.

It had been all he could do not to slip into her when the tip of his cock brushed her opening. One quick thrust and his job at Barrowdell would be irrevocably done.

Instead, he kissed his way down her neck, while his hand moved over her belly and into her soft folds. If he was going to take from her, the least he could do was give.

And he intended to give until she begged him to shred her maidenhead. If she implored him to ruin her, perhaps his conscience would stop flailing him over it.

She was so wet. Each silky layer of her was swollen and slick. The sweet perfume of her arousal went to his head. He nuzzled her breast while his fingers played a lover's game on her mound.

She writhed under him as he teased around her most sensitive spot without giving her relief. She made the most alluring little noises of distress. He so wanted to give her ease, but he needed her to plead for it. He had no other recourse but to draw out her journey into bliss to unbearable lengths.

When he moved his hand away, she nearly sobbed.

"Hush, love," he murmured. "'Twill be all right. You'll see."

Then he kissed his way down her body, lingering at her belly button, before nuzzling the curls between her legs. When he slipped his tongue between her folds, she gave a shuddering breath and arched herself into his mouth.

Rhys cupped her heart-shaped bum and feasted on her.

❧

Love. He called me "love." Olivia's heart pounded while she fisted the linens. Surely no man would do to a woman what Rhys was doing to her unless he loved her.

Joy rippled through her, radiating outward from the center of the universe between her thighs. The ache was sharp-edged now, the line between pain and pleasure blurred. A tear squeezed from her closed eyes and trickled into her ear, but she couldn't have borne for him to stop. If he did, she'd scream loud enough to wake the entire household.

She wouldn't have left the bed if it had been on fire.

Then she felt herself caught in a downward spiral. She arched her back but couldn't stop herself from unraveling completely. Could this be right? Surely she wasn't supposed to come undone like this.

Her insides convulsed. Then bliss spread over her whole body and threatened to shoot out her fingers and toes.

Oh, yes. This is definitely right.

She was halfway to heaven. How long she hung suspended between this world and the next, she couldn't say. When she finally came to herself and her heart stopped galloping in her chest, she felt Rhys's head pillowed on her flat belly, his warm breath streaming over her skin.

She reached down and ruffled her fingers through his lovely thick hair. She wasn't capable of more than that slight movement. Anything else might stop the warmth and light coursing through her body, and more than anything, she wanted that blessed sensation to continue.

But Rhys was capable of more. He moved up to cover her with his body again and kissed her, softly at first and then with more insistence.

The ache she'd thought was completely stilled flared to new life. And with it came a terrible hollowness, a longing to be filled.

"Rhys," she whispered as she pressed her pelvis against him. "I'm so empty."

He raised up on his elbows and looked down at her, his expression unreadable in the dimness of the room. "There's only one way for me to fix that."

She knew without him saying what that way was.

Her choices were plain. When her father and the Duke of Clarence arrived, the marriage deal would be brokered and she'd enter the rarified world of the royals. Even though her cage would be gilded, it would still be confining and she'd be doomed to a loveless match.

She might wear a diadem someday, but she'd never know what it was to give herself to a man in total acceptance and trust. She couldn't quite bring herself to add the "love" that Babette included in the list, though she didn't know what else to call the dizzying sparks of emotion crackling through her.

Her only chance to experience the joy of surrender to someone she cared for was if she gave herself to the man in her bed right now.

If she did, she didn't think it would undermine her match with the duke. Rhys wouldn't ruin that for her by telling anyone what passed between them. Even if Clarence was unhappy with her after the wedding, their marriage would never be anything more than a church-sanctioned business arrangement in any case. He would never return her, along with the forty thousand pounds a year that came to him as long as she was his wife.

Rhys kissed her again, a warm, wet kiss tinged with the desperation of longing. A line from a Shakespeare play she'd read last month flitted through her mind.

If thou remember'st not the slightest folly that ever love did make thee run into, thou hast not loved.

This was certainly folly. By circular reasoning, did that also make this love?

"Olivia," Rhys said, his voice ragged. "I want you so."

His need intensified her own. The ache would not be denied. She closed her eyes and bade being a cautious virgin adieu. "Then take me."

His plan had worked. She'd told him to ruin her. One thrust was all it would take. He'd kept his vow. He hadn't lied to her. He truly did want her with every drop of blood coursing through his body.

Then why did he hesitate?

Because you also told her to trust you, his conscience accused. He hadn't heard from it for years, but since he met Olivia Symon, its rasping voice was becoming all too familiar to his mind.

He'd deal with the pricks of his scruples later. Right now, he had a completely beddable woman under him and she'd begged him to take her.

How could he do anything else?

He kissed her again as he moved into position. The tip of him entered her warm wetness. She was all that was good and bright in his world. He couldn't wait for her to envelop him in her snug embrace.

'Twill be all right, you said.

Damn it, he had said that. How could shredding her maidenhead make it all right for her?

She moaned and squirmed under him, ready to take him in entirely.

He'd be gentle. He'd never bedded a virgin, but he thought the pain he was bound to cause her would be negligible if he was careful. The destruction of the symbol of her purity would be over in a blink.

What of the lasting pain of being publicly ruined?

To appease Mr. Alcock, nothing they did in secret could remain so. Olivia's lack of chastity would have to be shouted from the rooftops in order to scotch the deal with the Duke of Clarence.

It didn't matter. He had to go through with it.

Otherwise Alcock would drag him into the well of the House of Lords and accuse him loudly of war crimes that had only been connected to him in whispers until now. His father wouldn't be able to bear it.

Rhys started to slide into her by the slowest of degrees when the unthinkable happened.

His cock began to soften.

Concentrate, he ordered himself.

He pushed forward but it was no use. He was flaccid as an eel on the riverbank. It was like bringing a rope to a sword fight. For the first time in his life, Rhys Warrington could not properly bed a woman who was ready and willing for him to swive her silly.

He rolled off her and clambered out of bed as if the hounds of hell were after him. He couldn't bear for her to realize he was physically incapable of making love to her.

Even though he wanted to with all his heart.

Chapter 19

"RHYS, WHAT'S WRONG?"

He didn't answer. Instead he strode across the room and retrieved his discarded trousers. Keeping his back to her, he stepped into them and tugged them up.

Olivia climbed out of bed, letting the hem of her nightrail billow to the floor. Her shaking fingers fumbling with the buttons, she did up the front of her shift as she followed after him. She might not have much sensual experience, but even she knew something had gone horribly wrong.

"What just happened?" she asked in bewilderment. One moment he was making the sweetest love to her and the next he was flying across the room trying to put as much distance as possible between them.

"What do you think happened?" He sat in one of the wing chairs and struggled to pull on his boots. "I saved you from a very stupid mistake. Honestly Olivia, if you hope to be a queen one day, you really ought to use better judgment."

She flinched as though he'd slapped her. He hadn't meant any of it. The whole thing was some elaborate test, which she'd obviously failed. "But I thought—"

"That this was something other than a lesson from a libertine?" He pulled on his shirt and fastened it up at a blistering pace. "Where the devil did that button you tore off get to?"

She stared at him in disbelief. Her world was imploding and he was looking for a benighted button.

"Ah!" He found the lost button near the hearth and pocketed it. As he retied his cravat, he cast her a cynical look. "Close your mouth, Olivia. It makes you look like a cod. Surely you're not that surprised."

She couldn't have been more so if he'd told her he planned to sprout wings and fly out her window. Everything had felt so real.

"Haven't you any idea how close you were to ruin? You really are a silly little twit, aren't you? I confess I thought you brighter than that."

The way her stomach roiled, she feared she might be sick. But that would only mean further mortification before a man who'd seen her soul-naked, who'd *used* her for his own twisted purposes and now laughed at her. She couldn't bear more. She swallowed back the rising bile and straightened to her full height.

"Get out of my room."

"I would do so with pleasure, Miss Symon," he said as he retrieved his cufflinks from her vanity and reattached them at his wrists. "Nevertheless we have a small matter with which to contend. May I remind you there is still someone trying to do you harm?"

"More harm than you, you mean."

"Yes, more harm than me," he said testily, shrugging into his waistcoat and jacket.

"Since you think I'm a silly little twit, I have to wonder why should you care?"

"My dear girl, I am here at the behest of the Duke of Clarence. It would do my reputation with the royals no credit if something were to happen to you on my watch."

Nothing. What they shared in her bed meant nothing to him. She glared at him, taking refuge behind rage to avoid nausea brought on by total embarrassment. "With a reputation like yours, what's another stain more or less?"

He clasped a mocking hand to his chest as though she'd sent a dart into it. "There's a sting. Good. I was afraid you might turn into a weepy little puddle. But however you might feel about me at present, remember there is someone out there who seeks to do you ill. Until we discover who that person is, you're stuck with me in your bedchamber by night."

"Not for long. I intend to ask my mother to rescind her invitation for you to join the house party." She crossed her arms as if she might hold herself together with them. Her chest ached abominably, and this time the throbbing wasn't the least pleasant. She'd heard the word "heartache" but always thought it melodramatic in the extreme. She never dreamed it referred to pain that was all too real. "This is the last night you'll spend under Barrowdell's roof if I have anything to say about it."

"Fortunately, when it comes to your mother's social decisions, you have very little to say."

Drat the man. He was right. There was nothing she

could tell her mother, short of the truth, that would make her banish Lord Rhys Warrington. Even then, she wondered whose side her mother would be on. She whirled around and stomped back to the bed, trailing her dignity behind her like tattered wings.

"Stay away from me, Rhys Warrington."

"As you wish, milady," he said with false amiability as he settled into one of the wing chairs and propped his long legs up on the other.

She climbed into bed and pulled the covers to her chin. She bit back the sob that threatened to tear from her throat. She would not let the man hear her crying in the dark.

But that didn't stop the tears from coursing silently down her cheeks. Her heart hurt, pounding erratically. She'd nearly been dashed to pieces in that ravine, but she hadn't felt as close to death then as she did now, lying in the dark with her chest threatening to break open.

She replayed the interlude with Rhys in her mind, the intimate things he'd done with her, to her, the way she'd given herself over to him. How could he run so hot and then so cold? What had she done wrong?

Then she realized she hadn't done anything. *He* was the one who failed to do something. Now that she thought about it, she realized in the final moments of their loving his glorious thing had suddenly become inexplicably much less glorious.

There'd been a stallion like that at Barrowdell once. Mr. Thatcher tried every trick he could to interest the horse in a mare that was in season, but for some unknown reason, the stallion wouldn't mount. In the end, he was gelded and sold, and as far as Olivia knew, was still pulling a hackney cab around the cobbled streets of London.

She didn't want Rhys gelded, but the thought of him hauling around a cab with a bit between his teeth made her stop crying for a bit.

But men were not stallions. Rhys simply must not have wanted her after all and couldn't pretend he did for another second.

Shame burned her cheeks, and she buried her face in her pillow.

Deliver me, O Lord, from weeping women, Rhys prayed silently. Olivia tried to muffle it, but every other minute a hitched breath or small sob emanated from the bed. Each sound was a fresh lash to his conscience.

No wonder he couldn't make love to her. His insides were tangled in a knot. Even though he understood the reason, the fact that his body failed him made him feel like shite.

Even if he could have taken her maidenhead, there was no way he could have avoided hurting her. He was damned if he did and damned if he didn't.

If not for the very real threat from whoever had planted those thorns, he'd be long gone. New South Wales was supposed to be quite nice this time of year.

He laid his head back in the wing chair and stared at the heavily timbered ceiling. He was only fooling himself. He wouldn't leave. Like it or not, he couldn't abandon Olivia. He wasn't sure when it had happened, but somehow she'd attached herself to his heart as surely as her orchids were affixed to their hosts.

Rhys sighed and closed his eyes.

Against his expectations, he drifted into light sleep. When his head tipped forward, he jerked back to full wakefulness. He had no way to gauge how long he'd been asleep, but no sound came from Olivia's bed.

She's stopped crying, thank God.

The winter wind soughed outside the windows and drafted the chimney, stirring the banked fire into a small blaze. There was an occasional creak as the manor house settled on its foundations for the night. He could hear no other sound of human movement but the pounding of his own heartbeat in his ears. Even though sleep fled from him, the quiet was restful.

But then the quiet began to be oppressive. He was overwhelmed by the need to make sure Olivia was all right. He tugged off his boots again so his footsteps would be silent on the hardwood and stole over to her bedside.

Light from the three-quarter moon shafted through the window and silvered Olivia's face, tinting the hollows of her lovely cheekbones in shades of gray. Her breathing had settled into a soft, regular rhythm. Her lips parted in the relaxation of deep sleep.

But as he watched, her brows drew together as if she were in pain.

She must be dreaming.

Even though the anguished expression smoothed away almost immediately, his chest constricted at the sight.

He'd caused that pain.

He might be standing watch over her to keep her safe physically, but he'd hurt her heart. Badly. The stricken look on her face when he called her a silly little twit had made him want to punch his fist through the nearest wall and hope he broke his own knuckles.

But he'd had to say something that heinous simply to keep her at a distance. If she suspected his body had failed him and he *couldn't* bed her, she'd no doubt think it was somehow her fault.

Nothing could be further from the truth.

Olivia Symon wasn't like any other woman he'd known. Of course, she was desirable, but not only for her delectable face and form. He was captivated by her wit. He respected her intelligence. He was amazed at the courage and athleticism she'd displayed when her horse bolted, a situation that might have made a grown man wet himself.

That bothersome lump in his chest ached afresh.

Damn.

She trembled in her sleep even though she was tucked under the covers. She was obviously cold.

Moving with stealth, he lifted the counterpane and slid into the bed with her. He couldn't offer her much, but at least his body heat would keep her from shivering.

Still deeply asleep, she rolled toward him, nestled her head in the crook of his shoulder, and hitched her thigh over his. Her hand came to rest over his heart, her softness molded to his hard chest.

He breathed a sigh. He didn't know what the morrow might bring, but for now, it was enough just to hold her.

His body disagreed. His cock roused to an aching stand.

Traitor, he thought toward the offending member. *Where were you when I needed you?*

Chapter 20

EVEN THOUGH SUNLIGHT STOLE OVER HER, OLIVIA snuggled deeper into the linens. Her bed had never been so warm. The feather tick molded around her, holding her in a comforting embrace. She breathed in a deliciously masculine scent, a hint of leather mixed with citrusy bergamot. Then as she skimmed the surface of sleep, flirting with the idea of sinking once again into deep oblivion, she became vaguely aware that her hand was resting on a hard lump.

The lump moved ever so slightly and then swelled to a larger size. The surprising movement jerked her to full consciousness.

She opened her eyes and realized her head wasn't on her pillow. It was resting on Rhys Warrington's shoulder. The delicious smell was emanating from him, and the warmth streaming over her was from his regular breathing. More alarmingly, the lump under her palm was his male part. She jerked her hand away and sat up abruptly.

"What are you doing here?"

He stretched his arms to their full length and yawned hugely. "I *was* sleeping."

"You know what I mean," she hissed in exasperation. "You can't be in my bed."

"And yet, here I am, *ergo* I certainly can." He plumped the pillows so he was half-sitting up. Then he laced his fingers behind his head. "For an intelligent young woman you have a remarkably tenuous grasp on logic."

"I mean you *mustn't* be in my bed." Since he didn't seem inclined to move, she climbed out and shrugged on her wrapper, knotting the belt firmly at her waist. "Make up your mind, Rhys. Which am I? Intelligent or a silly little twit?"

"In all honesty, I think you're brilliant." He had the grace to look chagrined. "Unfortunately, I sometimes say things I regret in the heat of an argument."

"And I sometimes do things I regret in the heat of…" Well, it wouldn't do to mention the sort of heat she'd been in last night, but she might as well let him believe she wished she hadn't allowed him the liberties he took with her.

If only her body wasn't still singing about it.

"Wait a moment," she said. "Was that bit about my being brilliant your version of an apology?"

"If you like."

A low growl rumbled in the back of her throat. The man was infuriating. "What I'd like is for you to be gone."

"Perhaps that would be the wisest course for now." He glanced at the window where the morning sun streamed in and then swung his legs out of bed. "How early does your abigail usually arrive?"

"Not until I call her this morning." Olivia skittered over to retrieve his boots near the fireplace and brought them to him. If he was set on going, she meant to help him on his way. The sooner Rhys Warrington was out of her bedchamber—and out of her life, for that matter—the better. "Since I expected you to turn up here last night to take advantage of the wager you won, I left instructions for her not to disturb me."

"That settles it once and for all." He tugged on his boots and stood, trying in vain to smooth out the wrinkles left in his jacket from sleeping in it. "You're definitely an intelligent young woman."

"An intelligent young woman who'll be ruined if you don't leave now," she hissed.

"Not until you let me truly apologize for last night."

She opened her door a crack and peered into the corridor. There was no one to be seen. "Apology accepted. Now go."

"But I haven't apologized yet."

She closed her door with a soft snick of the latch and leaned against it. Sunlight tracked rapidly across her floor. Olivia had struggled with the mathematics her tutors tried to teach her, but she didn't need an equation to realize every second of delay meant the likelihood of their being caught increased exponentially. "Very well, Rhys. Apologize, but be quick about it."

To her surprise, he pulled her into his arms. "I've always felt actions speak louder than words."

He bent to kiss her soundly. She stiffened but couldn't remain unmoved as his lips moved over hers. Her body remembered him, clamored for him, even though her heart was still wary. Before she knew it, she was answering the blasted man's kiss as if the hurts of last night had never happened.

When he released her mouth, he smiled down at her. "Now I feel forgiven."

She thumped his chest with the heel of her hand. She had no idea how she should feel. He made so many conflicting emotions dart about in her at once, and most of them didn't do her the least credit.

"Why did you…I mean, I still don't completely understand what happened last night," she said, unable to look him directly in the eye. The memory of his mouth on her and the way she'd come undone under him made her knees tremble.

Rhys slid a finger under her chin and tipped her face up. "I was a cad. That's what happened." He brushed her lips with his again in a soft sweet comma of a kiss, a delicious short pause before he went on. "But I needed to be one in order for you to greet the dawn still a virgin."

Against her better judgment, a grin lifted the corners of her mouth. "At least I'm now a knowledgeable virgin."

"Not quite yet." He cocked a brow. "But you're definitely getting there."

"And you're not leaving and you need to," she said, turning him and giving him a little shove toward the door.

"See you at breakfast," he said. "I'll try not to let my hand drift to your knee under the table."

"It better not," she agreed, though part of her thought that would be better than extra clotted cream on her scone. What would it be like to try to sip her tea with her mother's guests all around while Rhys secretly caressed her in a spot much higher up than her knee?

Lord, what a wanton I'm becoming!

He kissed her once more and her body wept for him to stay.

"Go," she ordered in a whisper, proving however much her flesh might riot, her head was still in charge.

❧

Rhys opened the door and nearly plowed into an imposing man with graying temples and a salt-and-pepper mustache. He was standing in the hallway with his fist poised to knock on Olivia's door. His face twisted into a fierce scowl that wouldn't have been out of place on an English mastiff.

"What the devil!" the man said.

"Father!" Olivia squeaked.

"Mr. Symon—" Rhys began.

"I know who I am, young man. Who in blue blazes are you, and what in the name of perdition are you doing in my daughter's bedchamber?" Horatio Symon roared, obviously not the least concerned over who else might hear him.

Several doors up and down the corridor opened slightly, and curious guests peeped out through the cracks.

"Papa, this isn't what it seems," Olivia said in a meek tone Rhys had never heard from her before.

"Ballocks!" Mr. Symon roared. "Whatever else it might be, what it *seems* is bad enough. In fact, that's all that matters. Olivia, put some clothes on and I'll be back to deal with you directly. And as for you!" He poked Rhys on the center of his chest. "Come with me, you hairy-legged honyock."

Mr. Symon turned and stomped down the hall, leaving Rhys no choice but to follow. He'd have sooner faced a French firing squad, but he was well and truly caught by Olivia's father and now he was going to have to pay.

Symon didn't speak another word, but Rhys sensed fury roiling off him in waves as he led the way down the long, curving staircase. He wondered if the old man would choose pistols or swords. Pistols, probably. Not many men of Horatio Symon's years kept up their sword arms well enough to take on someone half their age.

Firearms were a great equalizer.

Mr. Symon didn't stop until he reached a room Rhys hadn't seen before. He drew a key from his waistcoat pocket and unlocked the door. Then he banged through the portal, letting the heavy oak slam against the adjacent wall.

"Get in here," he said gruffly.

Rhys followed. The study was richly appointed with floor-to-ceiling mahogany shelves on one wall, a row of windows on another, and a marble fireplace on a third. A massive burled walnut desk with ornately carved legs and corners occupied the central position in the lavish space before the tall windows. A globe mounted on a tripod stood in one corner. A collection of hunting rifles were displayed, within alarmingly easy reach, above the fireplace mantel. The skin of a tiger had been turned into a rug and stretched menacingly across the polished marble floor. Mr. Symon took the seat behind the desk like an Eastern potentate mounting his throne.

So Daniel must have felt as he was about to enter the lion's den. Of course, Daniel was innocent and Rhys had been caught red-handed. He deserved whatever sort of mauling Mr. Symon chose to give him. Nevertheless, he strode forward and stopped before the desk, clasping his hands behind his back and standing tall.

"Sir, I want you to know—"

"And I want you to know I expect you to answer my questions and nothing more." He leaned back his chair and narrowed his eyes at Rhys. "Olivia is my little lark. She's always up early, so when I arrived home this morning and she wasn't out and about, I assumed she must be ill. The last thing I expected to find was a man in her chamber."

"I can explain—"

"Did I ask a question?" Mr. Symon interrupted with hand upraised. "Didn't think so. Keep your teeth together until I do. Now, what's your name?"

Rhys decided his courtesy title would never be more useful. "Lord Rhys Warrington."

The man's nostrils flared as if he'd caught a whiff of raw sewage. "Son of the marquis?"

Rhys nodded. "His second son. As far as I know, my older brother is in the best of health, and I trust God will grant him the full three score and ten."

May as well let Symon know straight out that I have few prospects.

"A spare, eh? I know the breed, and let me tell you, you've run the wrong vixen to ground. I have no plans to let Olivia's future husband take control of her dowry. It'll all stay in trust for her use alone. If you thought you'd come to Barrowdell to find a rich wife—"

"No, sir." Even at the risk of angering him further, Rhys had to break in. "I came to help the Duke of Clarence find a rich wife."

Mr. Symon frowned. "Explain yourself."

Rhys ran through the same basic rationale for his presence that he'd given Olivia the first time they'd met. "So you see, my purpose for being here is to get to know His Highness's intended—"

"I doubt Clarence commissioned you to get to know her in the biblical sense," Mr. Symon said dryly.

"No, he didn't and I haven't."

"Do you expect me to believe that?"

"Believe what you will; Olivia is still a virgin. You have my oath upon it. But even if you can't trust me, you should trust your daughter. Ask her."

Mr. Symon made a noise somewhere between a snort and a chuckle, and the anger that had reddened his neck sloughed off him. He steepled his fingers on the desk before him. "Then what in God's name were you doing in her chamber?"

"I was protecting her." Rhys told Horatio Symon how Molly's saddle had been tampered with and about the death of Mr. Weinschmidt in the hothouse. When Rhys explained that the two incidents were linked by the unusual thorns, Mr. Symon's florid complexion blanched to the color of day-old porridge. "Someone has made two bungled attempts on your daughter's life. I didn't want the third time to be the charm."

Mr. Symon frowned in concentration as he digested this new information. "I know a father isn't supposed to have a favorite among his offspring, but Olivia is the apple of my eye. And I'm afraid everyone knows it. If you've been protecting her, I thank you"—he cleared his throat as if the next words were stuck in it, "my lord."

"Warrington will do. Or just plain Rhys, if you prefer." Rhys inclined his head in acknowledgment and began to hope he'd escape this interview without ending up like the tiger on the floor.

"A common touch. I like that. Just plain Rhys it is then, and you should call me Horatio. Take a seat," he said, indicating the tufted Sheraton chair Rhys was standing beside. Then Olivia's father stood and crossed to the bookshelves. He pulled out a thick copy of Adam Smith's *The Wealth of Nations*. "Not all the wisdom in the world is to be found in books. Sometimes we find enlightenment in a bottle."

The tome turned out to be hollow. Within its binding, *Wealth of Nations* hid a flask of spirits and two tumblers. Horatio poured up two fingers of green liquid and handed one to Rhys. The strong smell of anise wafted up from the drink.

"Some folk might say it's too early in the day for spirits," Horatio said. "But they'd not say it if they learned their darling daughter is the target of an assassin."

Symon clinked the rim of his tumbler with Rhys's and downed the contents in one swallow. Rhys followed suit, letting the liquor burn a trail down his empty gullet. Rhys prided himself on holding his drink, but this stuff was potent enough to make his eyes water.

"Who else knows of your suspicions?" Symon asked as he refilled Rhys's glass and then settled into his chair.

"No one but Olivia."

"Good. Let's keep it that way. Mrs. Symon means well, but she'd go to pieces if she learned of this. Drink up, son."

Rhys felt himself relax a bit, whether from the spirits

or from having someone else to trust with Olivia's safety, he wasn't sure. Either way, it was a welcome turn of events.

"Have you any idea who's behind the attacks?" Rhys asked.

"How should I know?" Horatio said. "I've been at court these past months."

"Then you might know who would be upset enough over Olivia's match with the royal duke to take such drastic measures to stop it."

"I don't think we need worry on that score," Horatio said as he reached across and refilled his and Rhys's glasses. Then he downed his own portion in a one gulp. "Where do you intend to live?"

Rhys frowned and, even though he was at least one drink up on Olivia's father, he was not to be outdone by his host. He knocked back the liquor. *What difference should it make to Horatio Symon where I go after I leave Barrowdell?* "I don't understand the question."

"Where will you take Olivia after the two of you marry?"

Rhys stood. "Now wait a moment. Weren't you listening? I'm here on behalf of the Duke of Clarence, and besides, Olivia is still a maiden."

"I heard you, and I must confess it makes me wonder a bit about you, young man." Horatio shook an admonishing finger at him. "But after the scandal you caused this morning, my little girl needs a husband and you're the logical choice."

"But the Duke of Clarence—"

"Is no longer pursuing a match with her," Horatio admitted. "Seems Parliament put its foot down. The

House of Lords will not countenance a commoner princess, no matter how well dowered, no matter how badly the prince's purse wants her." He rubbed the back of his neck. "Her mother will be crestfallen, but in truth, I'm not sorry the match fell through. Clarence would not have made my little girl happy. But I didn't know how to tell Olivia she's been rejected on account of something over which she had no control. Now I won't have to. That's why it'll work out perfectly for you to marry her. Mrs. Symon will be inconsolable about losing the chance to have royalty in the family, but only until I tell her Olivia will still have a titled husband. Cheers."

He clinked the rim of his tumbler to Rhys's. When had Mr. Symon refilled them? No matter. Rhys was obliged to drink. The burn wasn't as noticeable now, but the top of his head felt appreciably lighter.

"But mine is only a courtesy title."

"Still counts with Mrs. Symon, and that's what matters to me," he said, rising again and coming around the desk to clap a hand on Rhys's shoulder.

He refilled Rhys's glass and they both drank. This time Rhys's vision almost tunneled.

What the hell is this stuff?

"So if you have no ideas about where you might live," Horatio said, "I'll send word for my man of business to see if there's a suitable townhouse in London near our Mayfair address and have him purchase it."

"I don't want you to buy me a townhouse."

"Let's set matters straight right from the outset. I'm not doing this for you," Horatio said gruffly as he refilled both their tumblers. "I'm doing it for Olivia.

It'll be her house. Not yours. Behave yourself well enough and she might let you live there."

Horatio knocked his drink back and raised a brow at Rhys's full glass. Rhys drained his as well. The whole world seemed to soften a bit around the edges as if he were peering through thin gauze.

"Fine." *Fine?* He should have bitten off his tongue before he made any noises that sounded like he agreed with this nonsense. "No, I mean, not fine. No, it's not necessary to buy a townhouse for Olivia because I won't be marrying your daughter. I'm not the marrying kind."

Horatio's eyes held a faintly sympathetic light. "No man is, son, until he meets the woman who turns him into the marrying kind."

Rhys could do far worse than Olivia. But she could do far better. Her standards were so high; she hadn't even consented to wed a royal duke when most women would have fallen over themselves to snag one. "She may not accept me."

"I think she will."

Rhys was beginning to warm up to the idea. Horatio poured another helping of liquor into Rhys's tumbler, though he neglected to refill his own. This time when he downed it, Rhys wondered why he'd ever thought the liquor strong, though he did have the sensation that his feet were about to leave the floor.

"I could ask my father to procure a special license for us. He's a marquis, you know," Rhys said confidingly. "He could do it like that."

Rhys tried to snap his fingers, but they didn't seem to want to obey his commands. Still, a special license was a good idea. That way they wouldn't have to wait the interminable weeks for the banns to be read each Sunday. If he was going to marry Olivia in any case, why delay?

"No, I think it's best if the pair of you head out for Gretna Green now, this very day. Honeymoon for a month in Scotland, and by then we'll have that townhouse business settled," Horatio said. "Besides, if you're concerned for Olivia's safety, you'll want to take her away from Barrowdell as soon as possible."

"That's right," Rhys said. "As shoon as poshible." He waggled his empty glass at Mr. Symon. "What is this shtuff, by the way?"

"Absinthe. Mostly. Among my many business interests is a little distillery that makes a fortified version for me. Don't make a habit of it or you'll go blind," his future father-in-law advised. Horatio put his arm around Rhys's shoulders. "Have I told you about my tiger yet?"

Rhys looked down at the fur beneath his feet. The black and golden stripes seemed to waver like tall grass in a breeze. He shook his head and the wavering sped up as if a gale had suddenly blown in.

"It was a notorious man-eater. Killed seventeen villagers before I led the hunting party that bagged him." Horatio puffed out his chest like a peacock doing a mating dance. "Made me mad, him dragging people off like that. Got him right between the eyes."

Mr. Symon tapped Rhys on the forehead.

"Don't make me mad, Warrington. You treat my little girl right. Make her happy."

Rhys nodded. Of course he would. He'd treat

Olivia like a princess. No wait, she wasn't going to be a princess anymore. He'd have to think of something else. Something better.

Thinking hurt.

He squeezed his eyes closed because the room was starting to spin.

He'd mucked up so many things in his life—his military career, his family, and now poor Olivia was going to have to marry him.

"What if I don't make her happy?"

The tiger fur seemed to be rushing up to meet him, but it might have been that he crumpled to the floor. The last thing he heard before he let the gathering blackness envelop him was Mr. Symon saying, "See that you do, boy. I'm still a damn good shot."

Chapter 21

"AT LEAST I'M BEING SENT INTO EXILE IN STYLE," Olivia said to no one in particular as the sumptuously padded coach lurched along the frozen road. The only one who might have heard her was Rhys, but he was slumped on the opposite squab, snoring like a two-man saw.

It was bad enough that her father felt it necessary to bundle her off before breakfast, without even giving her a chance to say good-bye to her mother or sisters.

"That would defeat the purpose of an elopement," Papa had argued. "The whole idea is to steal away without anyone's notice."

Not that they'd been particularly successful in that respect either. She was sure most of the guests quartered near her chamber were aware that Rhys Warrington had been caught there with her in a compromising situation. No one could have slept through Horatio Symon's roaring. By now, the tale had surely lost nothing in the telling.

And word of their flight certainly swirled through the servants' wing of the great house once Mr. Thatcher and Davy were ordered to hitch up the matched set of bays to the Symon's best traveling coach.

"But I'm still a virgin," she'd told her father, grateful now that Rhys had made sure she remained one.

It didn't matter. Papa had come to a "gentlemen's agreement" with Lord Rhys over copious amounts of spirits and that was that.

The worst of it all was for the first time her father refused to listen to her. He wouldn't be swayed when she pleaded with him not to send her away with a drunken lord. Until today, she'd have said she was a little bit his favorite among all his daughters, but his face was set like stone.

It had softened for just a moment before he closed the carriage door. "Be careful, daughter, and write your mother once everything's settled good and proper," he said. "Lord Rhys gave me his word he'll try to make you happy, and we already know he is particular about your protection. If anything happens to you, I…"

Her gruff father found he needed to blow his nose and did so loudly after the door clanged shut.

Barrowdell was within a hard day's drive of the Scottish border, so word of fleeing couples who were bent on taking advantage of the liberal Scottish marriage laws came to her mother's notice with frequency. Beatrice Symon always made a tsking noise when they did.

"It smacks of seediness and poor upbringing," she'd say. Words like "shockingly fast," "loose morals," and "bun already in the oven" were burned into Olivia's memory.

Even though she was ashamed at being hustled away

to be married on the quick, part of her still might have been glad to run away with Rhys.

If only he hadn't been rolling on the floor drunk.

He'd roused once or twice and demanded they stop so he could heave in the bushes alongside the coaching road. Each time he'd looked so pale and drawn afterward, she hadn't the heart to berate him for his disgraceful condition.

Now that he was sleeping soundly again and his skin had regained a healthy color, she thought a good berating was exactly what he deserved for ruining what by rights ought to have been an exciting adventure. An eloping couple should have spent this coach trip laughing together and enjoying the splendid Lake District sights. Maybe even indulging in a little naughtiness in the rocking conveyance, which would shortly be state- and church-sanctioned naughtiness after the words were said over them in Gretna Green.

Instead, though their flight was encouraged, forced even, by her dear father, Rhys's drunkenness made the escapade feel tawdry.

He hadn't even *asked* her to marry him.

Her chest constricted. Was he drunk because he couldn't bear the thought of marrying her while sober?

The coach dipped in a pothole, and Rhys was startled awake. He groaned like a wounded bear, but he opened his eyes and made a manful attempt at sitting upright. He managed it on the second try.

"Decided to join me, did you?" Olivia said in a clipped tone.

He stared out the window of the coach through bleary eyes. The Blencathra and Caldbeck Fells rose in the distance, a blue blur capped with snowy peaks towering over the lower hills. "Where are we?"

"More than halfway from Penrith to Scotland," she said. "I saved you a bit of my luncheon. We have cold chicken and liver pate—"

"Ugh. Don't mention food."

"So sorry, milord. I neglected to pack any liquor, since we embarked on this journey with such short notice," she said snippily, "but in your case, I doubt even the 'hair of the dog' would help."

He leaned forward and cradled his head in both hands. "If ever again I touch absinthe, or any derivative thereof, I beg you to shoot me. But in the meantime, will you please stop shouting?"

"I'm not shouting," she said, making a conscious effort not to do so.

"It sounds like you are from in here." He tapped his temple and grimaced. Then he reached over and lowered the curtains, throwing the interior of the coach into semi-darkness. "That's better."

They rode in silence for a few minutes.

"Do you even know where we're going?" Olivia finally said, crossing her arms over her chest.

"Of course I do." Rhys raised his head and looked at her. "You just said we're halfway to Scotland, didn't you?"

Then he muttered something about how women never think men listen when clearly they do and a few other less decipherable sentiments along with an expletive or two about absinthe. She thought he also may have cast aspersions on the legitimacy of Horatio Symon's birth, but as his words were fairly garbled, she decided to give him the benefit of the doubt on that score.

She was none too pleased with her father either.

"Do you remember why we're going to Scotland?" Olivia asked.

"Horatio said we need to get you away from Barrowdell to keep you safe."

Horatio? Not even her mother called her father Horatio. "When I last saw you with my father, you were not on such pleasant terms."

"After a few jiggers of that devil's brew he calls absinthe, I'd have called him the pope if he'd asked me. What rotten stuff." He rubbed his temples.

Her father used his fortified liquor to gauge a man's mettle. He always claimed anyone who was still upright after three shots of the hellacious liquid was probably worth his time.

"How many drinks did you have?" she asked.

"Four, no, five, I think. Maybe a dozen," he said. "And on an empty stomach to boot."

Her father was, no doubt, impressed. Olivia was considerably less so.

"At any rate," Rhys went on without any noticeable slurs in his words now that he was more fully awake, "Horatio and I agreed that this was the proper course."

"This?" What was so hard about the word elopement? Why couldn't the man say it?

"Yes, this. Whoever threatened you at Barrowdell surely won't follow us to Gretna Green. Besides," he pressed a fist to his chest to stifle a belch, "the royal duke isn't interested in marrying you now, so there's no reason for anyone to try to hurt you."

"What?"

"Oh, I ought not to say it that way. How did your father put it? Something about the Parliament wouldn't let His Royal Highness's purse marry you because you're a commoner. No, that doesn't sound right either, but there it is," he said. "But if you want to put a fine point on it, I'm a commoner too, and I have no purse to speak of, so what do I care?"

"How very enlightened of you, Rhys." *What does he care indeed?*

"Yes, it is, isn't it?" He grinned soppily at her, pleased with himself.

Evidently, one of the side effects of too much absinthe was to render the sufferer immune to sarcasm.

"So once we arrive in Scotland, what are your intentions toward me?"

His grin dissolved into a puzzled frown. "I intend to make you my wife, of course."

"Have you asked me to marry you?"

He stared down at the tips of her slippers as if the answer to the question might be imprinted on their rounded toes. "I must have. You wouldn't be here with me otherwise."

"I'm only here because my father bundled me into the coach with you and sent us on our way," she said testily. "Luckily for you, I've never disobeyed my father."

"Didn't he tell you that you're going to marry me?"

Drat the man. "Yes."

"Well, then there you are."

She reached up and pounded the flat of her palm on the coach ceiling, signaling the driver to stop. Once it stopped moving, she shoved open the door. "And here I go."

She clambered out of the coach and started walking back in the direction from which they'd come. Her slippers were not meant for long hiking. She had no money. She had no idea how long it would take for her to make it back to Barrowdell, but she didn't care. Her only plan was to put as much distance between her and Rhys Warrington as possible.

"Olivia, wait," he called after her.

She didn't slacken her determined stride. Given the fact that light was like shards of glass to the eyes to someone who'd imbibed as much of her father's liquor as Rhys had, she was more than surprised when she heard his quick footfalls pounding behind her.

He caught up to her and fell into step beside her. "Slow down and I'll walk with you."

She shortened her strides by the smallest of measures.

"Where do you think you're going?" he asked pleasantly, as if they were off on a stroll.

"Back to Barrowdell." She pulled the hood on her pelisse closer against the wind washing down from the distant peaks. "If the Duke of Clarence no longer wants to marry me, then I'm no longer embroiled in royal intrigues. I'm reasonably safe from whoever tried to do me harm."

"You don't know that." Rhys started to reach for her, but when she glared at him, he shoved his hands into his pockets. "They may have had another motivation."

"So, you think I'm distasteful enough that someone wishes me dead."

"No, of course not. It wasn't because of you. Never." He put a hand up to shade his eyes. She was sure being in the open sunlight was excruciating for him.

Good, she thought waspishly.

"But your father is a very rich man. And rich men make enemies," Rhys continued. "In fact, if he makes a habit of introducing his associates to absinthe, I'll wager he's made plenty."

She stopped her ears with both hands. "No more wagers." Lost bets to Rhys Warrington were the beginning of all her troubles.

He swung around in front of her, stopping her in her tracks, and took both her hands, sheltering them between his. "Olivia, I only want to see you safe."

"Is that all you want?" she asked, her heart anxious about his answer, but not terribly hopeful. It seemed Rhys was only following her father's dictum.

"Well, no."

Now. If he's going to ask me to marry him, let him ask now. Oh, please, God, let him ask.

"I…" He paused as if stringing together words were an onerous task to which he wasn't sure he was equal. "I want to find out who made those attempts on your life and see them brought to justice. Someone has to pay for Mr. Weinschmidt, you know."

"You're right. Mr. Weinschmidt deserves better than he got." She tugged her hands free, her heart wilting inside. "Then the best place to find his killer is back at Barrowdell." She started to walk again.

"But your father says you need a husband."

"I also need a mare that isn't lame and a gardening assistant who's still alive, but we can't turn back time.

Don't worry about me, Rhys," she said. "I don't mind losing the match with Clarence. Court life would have been like prison to me."

"I'm glad you feel that way."

"And don't trouble yourself over being caught in my bedchamber this morning," she said, increasing her pace. He matched her easily with his longer strides. "I'm not the fashionable sort. I don't care what fashionable people say about me. I'll be perfectly happy to live out my semi-scandalous life in my father's house as an eccentric spinster."

"But what about my happiness?"

That made her pause for half a step; then she shook it off. "Your happiness? Why, I expect you'll remember very shortly that you're a libertine and a rake and glad to be one. Just because we were caught in a compromising situation this morning, you are not obligated to marry me, Rhys." The last thing she wanted was a man who felt required to become her husband. "I release you from whatever Machiavellian bonds my father and his absinthe placed upon you."

He caught her wrist and stopped her. "What if I don't want to be released?"

"You don't?"

"No, I don't."

"Then you do want to marry me?"

"I do."

It sounded so much like a real declaration her heart leapt up in joy. Then she remembered she was Horatio Symon's daughter. Her father lived for the art of the deal. "What did my father promise you if you married me?"

"He promised that I wouldn't be able to touch a farthing of your dowry, which is fine with me." His lips quirked in a quick smile. "Since I intend to continue to support myself at the gaming tables, it's probably best that I not have an infinite kitty from which to draw. Too much money in the hole makes a gambler sloppy. Rest assured that I will always provide sufficient funds to support you. I may be out of favor with my family, but they haven't cut me off financially. If we get in a tight patch, Warrington credit is good anywhere. Use your father's money for more orchids or horses or whatever pleases you. I won't touch a pence."

Forty thousand pounds a year would buy a lot of orchids. She'd have to look into founding some charities with her father's largess.

"Did *Horatio*—" she could still scarcely believe her father had asked Rhys to call him that, "promise you anything else if you and I wed?"

"He hinted that you might allow me to live with you in the Mayfair townhouse he intended to buy for you."

"I might," she said, "but you'd have to learn to behave yourself."

"That's what he said too, but I can't promise that," he said and bent to kiss her. Then he picked her up and twirled her around. "In fact, I'll never behave myself with you."

When her feet finally touched the ground again, she sighed. "But I can't marry you."

"Why not?"

"You haven't really asked me, have you?"

He nodded slowly. "Without doubt I have done,

and in the future will do, many things wrong. Allow me to attempt to do one thing right."

He dropped to one knee before her. "Olivia Symon, will you do me the supreme honor of becoming my wife?"

She almost asked why he wanted to marry her. After all, he hadn't said a word about love. Everything she'd read in the *Practical Guide for Young Ladies of Quality* led her to believe that courtship was the only time a woman might expect fair speech from her man.

But she thought she saw something that might be love shining in Rhys's dark, slightly bloodshot, eyes and decided not to push him for a declaration. Fair words weren't the be-all and end-all, were they? Besides, if a man had to be prompted to proclaim love, how satisfying could it be?

How real?

Perhaps just the fact that Lord Rhys Warrington, self-avowed rake, was willing to commit to a wedding was enough for now.

She bent down and kissed his forehead. "Yes, Rhys. I'll marry you."

Chapter 22

DARKNESS WAS GATHERING BY THE TIME THE COACH rattled into Gretna Green, painting the surrounding hills a dim purple in the fading light. Rhys had sobered considerably in the last few hours of the trip. They'd laughed and talked and engaged in a little naughtiness in the rocking coach.

"There are ways for a man to have carnal knowledge of a woman in a carriage without either of them undressing completely, you know," Rhys had told her.

"How?" she asked. "This may be your last chance to make a knowledgeable virgin of me."

"Yes, but I couldn't guarantee you'd remain one. Potholes can make for some spectacularly disastrous results. Besides," he pulled her close and whispered in her ear, "I want your first time to be perfect, and we really need a good stout bed for that. After all, it'll be your first chance to catch me without my stockings."

"That's right. I've yet to see you completely naked." They laughed together then. When Olivia looked at Rhys and closed her eyelids, the imprint of his profile was burned on the backs of her eyes. His broad brow, his fine straight nose, the mouth that tempted her to any amount of folly…

And he's mine. She hugged that delicious little fact to herself. If she lived to be one hundred, she'd remember him like this, ruggedly handsome, full of life and joy.

After seeing the coach and horses safely housed in the town livery and their driver given a place in the haymow for the night, Rhys lost no time locating the blacksmith's shop on the edge of town.

The way the laws of Scotland read, anyone could say the words over a willing couple and they'd be considered man and wife. Smiths took advantage of their prime locations at crossroads to offer their services as "anvil priests," leading couples to offer their marriage vows amid the soot and ironworks, and then re-shoeing the tired horses that brought them there in haste.

"O' course, I'll tie the knot for ye," the burly, red-haired giant said as he stepped away from the heat of the forge. "Only one thing first. Are ye a willing party to this marriage, missy? I'll no' be leg-shacklin' ye to this gentleman if ye're under compulsion of any sort."

Olivia shot Rhys a quick smile. "I'm willing."

"Weel, that's grand then, isn't it?" He swiped his sweaty neck with a grimy hand. "Are we in a hurry or d'ye think there's none followin' close enough to hinder yer intentions if I take a moment to wash up a bit?"

"We're not likely to be disturbed in the next few minutes," Rhys said.

The smith nodded and submerged his ham-sized hands in a nearby basin. He scrubbed mightily, but soot stains still clung to his fingernails.

"Calum," he said to the gangly bare-chested lad who

worked by his side. "Fetch yer mother and a clean shirt for me. Have a bit of a wash for yerself too whilst ye're in the house. Ye're sixteen now. Old enough to be witness to a wedding. Best ye make a presentable job of it. Oh, and light the fire in yer brother's cottage before ye do aught else."

While the boy disappeared into the thatched cottage near the forge, Olivia took stock of their surroundings. When she was younger, she'd imagined her wedding in vibrant detail. She'd envisioned the parish church fragrantly alive with blooms from her garden and hothouse. The choir of boys that populated the church school would sing their sweet little lungs out. She'd seen herself in an elegant gown, styled in simple lines to please her and sparkling with seed pearls and lace to please her mother. The sanctuary would be filled with her family and well-wishers from the village.

Only the bridegroom's face remained hazy in her maidenly imaginings.

Now her bridegroom's face was the only real thing. She'd never have been able to envision becoming a wife in a sooty blacksmith's shop. Even though her insides were jumping with excitement over marrying Rhys, a small part of her was disappointed to miss the High Church rite of her dreams.

"Angus MacDermot is me name," the blacksmith said. His son Calum returned with a grinning, gap-toothed woman who must have been the smith's wife in tow. "I'll be needing your names as well, and make 'em your true ones, mind, else the rite's no good."

"Lord Rhys Alexander Ford Warrington."

"Miss Olivia Marguerite Symon."

"Verra good, your lairdship, Miss Symon. Now stand ye here on either side of me anvil and clasp hands so." Mr. MacDermot joined their hands palm to palm, Olivia's right to Rhys's left. Then he took a length of leather strap from his pocket and bound their wrists together. "Ye've stated your names. Now state your intention."

"We want to be married, of course," Rhys said, his brows lifting a bit at being required to name the obvious.

"Aye, and so shall ye be." Mr. MacDermot cleared his throat and placed his hands on the anvil between them. "This anvil has forged many a fine blade for protectin' what a man wishes to hold. So may this marriage forge together these two souls and be a safe haven for both parties to it."

Rhys's dark eyes shone as he looked down at her. He had already proven his ability to keep her safe physically. Would he give her heart the same care? He was a rake, she reminded herself. It was a little late to have misgivings, but she couldn't help a small flutter of unease under her ribs.

"This anvil has forged a good many plowshares for tillin' the land. So also may this marriage between Lord Rhys Warrington and Miss Olivia Symon prove fruitful," MacDermot said with a wide grin.

Fruitful? Children, he means. Oh, dear. I didn't even think about that.

Rhys would have enough trouble adapting to the married state. What sort of father would a rake make?

"This anvil has wrought many needful things for the

making of a prosperous home. So may this marriage provide needful things for the happy couple—enough so they know no want, yet not so much that they forget to share."

It wasn't the Anglican rite, but Olivia found herself agreeing with Mr. MacDermot's sentiments.

"And may they never forget the most needful thing is love," Angus MacDermot concluded.

Mrs. MacDermot sniffed loudly at that and swiped her eyes on her sleeve. She smiled at Olivia and Rhys though tears still welled. The woman meant well, but since she didn't know them, the tears rang false. Olivia wondered if she hired out as a professional mourner when business as a professional witness was spotty.

"And that's the end of me speechifying," their anvil priest said. "Now I call upon Mary MacDermot and James MacDermot to witness and mark it well as ye make yer vows."

Silence reigned for half a minute. In the church rite, the vicar read the vow from his book of services and the couple recited after him. Rhys looked askance at MacDermot. "Aren't you going to lead us?"

"How should I know what ye intend to promise the lady?" He pronounced the word as if it were "li-dey." "I'm no' a real priest, ye ken. Speak but the words in yer heart, man, and I'll pronounce ye *marrit* when the pair o' ye reach an end of yer jawin'."

"Are you sure this is legal?" Rhys asked.

"Oh, aye. Folk been marryin' this way in these parts since the Flood. Once ye leave the presence o' the anvil, ye'll be marrit before God and man."

Rhys tipped his head in a gesture that suggested he

was still dubious about the whole process, but he was willing to proceed. He met Olivia's gaze directly.

"Olivia Marguerite Symon, I have nothing you could want. No fortune compared to the one you're leaving in your father's house. No title. Once my father dies and my brother ascends to the marquisate, I'll be plain Mr. Warrington." A frown marred his brow. "Come to think of it, I can't even offer you a good name because I've soiled mine rather badly up to this point."

He squeezed her fingers and gazed at her earnestly.

"So all I can offer you is myself and hope it's enough," he said, his voice husky with emotion. "I'll try mightily not to shame you with bad behavior, though you know as well as I, I've had little practice with good. I'll provide for your comfort as best I can and protect you as long as I have a beating heart. I'll stand by you, in sickness or in health. I'll love you with my body and honor you with all that is in me. And if by some miracle we reach old age together, I'll sit beside you as the shadows fall and hold your hand, until we are dust."

Olivia's mouth gaped a bit and tears trembled on her lashes. Mrs. MacDermot sobbed aloud, but Olivia no longer thought she was putting on her emotional response. Who would have guessed her rake had the soul of a poet?

"These things I vow. Am I enough?" he asked.

She nodded. "Oh, yes, Rhys Warrington. You're enough."

"Weel, then, that's grand, isn't it?" Mr. MacDermot said. "Now then, have ye a ring to seal yer promise with, yer lairdship?"

Rhys frowned. "No."

"No worries. 'Tis a rare couple as has thought that far ahead by the time they reach me shop. So I've prepared a few what ye might call placeholders for just such a situation. 'Tis only 'til ye can buy the lady a proper ring, mind." Mr. MacDermot squinted at Olivia's left hand for a moment, then rummaged along his workbench and retrieved a nail that had been curved into a small circle. "Reckon this'll do for the now."

He handed it to Rhys and motioned for him to put it on her. The iron circlet was surprisingly smooth and fit her ring finger almost perfectly.

"Speak the words, man. Ye ken the ones I mean."

"With this ring," Rhys said, "I thee wed."

Mr. MacDermot beamed at them. "I now pronounce—"

"Wait a moment," Rhys said. "Isn't she supposed to make a vow to me?"

"The lass consented to marry ye, did she no'? After that litany of what ye dinna have, I'm thinkin' a canny man might be wantin' me to hurry things along lest she change her mind," Mr. MacDermot said out of one side of his mouth, as if only Rhys could hear him. "If ye're still desirous of a promise from her, I'll help ye, but let's make it quick before she has a bit of a think about things." Then he went on, directing his speech to Olivia alone. "Tell me, lass. According to the laws of God and man, will ye be a good and faithful wife to this undeserving wretch of a man?"

"That's helping?" Rhys said.

"Whist, man. Let the lass answer."

"Yes, I'll be his good and faithful wife."

"Then the necessaries having been satisfied—trust

me, man. Her vow, simple as it is, will stand ye in good
stead. Women have more sense about the doing part of
being marrit than men do. She'll do ye proud, I'll be
bound. Where was I? Oh, aye, I now pronounce ye
man and wife."

Mr. MacDermot handed Rhys a dirk.

"Yer first task as her husband is to cut her free. Ye're
bound together yet, even though the strap binding ye
be gone, but after, when ye come to each other, 'tis
always of yer own free will."

Rhys slid the tip of the dirk between them, taking
care not to nick her wrist, and sliced the leather in a
quick stroke. Olivia's hand still wasn't free though. He
laced his fingers with hers and held her fast.

"Now ye can kiss yer bride," MacDermot advised.

Rhys didn't need to be told twice. He gathered her
close and kissed her deeply. The wedding ceremony
had had the hazy quality of a slightly comedic dream,
but Rhys's kiss was as real as life could ever be.

"Easy, man," MacDermot said. "Save a trifling for
the weddin' night."

Olivia's face flushed hotly.

Wedding night.

All those lovely, filthy things Rhys had done with
her were suddenly lovely, pure things. Didn't the Good
Book say Adam and Eve were naked and they were not
ashamed? If she had her way, Rhys would run around
without stockings or anything else all the time. Her imagination was already running rampant with some previously
wicked ideas that were now perfectly good ones.

They were the same things. How amazing that a few
words said over an anvil should change them so utterly.

"And speakin' o' the weddin' night," MacDermot said, "while it's true what we've done here is legal, a bedding makes it *completely* legal, if ye take me meaning. To that end, may I suggest that your lairdship might take his ease with his wife in yonder croft?"

On the other side of the forge stood another thatch-roofed cottage, as like the smith's home as two peas.

"It belongs to me oldest son, Seamus. He and his brood have gone to London in search of work. Calum started the fire in there afore we began the ceremony, so I'll warrant 'tis toasty warm now, and me missus keeps it clean enough to eat off the floor. Me son lets me lease it out to deserving couples such as yerselves for a fair reasonable price." MacDermot named a sum that bordered on highway robbery. "I can let ye have it by the month or the week, milord."

"We'll take it for the night. One night only," Rhys said. "But I'll pay you for the week if your good wife will bring us some supper in a couple hours."

Mrs. MacDermot bobbed a quick courtesy and scurried back into her home to make preparations while her husband handed over the iron key to the oak door of his son's home.

Rhys offered Olivia his arm. "I'm sorry you had to be wed with a nail for ring. I promise you a real one as soon as possible."

"I rather like this one," she said, holding her hand aloft and pretending to admire the lead-gray metal. "I suspect it will fit your nose well should I ever feel the need to lead you around by it."

Rhys threw his head back and laughed. "Come, wife. Like the man said, I'm ready to take my ease with you."

"Prepare yourself, husband," she said with a grin. "I plan on a little ease-taking myself."

Chapter 23

As they neared the cottage door, Rhys scooped Olivia up to carry her over the threshold.

"I had no idea you were so old-fashioned." She draped her arms around his shoulders and peppered his neck with kisses. Then she suckled his earlobe.

His eyes threatened to roll back in his head, but he somehow managed to hold her one-handed while he worked the key in the iron lock and threw open the door.

"Haven't you ever heard it's bad luck for a bride to trip on the threshold? If she does, the marriage starts with a bad omen."

"What if the bridegroom trips?" she asked.

"Then the bride realizes she's married a clumsy lout, but by then it's too late." Rhys set her down inside the tidy cottage. He'd barely closed the door behind him when Olivia wrapped her arms about him.

He placed an arm around her waist and drew her close. Then he caught one of her hands and pressed it against his chest, letting her feel the pounding of his heart. "You're stuck with me, Olivia, and I don't intend to let you think long enough to reconsider."

He'd meant to hold back, to wait for her to respond, but blood pounded in his ears, the drumbeat of lust. He claimed her mouth, nearly overcome by her sweetness. Her clean scent surrounded him, intoxicating him more thoroughly than that cursed absinthe. When she answered his kiss and pressed herself against him, the pounding in his ears grew so loud he thought she must be able to hear it. Then the drumbeat moved much lower, to his hard cock. It throbbed with the rhythm of his life in ever-quickening pulses.

Rhys knew he should be gentler as he cupped her bum and lifted her against him. This was her first time, for pity's sake. He ought to go slow. If he didn't hold back, she might shatter in his arms.

Olivia didn't seem to think she was that fragile though. When he started to release her, she pulled his head back down with a soft moan, urging him to stay.

Olivia nipped at his lower lip. His groin ached all the more. The desperate little noises she made at the back of her throat nearly drove him mad.

His hands roamed over her, finding and exploring each dip and valley, the exquisite line of her back, the curve of her bum. He gathered the bombazine of her traveling gown in his fists and worked the column of fabric up. She raised her arms in surrender, and he pulled the garment over her head.

Her hands were busy too, plucking at buttons here, shoving clothing out of the way there. She stepped out of her slippers and he toed off his boots, balancing one-legged all the while so as not to interrupt the drugging effect of her mouth beneath his. If he'd been capable of rational thought at the time, he'd have applauded his athletic prowess.

They moved together in a stylized dance of lust, garments dropping unheeded to the clean-swept plank floor as they worked their way toward their destination—the soft-looking string bed in the corner of the cottage's single room.

When Olivia stood before him in naught but her shift, he paused for a moment, drinking in the sight of her. Her pale skin was gilded with light from the fire, setting her aglow like some ethereal being. She was as out of place in the homely cottage as an angel in purgatory.

"You're not stopping?" she asked, her voice dusky.

"Not for worlds," he promised as he pulled the chemise over her head, leaving her bare as Eve in glory.

Her breasts shuddered with a sigh. Then her gaze swept down over him and she giggled.

"What's so funny?" He'd been so intent on seeing her naked, he hadn't realized she'd done a fair job of disrobing him at the same time.

"You're still wearing your stockings."

He bent down and yanked off the offending socks. Then he straightened and looked his fill of her. His conscience had flayed him while he tried to seduce her in her father's house. Now they stood before each other, man and wife, naked as God made them.

And for the first time in a very long while, Rhys felt no shame.

"Now what?" she asked.

"Now, my love, I show you that being even a knowledgeable virgin is overrated. Stand still."

Slowly, he reached out a hand. Starting at the base of her throat where her pulse fluttered like the wings of a hummingbird, he traced a lover's journey over her flawless skin. She shivered under his touch.

Oh, the feel of her, all warm and soft and willing!

He paused to dally in every crevice, the crease beneath her slender arm, the delicate skin at the bend of her elbow. Defying the urgency of his cock, he took his time, learning her by heart.

He ran his fingertip around the outline of her hands, to the deep base of each finger and threading his way around her knuckles. He taunted the soft curve beneath each breast. He thumbed her nipples and watched them tighten to hard little nubs.

"Rhys," she chanted his name with urgency. He couldn't tell if it sounded more like a prayer or a curse.

"Hush, now." He kissed her again. "It'll be all right. Trust me."

She absolutely could this time.

He drew circles around the shallow indentation of her navel. Then his touch dropped lower and he teased her legs apart. His fingers launched a gentle invasion, though his gaze never left her face. He wanted to watch as he pleasured her.

She was hot and slick and ready. That little spot had risen for him to stroke and torment. Need parted her lips and made her eyes go languid.

When she reached out to touch him as well, he stopped her. "Not yet, love. You first."

"No, Rhys." She lifted her hand again to press her fingertips against his lips. "You've given me pleasure and taken none for yourself before. It brought me such joy, but no ease. Because if I can't give to you, I think I'll burst. We go together into this madness or not at all."

Then to his deep delight, she smoothed her palm along his jaw and down his neck, her touch a balm and a firebrand at once. A slight breath of wintery air found its way in around the nearby window, cooling the fever heating his bare skin.

"I've enjoyed being a knowledgeable virgin," she said, her voice sultry as she eased his hand away from her soft folds, "but I think I'll enjoy being a knowledgeable wife far more. Now it's my turn. This time *you* stand still."

He had difficulty drawing breath as her clever little hands fluttered over him, tickling along his ribs, teasing his nipples into hard knots. Then she cupped his ballocks. Her gentle massage only sent his cock into a deeper ache. She ran her hands over his hard thighs and stepped close enough to reach around and cup his buttocks as he'd done hers. Her breasts taunted him with glancing brushes as she moved closer. Then Olivia stepped back a pace.

"You're a quick learner," he said huskily.

"I had a good teacher."

But she carefully avoided the throbbing shaft that yearned for her touch more than any other part of him. Instead she raked his ribs with her nails and splayed her fingers across his flat belly. When she finally grasped him, it was all he could do not to erupt in her hands.

"Olivia, I can't—" Rhys began, but then she surprised him by leaping up, hooking her hands behind his neck, and wrapping her legs around his waist.

"Can't what?" she asked with feigned innocence

as she pressed herself against him, her hot moistness tormenting the tip of his cock. "Seems to me you definitely can."

She lifted a brow at him.

"You've been close to taking my maidenhead before," she said. "Now there's nothing stopping you."

Not God. Not man. Not guilt over how he'd meant to ruin her. She was his, well and truly. Or she would be in another moment or two.

"I love you, woman," he said. Then he covered her mouth with his before she could make fun of him for being so maudlin. All his longing and hope poured into her through that kiss.

He'd finally settled on the true name for that expanding lump in his chest that ached at the sight of her. It really was love. He'd thought himself dead to that heart-pumping anarchy, and yet, here it was, surging through him like a rain-swollen river.

He loved her—Olivia Symon, gardener, equestrienne, relentless tease. She was either a gift or a curse. A gift because from the crown of her head to the soles of her delicately arched feet, she fit the wrinkles in his soul perfectly.

And a curse because, having once had her, it would kill him to lose her. He'd spend the rest of his life trying to be worthy of her.

But if he didn't take her right now, he'd die on the spot. Slowly, he pushed her hips down, gently impaling her on his rock-hard erection. He groaned, awash in the pleasure of her slick, hot flesh. When he reached the thin barrier of her purity, he didn't stop. With one quick thrust, he made her take all of him.

She cried out, but it didn't sound like pain. The gasp that tore from her throat was the feral sound of feminine triumph as she engulfed him completely.

He tumbled onto the bed with her. Once they came to rest with her beneath him, he moved inside her, reveling in her softness. Her skin was heaven against his; her responses added fuel to the flame in his groin.

He'd never have guessed she was a virgin if he hadn't felt the rending of her hymen. There was no hesitation in her. Olivia moved with him, meeting his thrusts in an undulating rhythm. Heart on heart, they joined in perfect concert. They strained against each other.

Pleasure was their goal and their guide as they took and gave in equal measure. He'd thought to teach her, but she was schooling him.

A touch here, a gasp there.

Stop. Start. Speed up. Slow down now. Oh, that. Yes, please God, yes.

Their hands, mouths, bodies, and hearts joined. If they stopped kissing, it was only to tumble into each other's eyes. When Rhys looked down at her, he was lost in the wonder of the connection they were building.

Rhys had known countless women. But he'd never let one know him. When Olivia looked up at him, with trust shining out of her, with acceptance in her tremulous smile, he realized he'd never truly made love before. He might have joined his body to another body, but he'd never joined his heart to someone else's, never committed that misshapen part of him to another's care.

Olivia made him feel it might be safe.

There is surrender in shared bliss, a kind of dying that the body welcomes like the faithful soul longs for its reward in the afterlife. They teetered for just a moment on the brink of the abyss, then plummeted over the edge together. He felt her contract around him in spasms of joy as his seed pulsed into her.

He didn't know how long it lasted. Didn't care. Eternal things aren't bound by time, and they'd done something that would stay with him for the ages.

He'd made Olivia his.

Unwilling to part from her until he must, he lay his head on the pillow beside her and inhaled her sweet scent. Her heart hammered under his. Gradually, their breathing fell into an easy rhythm together as the fever of lust subsided.

When he finally slipped out of her, he shifted to settle by her side. He nuzzled her neck, utterly spent.

There was no need for words. Anything he might say would seem redundant. Though he wouldn't have minded hearing her say she loved him too.

He wouldn't press though. Her body had said it. Love was in every hitched breath, every shuddering cry. It enveloped him, sending delayed shivers over his skin. It was in the air he breathed. With this joining, he'd claimed her forever.

She kissed the crown of his head and hugged him close, relaxing beside his body with the same lethargy that was stealing over him. In a few moments, her even breathing told him she'd escaped into sleep ahead of him.

He propped himself up on one elbow and gazed down at her. Her lashes quivered on her cheeks and he knew she was dreaming.

"Let it be a good dream," he whispered. He'd let her sleep for a while. Then after Mrs. MacDermot brought them supper, he'd torment her until she begged him to take her again. No point in having been a rake if a man hadn't picked up a few useful insights into feminine sexuality.

He also decided he'd never ask God for another thing for the rest of his life. He'd already received more than the full measure of happiness. Another drop of joy might be too much.

Olivia was his. It was more than a rake had a right to ask. More than enough.

Chapter 24

"I'M PERFECTLY CONTENT TO REMAIN HERE IN GRETNA Green for our honeymoon," Olivia told him over their breakfast the next morning.

Mrs. MacDermot had sent over a platter of eggs, fresh bannocks, and plenty of clotted cream with an assortment of jams. There was also a savory covered dish of hot, juicy, perfectly spiced sausages. Rhys suspected they'd enjoy them more if their true list of ingredients was not questioned.

"Mr. MacDermot said we could have this cottage for a month," Olivia said between sips of her tea. She darted an inquiring glance at him. "If we wish, of course. If it's a question of funds—"

"It's not a matter of money. Never fear. I'm sufficiently flush to support you for at least the next month." The day he couldn't afford to lease a simple Scottish croft for a goodly stretch of time was the day he'd cock up his toes. It irked him that she thought he might not be able to adequately house her.

They'd made love no less than three times last night and indulged in one quick swive this morning.

But while their bodies found perfect harmony, their breakfast conversation had been stilted and filled with awkward silences. They communicated just fine in the marriage bed, but now that they were out of it, the strangeness of their new situation made them skittish with each other.

Something was bothering Olivia, but she hadn't come right out with it. Rhys wasn't sure he wanted to know what it was.

Instead she'd been hinting around that they'd need to access her money sooner rather than later. The idea chafed him more than wearing wet socks.

And she still hadn't told him she loved him, which was beginning to irritate him more than he wanted to admit.

"Why should my bride sleep in a crofter's cottage when my family has a small estate near here?"

"Oh! I didn't know the Warringtons had Scottish roots."

"We don't."

Rhys slathered his bannock with clotted cream and bit into it. He was sure the warm bun was fine, but as long as he felt this niggling sense that Olivia was disappointed with him for some reason, he couldn't completely enjoy Mrs. MacDermot's baked goods.

"The marquisate acquired a Scottish holding back in the days of Edward Longshanks," he explained. "And since no Warrington has ever yielded a foot of earth once it came into his possession, my father holds it still. Though the family seldom uses Braebrooke Cairn for more than a hunting lodge, there's a decent manor house on the estate." He used the rest of the bannock to sop up his eggs. "Besides, I want to be able to send back your father's coach as soon as possible."

There should be at least one serviceable conveyance they could use at the Scottish Warrington estate. Besides, the idea of being indebted to Horatio Symon for anything curdled his soul. Especially after the man thought he'd have to get Rhys thoroughly foxed before he'd marry Olivia.

"I wonder how your family will take the news of our hasty wedding," Olivia said, biting her lower lip.

"I doubt any of the family will be in residence there if that's what's worrying you," Rhys said. "Father may be in London if Parliament has been called into session, but Mother will be in the country still at the ancestral seat. My sisters and brother are all married with homes of their own. No one in the family lives at Braebrooke Cairn full time."

"Oh," she said, chasing a bit of sausage around her plate without actually spearing it so she could eat. "Once the Season starts, should we plan to go to London so I can meet your family?"

"No. I mean, we may go to London. After all, I believe you're going to be the proud owner of a townhouse there shortly." He scowled at the thought of living in a home for which only his wife held title. If not for the fact that he needed a safe place for Olivia to live, he'd refuse his father-in-law's generosity. As soon as he was financially able, Rhys would arrange for his own townhouse and move Olivia out of the one her father was going to buy for her. A man had to have some pride. "Wherever we live in London, we won't be seeing my family."

"Why not?"

"They don't want to see me." One of the reasons he felt comfortable going to Braebrooke Cairn was because he was fairly certain only the estate's servants would be there.

"Nonsense. I'm sure they do." She cast him a smile that would normally have made him melt.

He stared at her until the smile left her lips. "Let it go, Olivia."

"I see." She dabbed her lips with her napkin and laid it beside her plate.

The silence became so oppressive he finally asked, "All right, I give up. What do you see?"

"You're ashamed of me."

"Now you're being ridiculous." On the contrary, he was ashamed of himself and the whole Warrington clan. His family had all but cut him off. And frankly, he feared a hasty wedding to a commoner, albeit a wealthy heiress of a commoner, wouldn't do anything to endear him to his rigid father. If the marquis wouldn't see his son when he was on what everyone supposed was his deathbed, he likely wouldn't hesitate to snub Rhys over marrying a commoner wife.

The last thing Rhys wanted to do was bring Olivia into that nest of briars. He didn't want her hurt. But taking her to Braebrooke Cairn was a calculated risk he was prepared to bear. He wasn't likely to see any of his family, though the steward would probably send word that he and Olivia had been there. A thrifty soul, Alpin Ferguson sent detailed ledgers of the estate each quarter without fail. He'd have to notify Lord Warrington that his second son and his new wife were at Braebrooke Cairn in order to account for the extra consumption of everything from butter and eggs to the burning of costly beeswax candles.

But at least at his father's Scottish holding they'd be surrounded by loyal servants and miles of rugged countryside dotted with crofters who owed their living to the distant Lord Warrington. It would undoubtedly be safer for Olivia there than this cottage in the middle of nowhere.

Now that he'd had time to consider it, Rhys wasn't so sure the attacks on her at Barrowdell happened because someone wanted her match with the Duke of Clarence to go away. Those thorns seemed like a message, and a more personal method of dispatch than a political assassin would use.

He rose, leaving the rest of his sausages untouched. There was nothing wrong with the hearty country fare. The thought of someone targeting Olivia made him lose his appetite. The sooner he had her firmly ensconced behind the gray granite stones of Braebrooke Cairn, the better.

"Gather up your things," he said. "We're leaving."

"Just like that?"

"What do you want? A trumpet fanfare?" Couldn't she see that he was just trying to spare her, both from his family's vitriol and a killer's further attempts on her life?

"What I want," she said, her eyes blazing, "is a husband who isn't an insufferable tyrant."

"Too bad. What you're stuck with is me. I'll be back with the coach and driver in a quarter-hour." He strode to the door. "Don't make me wait."

After he closed the door behind him, he heard the unmistakable crash of crockery on the heavy oak. No doubt Mr. MacDermot would add that to their bill.

Across the short distance between the cottage and the

forge, Mr. MacDermot called out to him. "Mornin', lad. I see yer lass has a temper. But dinna think ye suffer alone. Ye bear the pangs that have afflicted all men. No matter who a man weds, he wakes to find himself marrit to someone else."

Rhys wondered how he found himself married at all. *Oh, that's right*, he thought with a scowl. *Absinthe*.

Olivia stared out the coach window as they bumped along on the winter-rough road. It wasn't quite cold enough for the muddy ruts to freeze, so the conveyance's wheels were occasionally sucked into gelatinous goo. Fortunately the team of horses managed to keep their momentum going, though each time they slowed, she expected to be ordered out to lighten the load while the pair of bays struggled up increasingly steep grades.

The Scottish countryside was stark and misted with cold rain that occasionally found its way in around the isinglass. The moist breath of winter made her hunker beneath her woolen cloak and bury her hands deeper in her fur muff.

Still, she might have found the coach trip pleasing, because she always enjoyed seeing new places. But for the fact that she had to share the small coach with her new lord and master, Rhys Warrington.

Or at least that's what he seemed to think he was.

She sneaked a glance at him, but he seemed content to sleep away the journey. *Drat the man*. This was supposed to be their honeymoon. How could he begin their tenuous marriage first by bullying her and then by ignoring her?

"Checking for holes?" she asked in a loud voice.

He jerked awake and sat upright. "What?" Her new husband rubbed his hand over his damnably handsome face. "Holes in what?"

"Your eyelids, of course. You've had them closed for so long I assumed you'd discovered a flaw which required closer study."

He grimaced at her and then looked out the window. "Time goes by faster when a man sleeps."

"I find time has wings when I'm having fun," Olivia said, then muttered under her breath, "which accounts for why this trip feels so interminable."

"Sorry. I don't recall pledging to keep you entertained," Rhys said. "But I did promise to protect you, and that's what I'm doing."

He was certainly protecting her from meeting his family. She couldn't imagine a time or place when she'd be ashamed to have Rhys on her arm. He evidently couldn't say the same about her, and the sting made it hard to draw a deep breath. Why didn't he want to bring her into the Warrington fold?

Another gust of cold wet, air slipped into the carriage, and she shivered.

"You're cold," he said.

"How observant you are."

He moved over from the opposite squab to sit beside her and draped a long arm over the seat back behind her. "Come. I'll warm you."

"I'm fine."

"No, you're not." He scooted closer so his muscular thigh pressed against hers. "Your lips are turning blue."

Even through her cloak and the layers of her

traveling gown, chemise, and stockings, she could feel
the heat of him. "My lips are none of your concern."

"Yes, they are." He cupped her chin and turned her
head so she had to face him. "All of you is my concern."

What about her heart? Didn't he care that he'd hurt
her? Did he even know?

He leaned toward her and closed the gap between
their mouths, stopping just shy of her lips. He didn't
shut his eyes, didn't turn his head so their noses
wouldn't bump. He merely peered down at her like a
sleek tomcat by a mouse hole.

"If you meant to kiss me, you've miscalculated
the distance," she said without moving so much as
an eyelash.

"You called me a tyrant this morning. I'm just trying
to show you I'm not." He leaned back with a sigh and
stared up at the coach ceiling. "I meant to give you
opportunity to accept my kiss by meeting me partway."

A sob tore from her throat. "If you're too ashamed
of our marriage to introduce me to your family, why
would you want to kiss me?"

His face jerked toward her, and she read surprise on
his features. "That's what you think?" He palmed her
cheek. "Nothing could be further from the truth. I'm
very proud to have you as my wife."

A little candle of hope flickered inside her. Then he
dropped his hand and the flame guttered.

"I may as well confess to you now that you have
nothing to be proud of in your choice of husbands. I'm
in disgrace, Olivia. My family doesn't want to see me."

"Why?"

In halting sentences, he told her of the less than

honorable end to his military career and the disastrous battle near a small French hamlet called Maubeuge.

"There were even whispers of treason in connection with the defeat. I was suspected of espionage, along with two of my friends," he said dully.

"I don't believe it," she said staunchly. Rhys Warrington might have been a rake and a wastrel, but he was no traitor.

He smiled sadly at her. "Thank you for that. But it doesn't change the fact that there is a cloud on my name, a stain I haven't been able to scrub clean no matter what I try."

"If you're in such disgrace, how did you ever come to be the Duke of Clarence's representative to me?"

"God knows." A wall rose up behind his dark eyes and he heaved a sigh. "Actually, the devil may have had more to do with it than the Deity."

Did he regret the odd turn of fate that threw them together? "It's how you met me."

"For which I'm grateful, but I doubt you should be," he said. "I'm blacklisted by the ton, which hasn't troubled me much. I was always more at home with the demimonde. But I'm a pariah, Olivia. I haven't been received in my family's home since I returned from France."

Olivia bit her lower lip. Her father may have bundled her off to marry in haste, but she knew he'd welcome her back with open arms. Her mother, too. Once she got over the scandal of an elopement, Beatrice Symon would probably find ways to romanticize the tale of her daughter and the young lord fleeing to the Highlands together. Her family was odd in many ways, but she knew they loved her and would never reject her.

Everything she'd really learned about life until she met Rhys had come from her parents. She might have chafed against some of her mother's strictures and wished for her father to be home more often, but they still taught her that the world was a safe place and she could count on their support.

Rhys had been taught that the ones who should have trusted him didn't.

"So you see why I don't want to present you to my family," Rhys said. "I can't be sure of our welcome, and I would not subject you to that."

She palmed his cheek and turned his head so he had to face her. She felt his pain as if it were her own and realized suddenly why he'd become a libertine. If no one else cared about him, why should he care about himself? His family's rejection had sent him on a self-destructive downward spiral. She pulled his head down so their lips were an inch or so apart.

"I want you to be sure of your welcome with me."

He closed the distance between their mouths and claimed hers in a warm, sure kiss.

He wrapped his arms around her and pulled her over onto his lap. She melted into his embrace, giving herself over to the gentle assault of his tongue.

It was a potent reminder of how wonderfully they'd fit together in other ways. He was hard as iron where her hip pressed up against him.

"I believe you told me once that it's possible for man to have carnal knowledge of a woman in a moving coach..." she said with a sly smile.

Chapter 25

RHYS'S MOUTH ON HERS WAS A REVELATION. NOW tender, now demanding, inviting her to do the same to him. Her heart hammered so hard, she wasn't the least cold any longer. She suddenly realized his hand was under her cloak, and it heated her to fever pitch.

While his kisses distracted her, he'd unbuttoned the top three buttons on her traveling ensemble. He teased his fingertips over her skin, grazing the lacy edge of her chemise peeping above her corset. Her nipples ached at his hand's nearness. He kissed his way along her jaw and down her throat.

His finger slipped under the lace and brushed her nipple, softly at first, then with a more determined thrumming. Longing shot to her core. Her breath hissed in over her teeth.

Desire flared white-hot when he kissed the hollow between her breasts. With his teeth, he caught the ribbon that held her chemise closed and tugged it loose. He nuzzled the linen aside to bare her nipples above her stays. He closed his lips over one and sucked.

The creaking wheels and jostling coach faded around her.

All that mattered was the pounding need. She was hollow with longing.

He took her hand and guided it inside his jacket, down the front of his waistcoat.

He wants me to touch him.

She undid his waistcoat as a thrill of power shot through her. His warmth radiated through the fine lawn fabric of his shirt. The image of Rhys naked and ready rose in her mind. His chest was rock hard beneath her palm.

She slid her hand down to discover another part of him was too.

When she stroked him, wishing the woolen trousers didn't separate her hand from his hot maleness, Rhys stopped nipping at her breasts and raised his head.

"Aren't you the little minx?"

"Disappointed?"

His gaze sizzled into hers. "Never. What say I lift your skirts and swive you senseless?"

She nodded, too shocked to answer.

Swive.

The deliciously decadent sound of it shivered over her. Oh, yes, being swived senseless was just what she needed.

He slipped a hand under her hem and ran his palm up her leg. Her thin cotton stockings and pantalets were no shield against the shivers that trailed his touch. When he reached mid-thigh and found bare flesh, she gasped at the nearness of his fingers to her throbbing core.

"I didn't promise to obey you in our wedding vows,"

she said with a hitched breath, "but I'll do whatever you say right now if you promise not to stop."

"I'll hold you to that." His hand moved up to where her pantalets left her crotch bared. He covered her mound with his hand, holding her hot, moist center. A fingertip invaded her soft folds.

She closed her eyes and bit the inside of her cheek to keep from moaning. Then she realized no one but Rhys was likely to hear her over the pounding of hoofbeats and clatter of the coach. She let her delight slip out of her throat in helpless little sounds.

"That's it," he murmured, his voice a low rumble in her ear.

She ought to bridle herself. She ought to be the proper English wife. She ought to insist they wait for a bed and the modesty of nighttime coupling. Hadn't Mrs. Noddlingham advised that real ladies were merely supposed to tolerate their husbands' marital attention?

"One must think of the children that may come as a result. Think of the coming week's menu to distract one's self from the unseemly invasion. Think that it will be over all the quicker if one closes one's eyes and lies quite still," the worthy Noddlingham advised.

But when Rhys's fingers moved with exquisite slowness over her secret parts, all she could do was moan like a wanton. She didn't want it to be over quickly. She welcomed the invasion, and if children were on their horizon, they were the farthest thing from her mind at the moment.

The coach's shades were open, but as they were bouncing through open countryside, she didn't worry that anyone might see her cradled on her husband's lap.

Of course, there was always the chance that they'd pass by an observant goatherd. He'd get an eyeful if they did.

Her breasts were bared and her skirt hiked up around her waist. She spread her knees to give Rhys easier access to her secrets. Rhys's mouth covered hers, driving all thoughts of modesty from her mind. He swallowed her needy little sounds. His blessed, wicked hand was between her legs. Her world spiraled down to that heat, that friction as he laid bare her soul with each stroke.

Olivia hitched one knee up, hooking her heel on the seat to open herself wider to him.

"Lord, you're so sweet," he said, his voice hoarse with wanting. He dipped a finger deep inside her and she moved against his hand, controlling how hard and how fast the fleshy part of his thumb rubbed against her sensitive spot. "Where did you learn that?"

She pulled her knees together. "Am I being very wicked?"

"Yes, but I like it. You're so wet." He teased her knees apart and resumed sliding his fingers through her intimate valleys. "Besides, no matter how wicked you decide to be, you can't touch my level of decadence."

She decided it might be fun to try. "Is this very wrong, what we're doing?"

"Nothing you and I do together is wrong." He kissed her deeply, then released her lips and started back down to her breasts again.

The swaying coach, his mouth on her nipples, his hand on her mound—the disparate movements conjoined in devastating rhythm.

She was so wet, he'd said. But he *liked* it.

Her heart seemed to crowd her ribs. She'd been taught to feel shame about that part of her, but Rhys handled that bit of her as if it were special, precious.

And fascinating.

She was slick and swollen, desire licking over her in tingling lashes.

He traced around her nipple with the tip of his tongue while his thumb circled her sensitive spot. She whimpered into his mouth. The long finger he'd slid inside her slipped in and out as his thumb continued its torture.

Sauce for the goose, she decided and reached between them to cup his groin hard.

It was his turn to groan. Through his wool trousers, his balls bunched tight under her touch. Then she rubbed her palm over his hard length from root to tip, pressing harder than she thought she should, but Rhys seemed to like it. He raised his pelvis into her strokes.

He growled with pleasure and tugged at her nipple, sucking the needy flesh. Desire flashed like heat lightning between her breasts and the tender spot between her legs, but offered no relief.

Frustration made her jerk in his arms. She was reaching for something, straining toward that unnamable place he'd taken her to before, that blessed unraveling. Rhys drove her toward her goal with aching fury. She finally came undone under the weight of his hand and his mouth and his warm embrace.

After her slow climb, the surge of release came fast. It washed over her with no warning, a warm flood. Her limbs trembled with the force of her inner pulses, and her spirit seemed to leave her body, drawn into a realm where all was warmth and light and pure joy. When she settled back into herself, the last concentric rings of her release were fading and she was once again bouncing along the Scottish excuse for a road in a rattling coach.

And Rhys was kissing her again, his mouth soft on hers. Urging her to return from wherever she'd been.

Now it was her turn to torment him. She grinned wickedly, moved to the seat opposite him, and tugged off her gloves. If there was no wrong way to undress a man, then it stood to reason there was no wrong way to partially disrobe him. Then she undid his trouser buttons with agonizing slowness.

Chapter 26

THE FAINT SCENT OF ALYSSUM HE ALWAYS ASSOCIATED with Olivia wafted toward him, along with a strongly sweet muskiness. Rhys responded to both. When Olivia moved off his lap, her skirts had drooped downward and now covered her knees, but her cloak was thrown back and her pert breasts still peeked out of the open bodice.

A delight to his eyes and frustration to his cock. How he'd love to rub its full length in the sweet hollow between those lovely mounds.

Her brows knit in concentration as she worked on his trouser buttons.

It was the height of hubris for him to think he was going to teach her about all things sensual.

Everything she did was already more than enough to send his body into rock-hard urgency. He resisted the urge to tell her to hurry. He didn't want to break the spell. His knowledgeable former virgin took to carnal business like a fledgling highflyer. He clamped his lips shut and let her do as she would. She made short work of the fastenings on his trousers.

Olivia sat back suddenly and frowned at him. "You're wearing drawers," she said accusingly. "You told me you didn't."

"I'm not in dress clothes," he explained. "I only go without undergarments when the line of the trousers is in jeopardy."

He took her hand and guided it back to his groin, showing her how to find the slit in his undergarments that allowed his cock to spring free.

When her fingers found his bare flesh, Rhys released her hand, letting her explore as she wished. Even though his shaft was ready for action, she wasn't content until she'd eased his scrotum out as well. He leaned back and watched her through half-closed eyes while she studied his male parts.

Her pupils expanded, darkening her hazel eyes as she trailed a teasing fingertip around his balls. Every wiry hair stood at full attention. She knuckled his testicles and slid along the full length of his penis. She discovered the rough patch of skin just beneath the head.

Rhys shuddered with pleasure.

"So," she said, her voice a satisfied purr, "that's your special spot."

"One of them. Touch me anywhere and I'm a happy man." He willed the pressure in his shaft to drop, but a pearl of fluid formed on his tip despite his best efforts.

"I'm glad I make you happy," she beamed.

He reached to stroke her breasts, and her nipples tightened.

"I can think of something that would make me happier."

Her smile was luminous enough to light the dreariest

Scottish day. She lifted her gown and cloak as she climbed onto his lap again, settling herself near his groin. With the movement of the coach surging forward in bounds and swaying from side to side, it was a good trick, but she managed it. The soft warmth of the curls between her legs tickled against his shaft. He silently blessed the tailor who dreamed up crotchless pantalets. If Rhys were king, he'd elevate the fellow to a baronetcy at the very least.

"I married a mind reader," he told her.

"Not such a feat since the bent of a rake's mind is fairly easy to guess."

At that moment, the coach lurched into a pothole that sent them both airborne. When they came back down, his cock slipped into her in a single lucky thrust.

"Oh!" she said, her eyes wide.

"Are you all right?"

"Better than all right." She squeezed his length with her inner muscles and laughed. "That was a happy accident. I thought you said doing this in a coach could lead to spectacular disasters."

"It almost did." Rhys laughed with her, jubilant over the way she engulfed all of him. Not all his previous bed partners could. She was a snug fit, but she was so ready, he'd slid in hard without hurting her. He covered her mouth, her cheeks, and chin with kisses.

Then he moved to her breasts. She arched them into his mouth. He scraped his teeth over her nipples. Those little mewling sounds of pleasure she made sent his cock into near spasms.

She shifted her weight, grinding her hips on him, coating him with the wetness of her arousal. He wasn't ready for it to end so he bit his lip to keep from spilling his seed.

"Careful, you'll make it bleed." She leaned forward and kissed him softly, suckling his bottom lip so he couldn't bite it any longer.

He rocked himself under her.

She sent him a perfectly wicked smile and lifted herself on her knees until he was nearly expelled. Then she lowered herself on him again inch by maddening inch, luxuriating in her own arousal.

Rhys couldn't believe his luck. He was leg-shackled to a woman who reveled in the joys of the body as much as he did. He knew he didn't deserve her. He just hoped she wouldn't figure that out for a while.

He hadn't spoken to God in a long time, but he launched a prayer skyward, thanking Providence for giving him such a randy little wife.

"What a perfect devil you are," he breathed as she engulfed him in her hot, tight channel.

"Perhaps I have the makings of a lady rake," she said, setting their pace.

"Only with me," he said fiercely.

Her eyelids drooped languidly as she moved on him. Her lips parted in pleasure. She raised her arms and steadied herself with splayed fingers on the coach's ceiling.

"Only with you," she promised.

Rhys reached between them to spread her soft folds and circle her spot again. She might be setting the pace, but he wanted to give to her as well. He liked the control of pushing her to another pinnacle.

Her head fell back, her cloak slipping off her shoulders. She arched her back and quickened her rhythm.

Rhys groaned.

He wished for a bed so he could spread her out and torment her properly. He'd make her beg.

But now he was near to begging himself. She brought him to the brink, then slowed her pace, denying him release. At least at the slower rhythm, Rhys could stroke her more deftly, using feather-light touches that had her panting.

She moved faster again, but he kept up the pressure she seemed to need. A low growl of feminine desire rumbled out of her.

He was close, perilously close. He really ought to pull out. He hadn't done so on their wedding night, but he'd silently berated himself for it several times since. Children were a complication their already complicated marriage didn't need. He should be more responsible. He ought to make it a firm policy that he'd do the gentlemanly thing and withdraw.

But he couldn't bring himself to sever their connection. He ached to feel her come around him. He arched up, penetrating her as deeply as he could. She cried out.

Her first spasm fisted around his cock. He teetered on the brink of control. She pulsed hard, squeezing him in sudden little contractions. The spurt of his semen rushed upward and it was suddenly far too late to do the gentlemanly thing.

He pumped for half a minute, clasping her close, wallowing in the fierce pleasure of release. His breathing was still ragged when the last pulse died.

Her arms wrapped around his neck and he could feel her heart pounding against his chest. Her heart rate finally slowed from a gallop to a canter.

"I'm sorry," he said.

She leaned back and cocked her head at him, a puzzled frown marring her brow. "For what?"

Guilt gnawed at him. Childbed was no light matter. Churchyards were littered with the graves of young mothers. Why hadn't he thought of that before he swived her willy-nilly?

"For not withdrawing at the last moment," he said.

Her cheeks paled. "Why would you do that?"

"So I don't get you with child, of course." She was so damn trusting. Hadn't she learned yet that he didn't deserve it? "Honestly, did your mother tell you nothing?"

He hadn't meant it to come out like that. It was just that he couldn't bear the thought of her going through the pain and danger of childbirth because he let his body make the wrong decision.

The selfish decision.

Olivia moved off his lap and slid over to the opposite seat, smoothing down her skirts. She fiddled with her bodice. Not meeting his gaze, she covered her breasts and tied the lace over them in a neat bow. She fumbled with her buttons.

"Let me help," he said softly.

"I'm perfectly capable," she said, her voice tight.

He was plagued with an odd sense of loss. For a brief moment, when he and Olivia were joined, he wasn't alone. He was part of a glorious "us." Now his soul was his own again and he was already tired of his own company.

"Are you angry?" he asked.

She glared at him. "Shouldn't I be? You've just told me you don't want me to bear your child."

"I didn't mean it like that."

"How else could you possibly mean it?" She pulled her cloak tighter around her.

"I didn't know you wanted children," he said. She'd never mentioned it. Of course, it wasn't a subject a rake usually broached with a woman he intended to ruin. It occurred to him that he could report success to Mr. Alcock now, but since the Duke of Clarence had already cried off, Rhys's deal with the Member of Parliament was probably a moot point. Guilt strafed his soul afresh.

"One of the reasons the Duke of Clarence courted me, aside from my dowry, is because I come from a fertile family. I've never considered *not* having children."

"Well, fine then." If she was willing to take the risks, who was he to deny her? Some women wanted a baby more than breathing. "If you feel that strongly about it, of course we'll have children. Avail yourself of my services at any time," he said, trying to inject some levity into a conversation that had veered badly into the serious range. They were supposed to be on their honeymoon, for pity's sake. Surely any serious disagreements should be tabled until they returned to society and real life descended upon them. "I am at your disposal, madam."

"I think not." She pulled her cloak's hood up, obscuring her face. "Not with a man who doesn't want to get me with child."

Rhys rearranged his own clothes as the coach made a lumbering turn and slowed. He started to reach for her. "Forget I said that."

She batted his hand away. "I'll never forget you said that. It changes everything."

Chapter 27

AT HER DISPOSAL. READY TO SERVICE HER, WAS HE? As if she was a mare in season.

Olivia huffed loudly and moved back to the forward facing squab. Sidling closer to the door so not even the hem of her cloak touched Rhys, she feigned interest in the quaint rock bridge arching over the tumbling brook, which the coach would be crossing shortly.

What did the man think they were doing?

She wasn't just another one of his conquests. She was his wife. And they weren't animals. When they came together, it wasn't just a coupling, a servicing, a swiving—oh! How she detested that wicked word now. What they did in the bedchamber—and out of it!—was supposed to *mean* something.

It had meant something to her.

How strange that something so intimate could be accomplished without really knowing what was going on in the mind and heart of the other person. Her chest ached that he could be so flippant about something so precious. So…sacred.

"Would you mind not scowling so?" Rhys said.

"Why? Are you afraid my face will grow that way?"

"No, but I am afraid you might scare the servants at Braebrooke Cairn. We've turned down the lane already. As soon as they see a coach coming, they generally turn out to welcome any of the family back."

She rolled her eyes. "Heaven forefend I terrorize the help."

"Olivia, if you want to be angry with me, be angry, though God knows, I don't understand why. All I ask is that you don't harm any innocent bystanders."

"Never fear." She shot him a poisonous glance. "I make it a policy only to harm the guilty."

"Let it go for now, would you please?" Rhys said as the coach lumbered to a stop at the top of a circular drive. "We're here."

Here turned out to be a gray stone tower that looked as if it might have sprung naturally from the rising wall of rock behind it. There was an adjoining manor house of the same weathered stone, though it looked to be several centuries newer than the tower.

Which means it's only slightly younger than dirt.

Braebrooke Cairn boasted no moat. However, it presented as forbidding an aspect as any castle. The riotous brook they'd driven over earlier burbled along before the house with only a stone footbridge spanning it. Since the property's rearguard was that sheer rock wall, it was as defensible a position as any fighting man could wish.

She sneaked a glance at Rhys as he handed her down from the coach. The way his jaw was set, she judged he was ready to continue their fight whenever she was ready to begin it again. But she couldn't fault his stilted courtesy. He placed a hand at the small of her back and shepherded her over the footbridge as if harsh words had never been spoken.

A row of servants formed up on either side of the massive oak door. The maids nervously adjusted their mobcaps and dipped in jerky curtseys as Olivia and Rhys passed them by. Rugged menservants, fresh from the stable, doffed their caps and shifted restlessly from one foot to the other. There were no gilded-lily liveried footmen or formally attired butlers, no lady's maids with starched aprons. But when Rhys called them each by name, the servants of Braebrooke Cairn grinned shyly back at him.

Only one old fellow didn't fidget like the rest. Despite the iron gray hair and beard, he stood tall, with his hands clasped behind his back, his brown and green kilt hanging unevenly to just below his knees. Rhys walked toward him.

"Hello, Mr. Ferguson."

"Master Rhys." The man nodded in acknowledgment, meeting Rhys's gaze steadily as though he considered himself any man's equal. "Welcome back to Braebrooke Cairn, laddie. Ye've been away too long."

"He's known me since I was in short pants," Rhys said to Olivia as an aside. "As far as Ferguson is concerned, I'm still a youngster."

"That ye are. And as green a twig as they come. But ye've a right sweet blossom on yer arm." Mr. Ferguson sketched a bow that would have been deemed elegant and courtly a generation earlier. "Alpin Ferguson, at your service, miss."

"It's missus," Rhys corrected. "May I present my wife,

Lady Olivia? Olivia, this is Mr. Ferguson, Braebrooke Cairn's steward."

"Ah! Lady Olivia, is it? A thousand welcomes, then. Tell me now, how did this blatherskite manage to sneak up on a pretty little thing like yerself?"

Olivia's mouth dropped open. Her mother would never have countenanced such familiarity from a servant.

"In case you hadn't guessed, Ferguson doesn't stand on ceremony," Rhys said.

"No need of it, this far back of beyond." Mr. Ferguson waved a hand toward the door to usher them inside. "Will ye be pleased to come in and rest in the parlor whilst we're about preparing your rooms?"

"Room," Rhys corrected. "We're on our honeymoon."

Mr. Ferguson smiled, displaying a mouthful of horse-sized teeth. "Weel, now, isn't that grand?"

They started into the manor house with Mr. Ferguson and the rest of the servants in their wake. Olivia had one foot on the lowest step leading up to the door when a voice from just inside stopped her.

"Rhys! Is it really you?" A pretty young woman appeared framed in the doorway. She patted her honey-blond hair, swept up in a bun that seemed to have come half-undone. Several tendrils teased her chin and dangled at her temples. The effect framed her oval of a face as artfully as if it had been planned. Her cheeks glowed with robust health. The high waist of her gown did nothing to disguise the growing bulge in her belly. Olivia wished she could look as good on purpose as this woman did by seeming accident.

"Sarah!" Rhys bounded up the steps, picked her up,

and swung her around. Their laughter echoed off the nearby tower and set Olivia's teeth on edge. Surely he wouldn't have kept one of his previous lovers at his family's Scottish estate.

Then she reminded herself that she really knew very little about her new husband.

Who knows what a rake might do?

When he finally put the strange woman down, she palmed his cheeks and kissed him squarely on the lips.

"Excuse me," Olivia said, stomping up the steps to join them at the threshold. "I'm Olivia Warrington, and that's my husband you're kissing."

Sarah's rosebud of a mouth formed a perfect "oh." "Rhys, you're married! Well, isn't that wonderful? And she's so pretty, too."

The woman threw her arms around Olivia and kissed the air by both of her cheeks.

"Olivia, may I present my baby sister, Sarah? Or should I say Lady Blakesby?" Rhys said with formality. "Sorry I missed the wedding."

Sarah reached over and squeezed his hand. "I understood and, in the interests of family harmony, I appreciated your thoughtfulness. Father would have been...difficult otherwise." She sighed and her eyes glistened, but she blinked back the unshed tears. "But my wedding didn't seem right without you." Then Rhys's sister turned to Olivia and hugged her tightly. "No titles between the two of us. Please call me Sarah and I shall call you Olivia."

"Sarah's a demonstrative sort," Rhys said with a laugh, "but we tolerate her pretty well in any case."

"Tolerate, indeed." She gave his chest a playful

swat. "I'm your favorite sister and you know it. Don't keep your bride standing there in the cold, you big oaf. Come in, come in. Your teeth are chattering, Olivia. Honestly, men never think of practicalities, do they?" Sarah said, waving them in.

Once they were all inside, she linked arms with Olivia and steered her out of the cold foyer and into a cozy parlor where a fire crackled merrily, driving away the eternal chill of the gray stone walls.

If the exterior of Braebrooke Cairn was forbidding, the interior was designed for homey comfort. The room was furnished with serviceable pieces instead of fashionable ones. The chair by the fire was overstuffed and, after their jostling coach ride, Olivia longed to sink into it and disappear into its softness.

Stacks of books graced the side tables. A slightly shabby settee was draped with a multi-hued blanket, and a tea service, whose elegance was out of place in the rustic parlor, was laid out on a low table before it.

"Here's what's wanted to warm you up." Sarah settled herself near the tea service and poured out. "One lump or two?"

"Two, please," Olivia said, thinking an extra helping of sugar would warm her all the quicker.

"Ah, that's how I take it too. I wonder what else we have in common besides this rakehell," Sarah said, lifting a brow at her brother. She grinned at Olivia as she plopped two brown lumps into her cup. Then she stirred in enough milk to turn the tea creamy-looking and handed the delicate cup and saucer to Olivia. "And of course, Rhys takes his with one lump. Oh, how he's needed a woman to take him in hand and teach him how to enjoy civilized pleasures. I suppose I needn't tell you he's already mastered the uncivilized ones."

She actually winked at her. Olivia decided she liked Rhys's quicksilver sister very much indeed.

"Because he's mastered those uncivilized pleasures, I believe it proves he's trainable," Olivia confided. "I have hope for him."

Rhys snorted, but Sarah laughed.

"I do too," she said. "Oh, Olivia, I'm so glad to meet you. Now, Rhys, there's someone I want you to meet, too." She twisted her ungainly form around and directed her next words over the back of the settee. "Alex. Hide-and-seek is done for the moment. Come out, lovie."

A rustling came from behind the cushioned settee. As Olivia watched, a child emerged, little bum first, then a pudgy body. Finally, a golden head wiggled out from its hiding place. The little boy scrambled to his feet and stood clutching the arm of the settee. He stared at first Olivia, then Rhys, thrusting a thumb into his mouth for reassurance.

"Alex. My firstborn," Sarah said with pride.

"Alex." Rhys squatted down so he was more nearly at eye level with the lad and smiled. Then he looked back up at his sister. "You named him Alexander?"

That was Rhys's middle name. Olivia remembered hearing it at their wedding ceremony.

"I did." Sarah sniffed and swiped a quick tear from her cheek. "I guess it proves you're my favorite right back."

"Didn't your husband object?"

"A wise man doesn't cross the woman who's just

brought his heir into the world," Sarah said, folding her arms across her chest.

Olivia would have bet that Sarah's husband, whoever he was, didn't cross her on much of anything. Then she reminded herself that she'd sworn off gambling of any kind. Intemperate wagers were the reason she now found herself married to a man she barely knew, after all.

Sarah turned her attention back to her son. "Come now, say hello."

The child took his thumb from his mouth long enough to wave, then popped it back between his rosy lips.

"Hello, Alexander," Rhys said to the boy. "I'm your uncle Rhys."

He extended his hand to the child.

"We've been practicing this. Go on, son," Sarah said. "Shake your uncle's hand like a big boy."

The toddler waddled over and put his small hand in Rhys' large one. Then he pumped it three times. The expression on Rhys's face was one of complete fascination.

Olivia's chest ached. That look proved he'd be a good father. He genuinely seemed to like children.

He just didn't want hers.

"That's excellent, lovie," Sarah said with a little clap. "Now you can go hide again. Father's probably done counting by now and he'll be looking for you."

Rhys stood as his nephew turned and scuttled back behind the settee.

"Lord Blakesby is here too?" he asked.

"I wouldn't very well venture to Scotland with a toddler at my skirts and one on the way without my husband, would I?" she said, patting her swelling belly. "Blakesby has a keen eye for architecture, and Father

wanted him to take a look over the place to see if
Braebrooke Cairn could do with some updating. When
could it not, I ask you? But when the marquis decrees,
the world must obey, so here we are. Oh, Rhys." She
stood and hugged him again. "I'm so glad to see you."

"That had better be your long lost brother," came a
masculine voice from behind them. A handsome sandy-
haired man with a prodigious mustache strode into the
room and extended a tentative hand to Rhys. "Jonathan
Blakesby. You must be the infamous black sheep."

"Guilty as charged, my lord. I'll try not to taint your
family while I'm here." Rhys shook his hand gravely.
Both men were trying to make light of the fact that
Rhys was not received by his family, but nonetheless,
a ripple of unease circled the room. Rhys turned to
Olivia. "My wife, Lady Olivia."

She stood and dropped a curtsey. "Lord Blakesby."

"Charmed." Lord Blakesby flashed a genuine smile and
made a correct bow over her hand. "Blakesby will do."

Silence reigned for a few heartbeats, and Olivia felt
a frisson of the tension between her husband and Lord
Blakesby. Rhys had told her he was in disgrace, that his
mere presence with them would render his family equally
unacceptable in the eyes of Polite Society. If little Alex
was connected with the uncle who was rumored to have
been a traitor, it could dim his prospects considerably.
Even the sister who loved him best wasn't immune to
the pressure for the sake of her son's future. No wonder
Rhys hadn't wanted children of his own.

Rhys's dishonor hadn't seemed real until this moment
when she saw with her own eyes the not-so-subtle
shunning he suffered.

"We didn't realize any of Rhys's family would be here," she said, crossing over to stand beside him. She slipped her hand into his and he squeezed it gratefully. Olivia decided perhaps she'd been fortunate not to grow up in a fashionable aristocratic family if even Rhys's own siblings were obliged to treat him as if he bore the pox. "Perhaps we should return to Barrowdell."

"Nonsense," Sarah said. "This is Rhys's home as surely as it's mine. Besides, who will know that we've even seen each other, much less lived under the same roof? I certainly don't feel the need to tell Father, if you don't." Then she fished her hiding son from behind the settee and scooped him up into her arms.

"It's time for your nap, your lordship," she said to the wiggling boy. "Would you care to join me, Olivia, while I bed this little fellow down? Surely after that, Mr. Ferguson will have your rooms ready."

"Room," she heard Rhys grumble as she followed Sarah out. "Not rooms. Blast it all, doesn't anyone remember we're on our honeymoon?"

Chapter 28

AFTER THE WOMEN LEFT, BLAKESBY HAD STOOD RHYS to a drink. Good Scottish whisky was a welcome change after Mr. Symon's demonically high-proof absinthe, but the conversation with his brother-in-law left a good deal to be desired. Unlike his jocular discussion with Horatio Symon over shared liquor, there were long bouts of silence, punctuated by awkward attempts on Blakesby's part to ferret out the truth of what happened to end Rhys's military career.

Finally, Rhys had said bluntly, "Whatever you've heard about my time in France, I didn't do it. However, I've undoubtedly done worse since." He upended his jigger on the serving tray. "Don't worry. Olivia and I will be on our way tomorrow."

Blakesby had protested and insisted they stay. Braebrooke Cairn was a rambling big estate. There was plenty of room for two families to be in residence, but Rhys knew the baron was merely being polite.

He supposed he couldn't blame Blakesby. If their roles had been reversed, he'd try to shield his family from association with scandal too. Maybe if Blakesby had been a duke or a marquis, someone a bit higher up on the aristocratic social scale, he'd have been willing to backhand convention and embrace his wife's wayward kin.

But Blakesby was only a baron, a lord on the bottom rung of titled nobility. If he hoped to expand his family's influence and wealth for the next generation, he needed to present a spotless face to the beau monde world in this one.

A face that wouldn't bear connection with a possible traitor. It didn't matter to Polite Society that Rhys was innocent. The mere whiff of scandal was enough. Blakesby didn't come right out and say it, but the man fairly tied himself into pretzel-like knots trying not to.

After that, Rhys had stomped out to the stable, hoping to ride off his frustration, but the only horses in the stalls were sturdy little Highland ponies. They were hardy, hill-bred stock and were supposed to be unmatched for surefootedness on rough terrain. But he was used to riding Duncan, his big Thoroughbred gelding, a generously sized horse even by the large breed's standard. Rhys suspected he'd feel as if his feet were about to drag the ground on one of the ponies.

He wished his father-in-law had thought to send along a groom to act as an outrider for the coach. He could have brought Duncan along. He hoped Mr. Thatcher was taking good care of him back at Barrowdell, but it didn't do Rhys much good here at Braebrooke Cairn. A reckless gallop across an open meadow or a hell-for-leather dash along a wooded path was what he needed to blow out the cobwebs and clear his head. Unfortunately, it wasn't to be had.

Finally, he took down a saddle from one of the hooks and began to clean it with the special blend of saddle soap Mr. Ferguson mixed up himself and kept in a stone crock in the stable. Rhys had tried to wheedle the secret recipe from the steward once, but Ferguson would only say, "Each man must make his own way of cleaning up the soiled patches in his life."

"And haven't I done a cracking job at that?" he muttered as he worked the creamy mixture into the leather.

"Cracking job at what?" came Mr. Ferguson's voice from behind him.

"Never mind," Rhys said. "It's not important."

"Aye, I can see how unimportant whatever it is to ye from the way ye're wearin' out that pommel." Mr. Ferguson handed him a clean cloth when the one he was using became too damp. "We've a canny stable lad as sees to the saddles, ye know."

"I know." Rhys clamped his tongue between his teeth in concentration and continued to rub the leather.

"An' ye dinna mind me sayin' so, ye've a long face for a bridegroom," Mr. Ferguson observed.

Rhys stopped rubbing and looked at the old man. "Maybe it's because I realize I've done my bride a disservice by marrying her."

"I dinna think the lass would agree with ye."

She would if she knew the whole truth. If Olivia ever learned he'd descended on Barrowdell with the express intent of ruining her, she'd despise him for it as much as he despised himself. True, he'd been motivated by the hope of clearing his name and reclaiming his place in his family, but now he realized his conscience wouldn't allow him to purchase his reinstatement at that cost.

It wasn't worth it. He never should have made that deal with the devil incarnate, Fortescue Alcock. He re-attacked the leather with vehemence.

"Ye'll wear a hole in it like that," Mr. Ferguson said. "Easy strokes, in a small circle like I taught ye when he were a wee lad."

Rhys grumbled, but he followed the steward's advice. The circular motion seemed to uncoil his frustration and he breathed in a relaxed lungful, taking in the aromatic smells of lanolin and beeswax, leather and dusty horse.

"I dinna think ye're troubled about yer lass exactly," the old man said. "I think this has sommat to do with that difrugalty ye met with when ye were over the water a while back."

"I've been dishonored, Ferguson."

"Did ye do something to warrant being shamed?"

Rhys had second-guessed himself plenty of times. He replayed the events leading up to the ill-fated battle, scrutinized all the decisions he made in the thick of the action, his vision obscured by the smoke of French cannons drifting over the field. But even he had to concede he couldn't have done any differently, given the information he'd had at the time.

Except maybe for Lieutenant Duffy. He still castigated himself for spending his last round on his dying horse instead of ending the suffering of the gut-shot lieutenant.

"No, I didn't do anything wrong."

"Then no man can truly shame ye, unless ye allow it," Ferguson said. "If yer conscience dinna condemn ye, what right has anyone else to name ye dishonored?"

"That's fine for the Highlands, Ferguson, but in London, the rules are a bit different."

"Good thing ye're no' there, then, aye?"

"Aye," Rhys agreed, echoing his old friend's brogue. "Good thing."

"Why d'ye no' let me finish this saddle whilst ye see to that lovely young wife o' yers?" Ferguson eased the cleaning cloth out of his hand. "Women have a way about 'em as makes whatever's wrong with a man's world turn right somehow."

The steward's round little wife had served as the estate's cook as long as Rhys could remember. "Mrs. Ferguson does that for you?"

"Aye, so she tells me, lad. Every bleedin' day," he said with a grimace. "But never underestimate the power of a woman's apple pie. Now go on wi' ye."

"Only one thing wrong with that, Ferguson. I don't think my wife can cook."

❧

But Olivia could organize like an army of ants. When he entered the chamber that had been prepared for them, he found her ensconced at the escritoire near a large window.

"I've written a letter to my mother to let my parents know where we are. The driver can carry it for me when he returns the coach to Barrowdell tomorrow," she said as she displayed the stack of correspondence she'd completed. "I also took the liberty of writing to your parents."

"My parents?"

"No matter what your situation with them, I gather they'd rather not learn about your marriage from reading about it in the *Times*," she said. "And speaking of which, here is the announcement for the paper."

He glanced at it. "So the happy couple will make their home in Mayfair, will they?"

"That's where Papa's buying a townhouse for us."

He stalked over to the window and frowned out at the ice-rimed brook. Where they'd live was a fight he didn't want to have just now. Not when remnants of their last argument were still swirling in the air above their heads.

"What did you write to my parents?"

"You may read it if you like," she said, handing the foolscap pages to him. "I haven't a signet ring to seal it with. I was waiting for you to put your stamp on the wax."

He unfolded the pages. Olivia's script was neat and precise.

Just like her.

She had introduced herself, and then went on to describe their "whirlwind courtship" and hasty marriage in the most glowing of terms. She even included a brief account of the way he'd saved her life when her horse bolted. Though Olivia's father had given their elopement his blessing—hell, he was the scheme's sole architect—Rhys knew *his* straight-laced father would think the whole Gretna Green ceremony tawdry and common.

But the next paragraph of the letter was anything but common. Olivia expressed gratitude to his parents. And of all unlikely things for which to thank them, she was thankful for *him*.

> You've raised a remarkable son. Rhys is a wonderful man—brilliant, courtly, and brave.

> *Given his attributes, one can only surmise he was*
> *blessed with equally wonderful parents. I thank you*
> *for the nurture which created his great heart. I am*
> *honored to be part of the Warrington family.*
>
> *Of course, I am cognizant that there is a schism*
> *between you and your son at present. It is a state*
> *of affairs which pains my husband deeply as I'm*
> *sure it does you. I can only hope the fact that he*
> *has taken me to wife will not further complicate or*
> *extend your estrangement. Rhys is too fine a man*
> *for you not to have him in your lives.*
>
> *When we have established our London home,*
> *I will write again. I hope to meet you soon. If,*
> *however, you decline, your wishes will be respected.*
> *Whether we meet in this life or the one to come, I*
> *want you to know that I'm thankful to you for the*
> *man who is now my husband.*

The lines on the page seemed to blur. Rhys blinked hard and the spacing resumed its proper form. That lump in his chest threatened to burst. Mr. MacDermot had assured him over the anvil in Gretna Green that women seemed to know all about the business of being married. The man was right. Olivia's staunch support overwhelmed him.

"Do you mean this?" he asked.

"Every word."

"Olivia, I do want us to have children," he said earnestly.

"That's a change. Is it accompanied by an apology?"

"More like the beginnings of an explanation. You know I admitted at our first meeting that I was a libertine."

"As I recall, it was a fairly titillating revelation," she

said, a smile tugging at one corner of her mouth. "You were without doubt the wickedest person I'd ever met and the most forthright about it."

And yet she was thankful for him. Was it any wonder she was a puzzlement to him?

"Be that as it may, even rakes have certain standards, and one of mine was making it a point of honor not to sire any bastards."

"A worthy goal given the preponderance of bastards in the world. In that, you have eclipsed the Duke of Clarence by a magnitude of ten."

"Then I suddenly find myself married."

"And no one is more surprised than you, I'm sure," she said, her tone turning prickly.

"True." He took one of her hands to soften his admission. "But before you take offense, let me add that I'm glad for it. I'm glad I married you. At our wedding, I'm pretty sure I promised to protect you. Childbed can be a dangerous place, and that's why I thought I should protect you from it."

The prickliness melted away and she reached a hand up to his face. "Oh, Rhys. That's sweet. If you'd told me that when we first argued, there wouldn't have been a fight about this."

If he'd thought it would have worked then, he would have said it. He wisely clamped his lips shut now but made a note that he didn't do his best thinking immediately after making love. He'd have to make sure Olivia didn't draw him into any more important conversations when all the blood in his body was still pooled somewhere besides his brain.

"If women began fearing childbirth, where would

we all be?" she said. "Besides, I saw you with little Alex. You'll make a wonderful father."

He was going to explain that he didn't think they should start a family until he was reconciled to his, but the words died on his lips. If he never patched things up with the rest of the Warringtons, it would be all right.

Olivia was his family now.

He drew her close and kissed her. It started as a sweet kiss, a grateful kiss, but quickly deepened into something tinged with more urgency. When he cupped both her breasts, she pushed against his chest.

"I didn't mean you ought to start siring a child now," she said.

"Why not? There's no time like the present." He nibbled on her neck the way he knew she liked, and she stopped pushing against his chest.

"I know we dallied in the coach on the way here, but"—she gasped when he bit down on her earlobe—"surely these things ought to be done by night in a proper bed with the lamps turned down."

"Not necessarily. How am I to see the sights with the lamps turned down?" He waggled his brows at her as he began unbuttoning her bodice.

"You're not taking this seriously."

"Of course I am. There's nothing more serious than when you and I come together. But that doesn't mean we have to act as if someone's died. Loving is supposed to be fun."

"Are you sure?"

"Trust me. It's one of my areas of expertise."

"Well, aren't you full of yourself?"

"Yes, I am." He picked her up and carried her to the

waiting bed. He laid her down on the thick feather tick and looked down at her. "But I won't be happy until you're full of myself too."

She laughed out loud then and lifted her arms to welcome him.

Chapter 29

HER LAUGHTER WARMED HIM TO HIS TOES. WHEN SHE ran a hand down his flat belly and cupped his genitals, the warmth pooled in another place. He leaned down, bracing himself on his palms, and nipped her earlobe as her palm slid over his groin. He was fully erect and straining against the wool. She waggled her brows at him and slanted him a sidelong gaze.

"I think I'm going to like not being serious with you," she said.

"As long as you seriously love me as much as I love you," he said with a laugh. Then his laughter died as he looked down at her. She hadn't said it outright, but it was suddenly something he needed desperately to hear. "You do love me, don't you?"

"Oh, yes, Rhys," she said, her eyes shining. "I think I loved you from the first moment I saw you and you took my breath away."

"I'll do my best to do that with regularity, madam." He stretched out beside her and they sank into the coverlet in a hailstorm of kisses.

~

Rhys was torn between wanting to draw this loving out and the desperate need to sink into her sweet flesh and find release.

She *loved* him. All his flaws. All his failures. She knew what he was and she didn't look away. The wonder, the grace of it, made him weak and strong at once.

She bleated a piteous little sound as he nuzzled between her legs, drunk on her scent. Her knuckles were white where she fisted the linens.

"Only a little longer, Olivia."

She groaned with wanting.

His balls tightened in response to her need. He wanted to give her the best, and to do that he knew, as she didn't yet, that delay would mean more delight. He'd taken his time undressing her and working every sensitive place on her body into a frenzy. But now he couldn't bear her sweet agony for another second.

Without even realizing he'd done it, he found himself positioned between her legs, his cock knocking at her gate, poised to slide into her.

His shaft throbbed at the nearness of her soft, wet core. Rhys could deny their need no longer.

He rushed in with one long stroke and she molded around him in a warm, tight embrace. Then his balls drew up into a tense mound, coiled for release. He held himself motionless, willing the urgency to subside so he could revel in the joy that was Olivia a little longer.

Only a little.

She wrapped her legs around him and hooked her ankles at the top of the cleft of his buttocks. His heart pounded in his cock, but he forced himself to be still.

Her mouth gaped. Her brows tented in distress.

He couldn't keep her suspended between need and completion any longer. He had to let her go.

He covered her lips with his and flicked his tongue in and out, loving her with his mouth and his cock in tandem. She rocked beneath him, urging him in deeper with little noises of desperation that threatened to shred his control.

He moved faster then. Rougher. She rose to welcome his bone-jarring thrusts.

A little longer, please. He was lost in the heat, the friction, the animal joy of rutting, but something else was happening inside him too.

The door to that sheltered part of himself, the part he'd never opened to anyone, was being battered down with every thrust. Olivia was suddenly in there with him, wrapping her sweet self around his secrets, guarding them, loving him in spite of them. All the scattered bits of himself, those pieces of his heart he'd carelessly given away, were zinging back into him. One at a time, Olivia put them back together until his heart was whole.

She pulled her lips from his and turned her head to the side. "I can't wait any—"

He felt it start. "Now, Olivia, now."

Rhys arched his back, driving in as deep as he could as his life shot into her in steady pulses. Her inner walls contracted around him.

It's like being born, he thought disjointedly. But instead of going out, he was trying to come in. Into her joy. Into her bliss. Into her love.

Pleasure, sharp as a blade, sliced through him, rending him soul and marrow.

Olivia's whole body convulsed around him, pulling him into her warmth, her light. He laid his cheek against hers as their connected bodies continued the mad dance of lust for a few more seconds.

When it finally stopped, his cheek felt damp.

He raised his head and looked down at her with concern. "You're crying."

She smiled up at him. "Only because I'm so happy."

He kissed her again, a soft shared breath. And he knew the years of wandering were over. Even if he was never received in his father's house ever again, it no longer mattered.

He was already home.

❧

Olivia had her way. The next morning, she'd sent her father's coach back to Barrowdell with all the letters and announcements she'd written. She and Rhys stayed on at Braebrooke Cairn. Each day, relations with Rhys's sister and brother-in-law improved. By end of the second week, they had formed a jolly house party during the day, though Sarah and Blakesby were careful to give the newlyweds time to themselves.

Little Alex was less thoughtful and latched on to his uncle fiercely. Rhys went galloping through the ancient keep with the laughing toddler on his shoulders. Of the two of them, Olivia didn't know which was having the most fun.

But Rhys and Olivia enjoyed plenty of privacy by night. And if by the end of their honeymoon she wasn't with child, it wouldn't be for lack of trying.

At the beginning of the third week, she was a little

distressed to see her father's coach lumbering back up
the long drive. Several large trunks were strapped to
the top of the conveyance. Surely even a busybody like
Beatrice Symon knew a man wouldn't welcome his
mother-in-law on his honeymoon.

Olivia needn't have worried. Only Babette and Rhys's
valet, Mr. Clyde, climbed out of the Symon coach, along
with Jean-Pierre and two of his best seamstresses.

"Your mother, she thought you would need a trousseau so she set Monsieur du Barry to work," Babette
said as she shook the wrinkles out of the new gowns
and hung them in Olivia's capacious wardrobe. "Now
all that's wanted is the final fittings, and *bien sur*, when
you and your bridegroom move to London, you shall
take the city by storm."

Her mother must have ordered the trousseau the day
after Olivia and Rhys ran off together. No doubt, she'd
driven poor Jean-Pierre and his seamstresses ragged to
complete so many pieces of a new wardrobe in so little
time, but she always paid them extra for quick work.
There was a new mauve traveling suit, a peacock blue
riding habit that would put all the other matrons who
rode on Rotten Row to shame, several dresses suitable
for receiving guests at home, and a breathtaking cloth-
of-gold gown that would outshine royalty.

As Olivia ran an appreciative finger over the exquisite satins and silks, she realized her mother had some
very fine qualities after all.

Rhys made himself scarce while Jean-Pierre and his
minions made short work of marking places where the
darts in Olivia's new wardrobe would need to be taken
in. But he was pleased to be present for a showing of the

new gowns, bonnets, pelisses, fans, and other fripperies. Then he dismissed the fawning Jean-Pierre so he could investigate Olivia's new stays, chemises, and stockings in private.

After a week of excitement over her new things, Rhys led her to the front parlor, covering her eyes. More than a dozen gaily wrapped boxes were stacked on the tea table.

"You were so taken with the trousseau, I decided it would be all right to wait a bit to show you these. Mr. Clyde was entrusted with seeing these wedding gifts safely here and has been fair to bursting for you to open them."

She settled on the settee and eyed the presents, feeling giddy as a child on Christmas morn, but she wouldn't touch a single ribbon until Mr. Clyde fetched a traveling desk. "We must have something on which to record each gift and who sent it so I can send thank you notes," she explained.

Lady Harrington sent a china chafing dish. Pinkerton and Amanda sent a collection of colorful scarves with fantastical beings possessed of a multiplicity of arms in unlikely poses on them. The Baron and Baroness Ramstead sent an ornate silver snuffbox. Neither she nor Rhys took snuff and weren't likely to start.

"But it's the thought that counts," Olivia said as she carefully set down a description of the useless gift for her records.

Even some of the Barrowdell staff sent simple home-spun presents—a woolen shawl from the housekeeper and a pressed orchid and progress report on her mare Molly from Mr. Thatcher. Olivia treasured them all.

But one of the last gifts she opened threatened to turn her into a hopeless watering pot.

"Oh, my!" she said when she unwrapped the heavy silver teapot. "It's Great-grandmother Gentry's tea service."

Olivia had only seen it once. Her mother had brought it out of storage and explained its significance when the Duke of Clarence first indicated interest in her. The tea set had belonged to Beatrice Symon's mother's mother, handed down from mother to first wedded daughter. Olivia knew her mother's family hadn't been wealthy. This tea service was the dearest thing they owned, and even though the family might have faced lean times, nothing would induce them to part with it.

The tea service wasn't as fancy as the ones the Symons used now. The surfaces were polished smooth with no intricate filigree, and a few of the handles were worn thin. But Great-grandmother Gentry's tea service signified an unbroken line of women whose goal in life was to make a proper home for their husbands and bring gentility to the menfolk who undoubtedly needed the civilizing influence.

When she'd first learned of the tea service, Olivia hadn't been impressed, but now she hugged the teapot to her breast. It was her mother's way of saying she understood about the elopement and wished her well.

"And this one's from me," Rhys said, pulling a small box from his pocket.

"When did you have time to go shopping?" And where would he have done it? As far as Olivia knew, there wasn't even a decent-sized hamlet nearby.

"I didn't. You're not the only one who can write a

letter you know." He settled beside her and pressed the box into her hands. "Mr. Clyde picked it out for me."

She gave the valet who'd stood in the corner while she opened gifts a broad smile.

"No credit to me," Clyde said. "Lord Rhys was most particular in his instructions."

The anxious expression on his face told her Rhys was also most particular that she open this present quickly, so she tore away the ribbon and raised the lid of the satin-covered box.

It was a ring. A lovely sapphire set with small diamonds round about winked up at her from its bed of pale pink velvet.

"Oh, it's beautiful."

"Not compared to you, but it'll have to do," Rhys said as he slipped the curved nail from her left hand and replaced it with the new ring. He started to put the nail in his pocket, but Olivia eased it out of his hand.

"I want to keep this one too," she said, putting it on her right hand. "So I'll always remember how we started."

Rhys pulled a face. "And here I thought you were keeping it to use for my nose in case you have difficulty leading me about."

"That too," she admitted with a laugh. Finally, there was only one box left. Rhys picked it up and gave it a shake. A rattling sound came from the package. "Who sent this?"

"I don't know. There's no card attached." Olivia took it from him and untied the lovely red ribbon. "Perhaps the sender put the note inside the box so it wouldn't be lost along the way."

Olivia lifted the lid and saw only cotton gauze inside.

She lifted a corner of it to see what delicate finery the cotton was cushioning. A small gasp escaped her lips and she dropped the box to the stone floor.

"What is it?" Rhys bent down and scooped it back up.

"Careful," she said, putting a hand to his forearm. "It's just like the others."

"Other what?"

"The other thorns," she whispered.

Rhys set the box on the low table before them and removed the gauze to bare the thorn to their gaze. He studied it carefully. "Not exactly like the others. It's not shiny like the ones we found with Mr. Weinschmidt. I think it's safe to assume this one is not tipped with poison. Someone is only sending a message."

"What does it mean?" she asked, her joy over the other gifts evaporating under the relentless heat of some unknown person's hatred.

"It means this is not over," Rhys said, pulling her into his arms. The attacks weren't motivated by her possible match to the royal duke. They were personal. "It means you're still in danger."

Chapter 30

Winter still held Scotland and the Lake District in its icy grip, but as Rhys and Olivia's coach neared London, the roads became increasingly muddy and rutted. Just outside the city, one of the wheels bogged down in the muck. Rhys was forced to disembark and put his shoulder to the side of the conveyance while the driver whipped the horses cruelly in order to get them moving again.

As a result, he was more than disheveled from travel. Rhys was an unholy mess, with mud caked from his boot tips to his elbows.

It was not the way he'd hoped to greet his father after more than three years in exile.

He had no choice.

Warrington House was the safest place he could think of, and though he detested asking the marquis for help, Olivia's security came before his battered pride.

Warrington House was a four-storied Georgian with rows of windows peering into the street from each floor. The panes were graduated in size, slightly smaller the higher in the house they were situated. The architectural trick gave the illusion that the imposing edifice soared even higher than it did.

A set of granite steps led up to the ornate double doors where stone statues of lions *en couchant* lay in wait for any who deigned to approach unworthily. When the Symon coach, which Rhys had commandeered without his father-in-law's permission, came to a stop on the elegantly curved Mayfair street, he experienced a moment's trepidation. His father might turn them away.

He couldn't allow that to happen, he decided.

Rhys climbed out of the coach and ordered Babette and Mr. Clyde to see to their baggage. They'd left the whining Monsieur du Barry and his seamstresses at Braebrooke Cairn. Sarah and Blakesby had promised to return them to Barrowdell after the designer and his helpers produced a small wardrobe of baby clothes for their coming new arrival.

Rhys helped Olivia down from the carriage. Her complexion was sallow from exhaustion. She hadn't slept well at the coaching inns at which they'd stopped, and Rhys hadn't wanted to chance veering off course to stay at the country homes of even his friends, Lord Nathaniel Colton or Sir Jonah Sharp. The fewer people who knew their destination, the better.

Putting a hand to her back, he guided Olivia to the door of Warrington House. He almost lifted a hand to knock, but then he realized the servants would be more likely to obey him if he acted like a returning son of the house instead of a wandering beggar.

He turned the brass doorknob and went in. It was almost sacrilege for him to tromp across the Italian marble foyer in his muddy Hessians, but there was no help for it.

The family butler heard their footfalls and appeared almost immediately. Mr. Tweadle had been with the Warringtons since before Rhys's father had come into the title, and the stiff-backed majordomo guarded the family honor as fiercely as the Tower Beefeaters did the crown jewels. Tweadle stopped midstride for half a second in surprise over seeing Rhys, but then he recovered and made a correct bow.

"Lord Rhys," Tweadle said, eyeing Rhys's disreputable appearance with a censorious expression. "Welcome. How may I be of assistance?"

"You can show my wife, Lady Olivia, to a guest room." He helped her out of her pelisse and handed it to Tweadle. Then he removed his muck-spattered garrick and loaded it onto the butler's waiting arms. "I assume my old chamber has been turned into a lumber room by now."

"No, my lord," Tweadle said. "Everything is exactly as you left it. Your mother's orders. But I wonder if Lady Olivia wouldn't be more comfortable in the parlor while I see if Lord Warrington wishes the linens aired first."

It was Tweadle's subtle way of letting Rhys know they wouldn't be accommodated without the marquis's approval.

Fair enough. No point in putting Mr. Tweadle in the crossfire.

"Where is my father?"

"His lordship is in his study, but—"

"Good. Wait here and Mr. Tweadle will see to your needs directly, my love," Rhys said to Olivia before starting down the correct hallway. Over his shoulder, he called to the servant, "See my wife to the parlor then, and I'll show myself to the study."

"But his lordship isn't receiving this morning." Tweadle scuttled after him, extending his arms before him so as to minimize his contact with Rhys's filthy coat.

"You mean he isn't receiving *guests*. Like it or not, I'm his son. He'll receive me."

"Perhaps you would prefer to freshen up first, Lord Rhys," Tweadle said, still scuffling behind him.

Rhys stopped and rounded on him. "Tweadle, clean boots won't make me any more acceptable in my father's eyes and, in any case, I cannot afford the delay."

If the marquis refused to shelter them, Rhys would have to make other plans quickly. He'd already decided to make for the dock at Wapping should the doors to Warrington House slam shut to them. If there were any passenger ships bound for New South Wales or Nova Scotia or, as a last resort, even America, Rhys and Olivia would take passage on the next available vessel leaving with the tide. Any place would be safer for Olivia than the British Isles.

But Rhys preferred not to flee. If Olivia were safe in his father's house, he could run the threat to ground and deal with it permanently. If they fled, he'd always be looking over his shoulder wondering if the assassin behind the thorns was still in pursuit.

He put a hand on Tweadle's thin shoulder. "See to my wife's comfort, if you please, Mr. Tweadle. We've had a long weary trip from Scotland. If you can coax her to eat something, I'll be grateful." Rhys jerked his head in the direction of his father's study door. "I'll make sure the marquis knows you tried to stop me."

"Thank you, my lord." A look of utter relief washed over the old servant's face.

His father must be in rare tyrannical form if even Mr. Tweadle was treading so lightly around him. Rhys silently vowed not to allow anyone else to be harmed when he bearded the old lion in his den.

"Very good, sir. I'll attend Lady Olivia immediately," Tweadle turned and hurried back down the hall to where Olivia waited, muttering under his breath as he went. "Cook has some fresh-baked scones that should be just the ticket. Oh, yes, quite."

Rhys put his hand to the crystal doorknob. On the other side of the door was the man he both loved and feared as he ought to love and fear God. It had devastated him to be cut off from his family. But this time, if the marquis cast him out, it wouldn't be only Rhys who suffered. Olivia would still be on the run and in danger.

He couldn't allow that to happen. Family had to count for something. Rhys straightened his spine, turned the knob, and went in.

At first, Rhys thought he'd made a mistake and stumbled into the wrong room. A wizened man was seated at the marquis's outsized oak desk, scratching away with a quill on the parchment before him. The top of his pate shined through thinning white hair. His stooped shoulders were draped with a shawl.

That dotard couldn't possibly be Rhys's father.

Then the man looked up. Illness had scraped all excess flesh from his face, leaving jutting cheekbones and sharp angles. He'd aged a pair of decades in a few short years. His complexion was ashen, but the marquis's cobalt eyes blazed under a pair of scrub brush brows.

Rhys's father replaced his quill in the inkwell and steepled his skeletal fingers before him on the desk.

"You have respected my wishes and not darkened my door for these past three years," the marquis said. "To what do I owe the dubious honor of your unrequested return?"

Rhys was normally never at a loss for what to say. In some circles, he was even counted a wit. But facing his father set his stomach churning and his tongue cleaving to the roof of his mouth. He blurted the first thing he could think of. "I've taken a wife."

"Damned irresponsible of you," his father said with a scowl. "And damned irresponsible of Tweadle to allow you in against my express orders."

"He didn't allow it. I bullied my way in," Rhys said as he approached his father's desk. "An unattractive trait, to be sure, but one I inherited from you."

"Insolent as ever." The marquis's scowl deepened, turning his lean face into a road map of wrinkles. "Taken a wife, you say. Unconscionable that you should do so without so much as a 'by your leave' from me. Especially since you're dependent on the largess of the marquisate for your living. I suppose now you'll want a raise in your allowance to support this doxie of yours."

Even though Rhys had been cast out of the family for all social intents and purposes, he had not been cut off financially. It wasn't due to any tender feeling on the marquis's part, he knew. Rhys was simply his responsibility, and Lord Warrington never shirked responsibility. Of course, to the marquis, the support of his youngest son was of no more import than any of several hundred retainers on the marquisates' far-flung estates who depended upon him.

Rhys's hands clenched into fists, then subconsciously clasped them behind his back in the same pose he'd always adopted for dressing-downs when he was a lad.

"I'm not here for your money," he said. "If you consult your man of business, you'll discover I haven't touched a farthing of it since I returned from France."

Lord Warrington's brow arched in surprised puzzlement.

"And Olivia is no doxie," Rhys went on. "She's the finest young woman I've ever known."

"From what I've heard, you haven't exactly gone out of your way to associate with fine women, young or otherwise, in the past few years."

So his father had taken note of his doings, just as Rhys had gleaned rumors of the major events in his family's life.

"That's correct, sir," he admitted. "I wasn't in search of a good woman, but one found me nonetheless. We were married in Scotland about a month ago."

"In Scotland. I should have expected as much." Lord Warrington snorted. "An elopement. Is the girl big-bellied with child then?"

"No, sir." But Rhys hoped she would be soon.

"Her name?"

"Olivia Symon."

"Horatio Symon's daughter?" Even though Mr. Symon wasn't part of the aristocracy, a man of his wealth hadn't escaped the marquis's notice. "Sit down, Rhys. It wearies me to look up at you."

His father hadn't said he was tired of looking at him, but the sentiment was close. Rhys sank into the

Sheraton chair opposite Lord Warrington, but he kept his weight forward, ready to rise if he needed.

"Seems to me I heard the Symon girl was going to marry Clarence. That monumental dowry of hers was supposed to clear out some of His Highness's confounded debt without further burdening the state with it."

Now it was Rhys's turn to frown in puzzlement. "Parliament forbade the match because she was a commoner. Weren't you there for the deliberations and vote?"

The old man's jaw went rigid. "Other considerations have kept me from the House of Lords of late. As my heir, your brother has taken the seat in my stead. I regret to say he apparently keeps me damned ill-informed." Lord Warrington arched a wiry brow. "No wonder you've no use for your allowance since you've come into a well-heeled wife."

"I didn't marry Olivia for her money, if that's what you're thinking. Her father set up a trust to which only she has access. I agreed with the arrangement," Rhys said. "It is how I would have wished matters in any case. I've managed to support myself. I'll support my wife as well."

"Yes, I've heard of how you've kept yourself. A man who gambles for a living is a fool."

"Only if he risks more than he can afford to lose," Rhys said. "I've been banished from your sight, yet you've made a point of knowing my business. Why?"

The question seemed to flummox his father. His jaw worked furiously, and there was a slight tremor to the hand that pulled his shawl closer. "Do not attach any significance to my interest in your activities. A man in my position must make it his business to be informed on a number of things."

Despite his words, Rhys thought he sensed a slight chink in the old bear's armor.

"Then let me inform you further," Rhys said. "I didn't marry Olivia for money. I married her for love."

The marquis made a derisive snort.

"And for her protection." Rhys told his father about the attempts on Olivia's life. The marquis listened without comment until he was finished.

"And to what do you attribute these attacks?" his father asked.

"I'm not sure. At first, I assumed someone wished to end her prospective match with the duke in the most egregious way. Since the last threat arrived after our marriage, it's more likely that her father has made a deadly enemy."

"The lady herself hasn't offended someone?"

"No. She's possessed of strong opinions, but only in private," Rhys said. "Until we wed, she was something of a wallflower."

"So what do you propose to do?" his father asked.

"Sir, I'm compelled to ask for your help. I propose to move her into Warrington House until such time as I can set up my own household and staff it with people who will help me protect her."

"And you think you're a good enough judge of character that you can hire fellows off the street to guard your wife from an assassin?"

"No, I wouldn't trust strangers," Rhys said. "I'll seek out members of my old regiment, the fighting men who served under me in France."

"The few who survived your command, you mean."

Yes, how good of you to remind me, you crusty old bastard. "They are few, but they're trustworthy and they'll be glad for the work."

His father leaned back in his chair and looked down his long nose. "And you think these men would take orders from you again?"

"They, of all people, know the truth of what happened at Maubeuge. They won't blink twice at my orders." After the battle, he'd made the rounds at hospital to find members of his command. To a man, the survivors thanked him.

All but Lieutenant Duffy.

"What did happen at Maubeuge?" the marquis asked.

Finally.

His father wouldn't let him tell his side of the story when he was first sent home. The rumors, the whiff of scandal, were heinous enough that the marquis was obliged to act decisively.

"A field surgeon must sometimes hack off a limb to save the man," his father had said in this very room three years ago before he banished Rhys from his sight. "A family too must sometimes set aside one of its members for the good of the whole."

And just like that, Rhys was an outcast. Without recourse. Without being given a chance to explain.

His father was giving it to him now.

"The tale of Maubeuge doesn't make for pretty hearing," Rhys said. "Someone gave us faulty intelligence that led my regiment into a French trap."

In halting sentences, he recounted the days of forced march leading up to the ill-fated engagement. At one point, his father rose and poured a jigger of whisky for each of them, waving a thin hand for Rhys to continue as they drank.

The British cavalry was lured into committing their forces, thinking surprise was on their side. The intelligence dispatches Rhys and his friends Colton and Sharp had received made no mention of the much larger French force hidden in the surrounding forest and behind the hills.

Rhys told his father the particulars, answering the marquis's questions without flinching.

But Rhys didn't confide the way the faces of the dying had risen in his mind to taunt him over the last three years—those who deserved death and, worse, those who didn't. He didn't share the blaze of light that would sometimes descend on his vision, the phantom screams of the wounded, or the way the ground sometimes seemed to shake under the memory of two hundred hooves pounding in unison.

The myriad details that used to torment him no longer dragged him back to that killing field. He hadn't been tortured by a full-blown episode when the world spun backward to Maubeuge since he met Olivia.

He didn't know why she grounded him in the present, but he thanked God it was so.

"I don't suppose you have copies of those fraudulent dispatches or any way to definitively clear your name?" his father asked.

"No," Rhys admitted. Since the Duke of Clarence withdrew his suit before Rhys succeeded in publicly ruining Olivia, he didn't think Mr. Alcock would deliver on his part of their failed bargain. "You have only my word for what happened."

"Perhaps," the marquis said slowly, "that's good enough."

Rhys sucked in his breath. With those few words, he was pardoned. He was suddenly restored and reconciled to his family.

And it didn't mean as much as he'd thought it would.

Olivia was his family now, but he'd certainly accept help from his old one to keep her safe.

"Thank you, sir. Once I have a guard set up for Olivia, I'll devote myself to uncovering the person behind these thorns and deal with him."

"Or her," the marquis said thoughtfully. "After all, poison is a woman's weapon."

"I hadn't considered that before. You're right." Rhys would have to revisit the guest list of the Symon's house party with particular emphasis on Baroness Ramstead, Lady Harrington, and Amanda Pinkerton. He mentally added another female name to the roster—Olivia's maid, Babette.

Rhys mistrusted all things French on principle, and the fact that this particular French woman had been associated with the suspected spy, La Belle Perdu, only added to his misgivings. Still, he hadn't seriously considered female involvement in the attempts on Olivia's life until now.

"Do you and your wife intend to be...*fashionable*?" His father's tone suggested keeping up with the bon ton was tantamount to considering becoming infected with the French pox.

"No, sir." How could his father imagine that Rhys

would be squiring Olivia to balls and the theatre when someone was trying to kill her? "The fewer people who know our whereabouts, the better."

"A wise decision." Lord Warrington stood. "I have sources of information not readily available to most. I'll make a few discreet inquiries and do what I can to determine who's behind these attempts on your wife's life. Do not consider establishing your own home at present. Warrington House is at your disposal for as long as you need it."

Rhys rose as well.

Then his father extended a tremoring hand. Rhys took it and gave it a shake.

"Welcome home, son."

Chapter 31

OLIVIA AND RHYS SETTLED INTO LIFE AT WARRINGTON House with a minimum of disruption to the staff or Rhys's family. His mother was overjoyed to see him and welcomed Olivia with open arms. The marquis was coldly quiet, but even though he was less demonstrative, Olivia caught him looking at Rhys across the dinner table with a satisfied glint in his eyes.

All in all, it was an agreeable arrangement until she and Rhys could set up their own household. Life fell into a comfortable rhythm. If not for the threat of the thorns and the way Rhys almost smothered her with protection, Olivia would have been perfectly content.

"My sister Calliope has finally gotten her way and escaped the nursery," she remarked to Babette, as the maid cinched her stays tight one morning.

Olivia had received word that her parents had moved their household to London and taken up residence in their Mayfair townhouse. Beatrice Symon was up to her elbows in plans for fifteen-year-old Calliope's "come out" once the Season started. The ton might try to bar the door against the Symon family on account of its lack of title and, what was possibly worse in the eyes of the mighty, its association with trade. But no one could keep such a well-dowered young lady as Calliope Symon on the sidelines of the Marriage Mart for long.

Besides, Olivia now sported a "lady" before her name. While the Symon link with the House of Warrington didn't carry as much weight as a match with the Duke of Clarence would have, Olivia's mother was reportedly milking her oldest daughter's aristocratic connections for all they were worth.

"Will you be calling on your family soon?" Babette asked.

"No," Olivia said as she lifted her arms so her maid could slip the muslin day dress over her head. The column of fabric draped to the floor in graceful folds. She might as well double as a Grecian statue. She certainly didn't have any more freedom of movement than one. "Rhys has made me a veritable prisoner here at Warrington House."

He meant extremely well, and she understood why he'd given orders for her not to leave the premises. He'd enlisted the help of the Warrington staff, and Tweadle especially trailed her like a bloodhound whenever she wandered too close to the front door. As long as she was under the marquis's roof, she was untouchable. Whoever sent those thorns must be pulling out their hair in frustration.

The only trouble was, Olivia was near to yanking out her own locks as well.

"Lord Rhys, he did not mean to cut you off from your family, *bien sur*," Babette said as she smoothed the counterpane on Olivia and Rhys's bed. He wouldn't hear of separate bedrooms, even though it fairly scandalized the help at Warrington House for them to share a bed.

Olivia was glad for it. Her days were filled with tedium while Rhys was out and about, tracking down information he hoped would lead to Mr. Weinschmidt's killer. She'd begged to come with him, but he was so certain the only way to keep her safe was to keep her at Warrington House, she'd finally relented.

"If anything happened to you, I couldn't bear it," he'd said, his voice catching. "I'd be…homeless."

So she stopped wheedling him about it, but she wouldn't budge when he tried to make her dismiss Babette as well. Warrington House was opulently comfortable and there were plenty of servants to be had, but Babette was her one link to her past life. She counted on Babette's gossip with the Symon servants for news of her family. She couldn't lose everything, even to keep herself safe.

"I could take a message to your parents, asking them to call on you here for tea," Babette suggested. Even Beatrice Symon didn't have the gall to knock on the door of a marquis's home without an invitation. "Do you wish it?"

"An excellent idea. Though between fittings with Jean-Pierre and putting Calliope through her paces, I doubt my mother could find the time unless I told her the marchioness would be pouring out."

But her father might come. It was worth a try. She was so hungry to see anyone outside of the staff and residents of Warrington House, she wasn't too proud to beg her father to visit.

"I'll just nip down to the library and write a note.

Then you can deliver it this morning," she said, leading the way out of the room she shared with her husband. Perhaps Papa would come this afternoon.

Mr. Tweadle met her on the first floor landing.

"A gentleman is here to see Lord Rhys, but his lordship is not at home. The caller claims to have something for your husband and will not entrust it to me. He will, however, give it to you. I wonder if you'd care to receive him?"

"Who is it?"

"Mr. Fortescue Alcock, Esquire," Mr. Tweadle read from the man's calling card. He added a sniff of disdain. "A Member of Parliament."

"I wonder that he didn't ask to see Lord Warrington then."

"The House of Lords has little truck with the House of Commons," Tweadle said crustily. "My lady may certainly send word that she is 'not at home' to Mr. Alcock, and I'll send the gentleman on his way."

"No, that's not necessary, Mr. Tweadle. If Mr. Alcock has something for my husband, I'll certainly meet with him," she said. Company of any kind was a welcome diversion from her days of isolation. "Please fetch some tea and bring it to the parlor, Babette."

Olivia had never been a social being. She hadn't ever felt alone while pottering about with her orchids or riding her mare, Molly, over the Barrowdell hills. There was a time when she would have reveled in the solitude she now enjoyed, but there was a difference between choosing her own company and being forced into it. Surely Rhys wouldn't begrudge her a chance to play hostess in his absence just this once.

She followed Mr. Tweadle to the parlor where he announced her to the tall, gaunt man who bent over her offered hand with correct deference.

"Lady Olivia," he said. "May I offer my felicitations on your recent marriage?"

"Thank you, sir. Please make yourself comfortable." Olivia claimed the central section of the settee and waved a hand toward one of the wing chairs opposite her. Mr. Tweadle hovered near the doorway, clearly intent on remaining unless she sent him away.

Babette appeared at the doorway, having set a speed record for assembling a tea tray. She bobbed a curtsey and then arranged the tray on the low table before Olivia. "Shall I pour out, my lady?"

Before she could respond, Mr. Alcock said, "I rather think you'll prefer to hear what I have to say alone."

Babette flashed a warning glance at her and waited.

"I trust my maid's discretion implicitly," Olivia said. Besides, she knew Rhys wouldn't want her alone with a strange man, even if he was an MP. "Whatever message you have for me to deliver to my husband will be safe in her hearing. Mr. Tweadle, you may go."

The butler pressed his lips in a tight line but did as she bade him. Mr. Alcock glared at Babette from under his wiry brows. Olivia was determined not to let him bully her into sending away Babette as well.

"As you wish," Mr. Alcock finally said. "Time is of the essence or I would have waited for Lord Rhys." He reached into his waistcoat pocket and drew out a fat parcel. "Enclosed, he will find copies of original dispatches that should have gone to him prior to the battle at Maubeuge. There is also a sworn statement from a Sergeant Leatherby that the dispatches were switched at the last checkpoint prior to being delivered to Lord Rhys."

Olivia's chest constricted. Mr. Alcock was offering proof of Rhys's innocence in that horrible debacle. "Did this Sergeant Leatherby reveal who switched the orders?"

"He wasn't willing to do so until he gets to open court, but I fear that day may never come. You see, I have it on good authority that the sergeant is at this moment preparing to take ship for Portsmouth at Wapping Dock. If your husband wishes to compel his testimony, I advise him to head for the docks before the next tide."

Mr. Alcock stood. "I regret I must decline this lovely tea, but business requires me to be elsewhere."

Olivia stood as well, clutching the packet of documents to her chest. "Thank you for this, sir. My husband and I are in your debt."

"No, it is I who would not be in his. A man must pay his debts of honor," Mr. Alcock said. "Even though your husband fulfilled his part of the bargain in a wholly unexpected way, I am still duty-bound to deliver on my pledge."

"His part of the bargain? What do you mean?" That smacked of a wager, and though her bets with Rhys had resulted in unexpected happiness, she was still suspicious of the practice.

"He didn't tell you? Hmph. I suppose I ought not either then. Ignorance is bliss, you know."

"Sir, I find ignorance an intolerable state. To what do you refer?"

"Very well, since you insist." His oily smile made

her realize he intended to tell her all along. He merely wanted her to beg. "I know you think Lord Rhys was sent to Barrowdell ostensibly as the Duke of Clarence's factor. His true commission, which I orchestrated, was to upset the match between you and the royal and keep it from coming to pass. Now, you mustn't take it personally. My reasons were purely political and had nothing to do with you."

Nothing to do with her? The man had just admitted to interfering with a possible marriage. Could it be more personal? Surely Rhys wouldn't have been a party to such skullduggery.

But now that she thought about it, Rhys hadn't been terribly complimentary to the duke. "And how did you expect him to stop the match with Clarence?"

"By doing what he does best, of course." Mr. Alcock popped his hat on his head. "Lord Rhys was supposed to seduce and ruin you, which I rather guess he did since your father forced him to marry you. Rather hard luck on him to be leg-shackled for life in exchange for information that could clear his name. Still, he could have done ever so much worse. You might have been a wart-ridden heiress with the squints."

Olivia's stomach cramped as if someone had punched her in the gut.

"I can see I've given you plenty to consider, Lady Olivia. I'll see myself out. Good day." Mr. Alcock strode out but stopped at the arched doorway and turned back to her. His practiced smile, the one Olivia suspected he used to disarm political opponents he intended to destroy, didn't reach his eyes. "You see, my lady, ignorance really is bliss."

❦

"Think, man." Rhys smacked his fist down on Horatio Symon's desk with a resounding thud. If Olivia had known he was paying her father a visit today, she'd have pitched a fit to come along. But since he was feeling rather less cordial toward his father-in-law than she'd have appreciated, Rhys was grateful he'd been able to put her off again. "Which of your wife's houseguests has reason to wish you ill?"

"A successful man of business makes enemies without even trying. Surely you can appreciate that." Horatio strolled over to his bookshelf, pulled out a thick volume, and took a flask of green liquid from between the worn covers. "Care for a drink, son?"

"No. May lightning strike me dead if ever I touch your vile brew again." Rhys sank into a chair and rubbed his temples. "You're not taking this threat to Olivia seriously."

"Of course I am." Horatio poured a jigger of the liquor for himself and knocked it back in one gulp. "I made sure she married you, didn't I?"

"If the threat isn't because of your business dealings, then the attack is personal. Why not target you directly?" Rhys wondered aloud.

"I expect the point is to cause me pain," Horatio said. "The dead feel none."

"If the aim of the assassin is to cause you pain, why not target Mrs. Symon then?"

Horatio cocked a brow at him. "You've met Mrs. Symon, I collect. Don't misunderstand. I love the woman, but she can be a bit much. Most people would think they were doing me a favor by ridding me of her.

Olivia, on the other hand…" He slumped into his chair again. "She's my own heart and I haven't been very circumspect about showing it. Everyone knows she's my favorite."

"So whoever is behind this knows that. Now, I ask again, which of your guests at Barrowdell has reason to cause you pain?"

"None of them. I was careful to help each of them during the time we all passed together in India. A stock tip here. A word of an impending unrest there. A man needs his friends all the more when he is far from Home, and he does well to keep them informed when something touches them." A shadow passed behind Horatio's eyes and he covered his mouth with his hand for a moment. Then he lowered it slowly. "I only exchanged harsh words with one of them and then only once."

"Who?"

"Dr. Pinkerton."

"What was the argument about?"

"It wasn't even my fault." Horatio went for another jigger of the green devil drink. "It's not as if I caused it, after all. I just pointed out the way of the world."

"What way of the world?" Rhys could almost see his father-in-law's jagged thoughts darting behind his eyes.

"So much time has gone by," Horatio said, his voice drifting to nothing, as if Rhys were no longer in the room. "No, it couldn't be that."

Rhys reached across the table and snatched Horatio's lapels. He yanked his father-in-law forward until they were practically nose to nose. "Confound it, start at the beginning and we'll decide together whether your suspicions are well-founded. Now what are you talking about?"

"I suppose…he might still harbor resentment against me for speaking an uncomfortable truth. Oh, God, if it all comes out, this'll touch Amanda too." Horatio buried his face in his hands. "What I'm about to tell you must never leave this room. Never. Promise me."

"I can't. Not if it touches Olivia's safety. But if it doesn't, I'm not the sort to carry tales. Now talk."

Horatio sighed and nodded. "Very well. It concerns Amanda's mother."

"Who died in India shortly after Amanda was born," Rhys prompted.

"Yes, but Gita wasn't a Greek lady as Pinkerton gives out. She was an Indian woman. A damned beautiful one too from up in the Khyber Hills. Nearly as fair-skinned as her daughter."

That explained Amanda's lush dark hair and large speaking eyes, Rhys thought.

"When Pinkerton and Gita married, I wished them well. Amanda was born just before I left India to return home. Beautiful child. The doctor told me he intended to bring his family to England as soon as Amanda was old enough to have a Season. 'That won't work,' I told him. It was all well and good to have a native wife in Bombay, but it would never fly in Brighton. And if folks in Britain ever discovered Amanda carried a touch of the tar brush, no well-bred Englishman would marry her."

"That was cruel of you to say."

"But it was the truth. Would he rather hear it from a friend, or have Gita and Amanda shunned by English society?"

Prejudice was an ugly truth, but Rhys still thought it was wrong of Horatio to point it out to Dr. Pinkerton. "And you think he means to hurt you because of what you said all those years ago?"

"I don't know. He was pretty angry, but we didn't come to blows or anything. After he settled down, we passed the rest of the evening pleasantly enough. I thought we were alone. We were smoking under the banyan tree behind his house, but what if Gita overheard me and was distraught...? Just before I took the boat home, I heard she'd died, but I never heard how." Horatio's eyes took on a slight glaze, and Rhys was sure he was seeing other times and places. "I didn't think much about it at the time because people were always dying of cholera or snakebite or some such terrible thing—strange place, India, beautiful and horrifying at once...You don't suppose she did away with herself, do you? You know, to spare her family from being ostracized when her husband returned to England?"

"If she did, Dr. Pinkerton would be justified in hating you. I'd hate you myself." Rhys disliked Horatio more than a little at the moment, but he could at least trust his father-in-law to try to help him protect Olivia. He rose and paced the small room. "As a doctor, Pinkerton would know which poisons are fast acting enough to use on those thorns. He'd have access to them as well."

"The man is a crack rider too," Horatio said miserably. "Pinkerton knows enough about horses and tack to have sabotaged Molly's saddle." He shook his head with vehemence. "No, I don't want to believe it."

"I think we must until we can prove differently."

Rhys headed for the door. "In the meantime, I want you to stay away from Olivia."

"But I'm her father. And this is not my fault. It's not as if I caused stupid people to be prejudiced. I simply pointed it out to Pinkerton. We must live in the world, I told him." Horatio spread his hands before himself. "The world is thus."

"The world is what we make it, Horatio." Rhys opened the study door.

"Wait a moment. All we have is conjecture. You can't go off and accuse my old friend when we really have no evidence. What do you intend, Warrington?"

"I intend to make the world safe for Olivia. By any means necessary."

Chapter 32

THE PACKET OF PAPERS SLIPPED FROM OLIVIA'S HANDS, fluttering to the hardwood like a flock of downed pigeons. Her knees gave way, and if she hadn't been so close to the settee, she'd have sunk just as surely to the floor.

Rhys had set out to ruin her.

"I don't know him at all," she murmured.

Babette retrieved the papers and stacked them neatly on the tea tray. "My lady, sometimes things they are not what they seem. The person you do not know is this Monsieur Alcock."

A rake was capable of several layers of deception. Had any of their unorthodox courtship been real? Or had Rhys merely been trapped in the spiderweb of his own making? When he made those heartrending vows over the anvil, was he only pretending?

She had to remind herself to breathe, and even then, there didn't seem to be any air in the room. Betrayal sucked up all the oxygen and left her none. "I have to go."

"Where, my lady?"

Home. If she were a bird, she'd fly away to Barrowdell and never leave its rolling hills. She'd ride her mare and grow her orchids, and the rest of the world could go chase itself.

But then she'd never see Rhys again.

Her chest ached. Love wasn't something she could turn off like a lamp. The glow of caring still flared inside her, burning hot and painful. How could he have done this to her?

"To us?" she whispered. Something inside her was dying. She and Rhys had formed a circle of two, a glorious "we." Now her soul hunkered by itself.

"My lady, you have not heard Lord Rhys's side to this tale," Babette said. "This is no time for the hasty decision. I urge you not to be doing something you will regret."

"Hasty," she repeated, the word calling up something Mr. Alcock had said. *Time is of the essence.* The man who could clear Rhys's name for good and all might be slipping away even now.

Rhys might have set out to ruin her, but she wouldn't see him permanently disgraced if she could help it. She'd remain loyal to him. Even if he didn't really love her, she loved him.

She'd be true to her own heart.

"Distract Mr. Tweadle for me," Olivia said, rising with purpose and swiping her glistening eyes before the first tear could fall.

"Why, my lady?"

"Because I'm going to Wapping Dock to find Sergeant Leatherby."

❧

Babette tried to dissuade her for a bit, but Olivia remained firm.

"*Ah, bien*," the maid said, shaking her head. "But after you are away, you must make to wait on the corner for me, and I shall slip out the kitchen and down the alley. A lady, she should not travel the city by herself. Besides, I shall bring your reticule and pelisse."

Olivia agreed, and after Babette led Tweadle away from Warrington House's front door, Olivia sneaked out. The sense of freedom would have been more invigorating if a cold wind wasn't whipping down the man-made canyons of Mayfair.

Or if her heart weren't still numb from Mr. Alcock's revelations.

Wrapping her arms around herself, she put her head down and walked into the wind until she reached a corner. She tried to hail a cab, but with no purse in evidence, hackneys simply rumbled past her.

She stamped her feet against the cold and glanced over her shoulder down the block. Babette was nowhere to be seen.

Then a carriage rumbled to a stop before her.

"God's garters! Olivia Symon, what are you doing out in this wind without a coat?"

Olivia looked up to see Amanda Pinkerton leaning out of the carriage window.

"I guess I should call you Lady Rhys Warrington. You slyboots, running off to Gretna Green with none of us the wiser! What have you to say for yourself?" She paused long enough to snatch a breath. "I can see the cold has your tongue. Well, come then. I've a heated brick at my feet and I'm glad to share."

At her signal, Amanda's footman leaped down from the rear of the carriage and opened the door for Olivia. She let the servant hand her up into the conveyance, grateful to be out of the wind.

"Here you go," Amanda said as she tucked a bearskin blanket around her. Then she rapped on the carriage ceiling to signal the driver to move on. "You'll catch your death out there like that, I shouldn't wonder. Now where can we take you? Are you staying with your parents or have you and Lord Rhys set up housekeeping somewhere?"

"I need to go to Wapping." Olivia knew she ought to ask Amanda to wait until Babette arrived, but if she could catch a quick ride to her destination, she'd brave the docks alone. Sergeant Leatherby might be boarding the ship for Portsmouth this very moment. "Can you take me there please?"

"Don't tell me you're running away from your husband and intend to take ship. First an elopement; now this!"

"No, I'm not running away from Rhys," she said, though she doubted she could bear seeing him. "Will you take me to Wapping or not?"

Olivia didn't care that she sounded snappish. She didn't have time for a gossip's prying questions. Besides, she was trying very hard not to think about her husband at the moment. Her chest might split open if she did.

"Of course I can take you to Wapping. The docks aren't so far from the home Father leased for us," Amanda said without the slightest show of offense. "It's not Mayfair, but you just won't believe what a cunning little place it is. Why, it even has a tower, and Father says there used to be a moat."

Olivia listened with half an ear. The way Amanda chattered on made Olivia realize she probably didn't have many people to talk to in London. As a doctor, her father wasn't considered "in trade," but neither was his blood blue. That placed his daughter on the fringes of Polite Society. In her way, Amanda Pinkerton was as isolated as Olivia.

When the forest of masts bobbing at Wapping Dock rose up in the carriage windows, Olivia asked Amanda to signal for a halt.

"And let you wander Wapping by yourself and without a coat? Not likely."

"But I have to find someone before they take ship. A Sergeant Leatherby. It's most urgent."

The coach slowed and stopped before a gray stone house of venerable age. It did indeed have a tower that listed only slightly to the right. Olivia suspected the ancient edifice had been overlooking the Thames back when the Danes flooded into England.

"Oh, that's easily done. I'll send our man Hector round to find this Sergeant Leatherby for you." Amanda climbed out of the coach and waited while her footman helped Olivia down as well. She gave the footman orders to scour the dock for the ship bound for Portsmouth, apprehend Sergeant Leatherby, and bring him back, willing or not, to meet with Lady Rhys Warrington. Then she linked arms with Olivia companionably. "You and I will take some tea while we wait for Hector to come back. I'm so longing to hear about…Scotland."

The plan did seem a good one. Better than wandering about the docks on her own. An unescorted woman would be easy prey for unsavory elements. Now that she had time to consider it, Olivia realized she wasn't thinking clearly when she set off on this quest. "Tea sounds lovely. Thank you, Miss Pinkerton. Or may I call you by your Christian name?"

"Of course, if we take it turn and turn about, Olivia." Miss Pinkerton dimpled prettily and led the way into the stone house. Given the severe exterior, Olivia expected heavy Tudor furnishings, but the parlor off the entrance hall was dotted with elegant mahogany and ebony side tables. The fashionable wing chairs were covered with tiny fleur-de-lis-patterned fabric.

"We live simply here," Amanda said as she hung up her own coat on a peg by the door. "It's Cook's half-day off, and besides Hector, we have no other servants. Even the coach is hired." She sighed. "It's not at all like India. We had servants for everything there. Do you know we even had one who did nothing but fan us on hot days?"

"I expect there are many differences between here and India."

"Oh, yes. For one thing, there were no rooms in the house in India where I wasn't welcome," Amanda said. "Here at first, Cook tried to keep me out of the kitchen completely."

The aroma of fresh bread wafted down the hall toward them. Amanda sighed. "Mrs. Pennyworth must have baked this morning. Come."

They followed their noses toward the source of the yeasty scent.

"Fetch me a cup of milk from the crock, if you

please," Amanda said as she lit the hob and filled the kettle at the hand pump by the sink. "The larder is through there."

Olivia was strangely comforted by the lack of ceremony. Friends would be so informal with each other. At least, she suspected they would be. Beatrice Symon had so regimented Olivia's life, she'd never had opportunity to make many true friends. She found the stone crock where the milk was stored and ladled up a dipperful. She delivered it to Amanda, careful not to spill a drop. "Will this do, you think?"

"Perfect." Amanda gave her a quick hug. "We really didn't get the opportunity to know each other while Father and I were visiting at Barrowdell. I hope we can rectify that here in London. Please sit down while I fix our tea."

Olivia settled at the long oak table while Amanda chattered about being invited to a ball at Sir Nigel Cavendish's lavish town house a fortnight hence. Amanda let slip that she was a trifle old for a debutant, and Olivia knew she was a couple years her senior, but Amanda hoped her exotic upbringing would render her "interesting" to the ton.

"Of course, I'm not truly 'out' yet," Amanda said as she cut the fresh loaf into thick slices and slathered each with clotted cream. "I haven't a voucher for Almack's, but Sir Nigel's ball will be almost as good. Father assures me I'll meet lots of eligible fellows there and I so love to dance. Don't you?"

Her mother engaged several dancing masters, but Olivia never moved with enough grace to please Beatrice Symon. "I'm afraid I never learned."

Amanda's eyes went round. "You're joking."

Olivia raised a mock solemn hand. "As I hope for heaven, I swear that I have two left feet."

"Well, that is something we shall have to fix. Perhaps I'll teach you. After we have tea, of course."

Amanda brought over two steaming cups. "Humor me and try these scones, will you? Cook made them yesterday with a new recipe."

Olivia nibbled at the delicate pastry and pronounced them heavenly. The tea revived her spirits considerably. Hector would find Sergeant Leatherby. She'd give Rhys a chance to explain himself on the matter of Mr. Alcock's pernicious bargain. And she and Amanda would become friends in a city where both of them needed one.

"Now, tell me what it was like to run away to Scotland with that handsome husband of yours." Amanda sat down opposite Olivia with her own cup of tea.

Olivia found herself relaxing, telling Amanda about her unorthodox wedding over the anvil. She recounted her meeting with Rhys's sister and brother-in-law. Amanda laughed at the tale of Rhys playing hide-and-seek with his nephew in old Braebrooke Cairn.

Whether it was relief at seeing a friendly face or the drowsy warmth of the kitchen, something compelled Olivia to tell her why she sought Sergeant Leatherby and how she hoped to help Rhys clear his name once and for all time. It all tumbled out of her like water gushing from a break in a dike.

"Just imagine," Amanda said as she poured out another serving of tea for Olivia. "Proof that Lord Rhys is guiltless in that unfortunate French affair may be walking the docks at Wapping this very moment. But I confess to a bit of puzzlement. My father says politicians don't even sneeze unless it benefits their position. Why did Mr. Alcock deliver those documents to you now?"

Olivia gulped the second cup of tea and grimaced. It was much sweeter than she liked.

"I put three lumps in this time," Amanda explained. "Drink up, dear. You really have very little meat on your bones, you know. So what about this Mr. Alcock business?"

"Well, it was because—" Olivia covered her mouth with her hand. She almost admitted that the MP delivered the documents because Rhys had fulfilled his commission to ruin her. Her vision faded for a moment, nearly going black. She blinked slowly, trying to make her eyes focus. Light streamed in the high kitchen window in a long shaft, illuminating countless little dust speck worlds. She gave herself a shake to keep from being pulled into orbit with one of them. "They had a business arrangement. Oh, me! I can't seem to…"

Her brain felt so fuzzy, she couldn't put another two words together. Amanda smiled and leaned toward her. The room tilted strangely, and suddenly Olivia's head was too heavy for her to hold up.

Darkness gathered at the edges of the room and then rushed in on her. She blinked into nothingness, as suddenly and completely as a pinched-off candle.

Chapter 33

RHYS WAS COLDLY FURIOUS WITH TWEADLE FOR letting Olivia slip out of Warrington House undetected.

"But she had help, my lord," Mr. Tweadle said. "That French maid of hers drew me away from my post and then sneaked out the back after her. However, Lady Olivia must have given her the slip as well. She came skulking back, with your wife's reticule and pelisse in tow."

"Where is Babette now?"

"I had Dirkwater shut her up in the cold larder until you returned, sir. Shall I summon the authorities?"

A Bow Street Runner would merely take statements and file a report. By the time someone might think of where to start the search for Olivia, it would be too late.

"No, fetch her here," Rhys ordered. "And step lively."

When Babette appeared, she bore not only Olivia's things, but a parcel tied with a string.

"Where is she?" Rhys demanded.

"First, you must know the why my lady she made to disobey you." Babette dropped the packet on the marquis's desk and laid Olivia's effects carefully on one of the Sheraton chairs. Then in her stilted English, she described Alcock's visit in detail.

Rhys listened in stony silence, rifling through the much folded documents that would clear him if they could be substantiated by a witness. Then, with arms crossed over her bosom, Babette recounted how Alcock had revealed their cursed agreement.

Olivia now knew he meant to ruin her at first. The backs of his eyes burned.

"But even though you meant to do her the ill turn," Babette said with undisguised loathing, "my lady, she is on her way to Wapping Dock to find the man who can clear your name."

Rhys swore softly, then muttered, "I don't deserve her."

"This thought it is also in my mind," Babette said agreeably. "But if you wish to know where she might be now, you would do well to ask Miss Pinkerton. The last I saw of my lady, she was riding away in a coach with that young miss."

Rhys made for the door, but Babette stepped into his path.

"Take me with you, my lord. I can help."

Rhys chuckled mirthlessly. "Just because you were lady's maid to a French courtesan, it doesn't signify that you would be useful in a tight spot."

"I was not only a maid," Babette admitted. "I was a help to La Belle Perdu *in all her endeavors*."

Rhys frowned down at her. "The French spy."

"Not a spy, a double agent. Her father was French, but her mother, she was English. Just like me. My loyalty and La Belle Perdu's, it is to the British Crown."

"So she leaped to her death to prove it?"

"*Non*, she is in hiding yet. Only one man in the government knew she used her profession to pass disinformation to French contacts. When he died, she was named an enemy of the state by those who did not know the truth." Babette walked toward him, her gaze direct as a man's. "You, of all people, should know what it is to be accused falsely."

She had him there.

"Now my loyalty it is to your wife," Babette went on. "If my mistress is in trouble, I want to help."

Rhys studied her determined features for a few heartbeats. "Then come with me."

Olivia fought her way back to consciousness despite a pounding headache. She was so cold. Her first coherent thought was that Amanda had let the fire in the kitchen burn out and opened the windows in the last gasp of winter. Then the fog in her brain cleared.

She forced her eyes open. Her back was propped against clammy grey stone. The smell of vermin and filth and the clinging reek of ancient misery assaulted her nostrils. Her mind reeled.

The tea! Amanda must have laced her second cup with something to render her senseless.

"Where am I?" She realized shakily that Amanda was fastening a heavy iron manacle to her right wrist.

"In the *souterraine*, of course. I believe it's intended to be a root cellar, but I like to think of it as the dungeon," Amanda said with maddening calmness. "I told you what a cunning place this was. Weren't you attending?"

"Why are you doing this?" Olivia struggled to free herself, but the residual effects of the drugged tea made her weak. Miss Pinkerton bound her other wrist tightly as well.

"I'm just protecting what's right, that's all," the young woman said. "Your father did my mother a terrible wrong, and we're going to make him pay."

"My father wouldn't knowingly hurt anyone," Olivia protested.

"Words can wound, sharp as a blade," Amanda said, her dark eyes blazing. "My father told me all about it. Horatio Symon said my mother wasn't good enough for London, never mind that she was a pure woman from a good family and could trace her lineage back to Rajputana kings."

Olivia frowned up at her, trying to make sense of her words, but failing miserably. "But your mother was Greek."

"That's the lie my father put about to satisfy bigots like your father." Amanda paced the fetid space, her footfalls thudding on the flagstones with unnatural loudness. "But that wasn't good enough for Mr. Symon; no, indeed. And my mother died of a broken heart over it."

"How can you know that? Weren't you an infant when she died?"

"Father never hid my true parentage from me or why my mother died."

Olivia still couldn't believe Horatio Symon had been so heartless. He'd always been so kind to her. She hung her head for a moment willing her darting thoughts to settle. She had to keep Amanda talking.

"It doesn't matter who your mother was. You are who you decide to be, Amanda."

"Ha! You, of all people, should know the world doesn't work that way. The Duke of Clarence threw you over because you weren't wellborn. I don't have the advantage of a fortune behind me, but my father's profession is respectable enough. I'll make good, if no one finds out the truth. But if the ton discovers my mother grew up speaking Hindi instead of Greek, I'll be outcast."

"More shame to them," Olivia said.

Amanda put her hands to her ears. "That's the kind of thing Father told me you'd say. He's right about you, I guess. Still, it makes me sad to see you so, Olivia. In another world, we might have been friends." She worried her lower lip with her white teeth. "Father said I should ride the carriage up and down your block on the chance that I'd see you out and about, and…well, this is ever so much harder than I expected."

All the blood ran from Olivia's throbbing head. "What are you going to do?"

"It's up to Father now," she said, her voice flat and expressionless. Amanda stared at the floor, but Olivia didn't think she actually saw the straw-strewn stone. Then Amanda gave herself a shake. "Mercy me, I have another fitting for my ball gown. I'll be late if Father doesn't attend to you directly. I wonder what's keeping him."

She scurried away, hanging the key that would unshackle Olivia's bonds on the wicked hook by the door. She tugged at a pulley that elevated the chains binding Olivia's hands, not stopping until Olivia was forced to stand tiptoe. Then Amanda waved good-bye before climbing the stairs.

The door at the top of the stairs slammed shut with finality. There was very little light in that dank place, only one small hole high on the east side of the round room. Olivia tracked the patch of light thrown across the space as it crept downward, stone by stone. By the time the sun reached its zenith even that small comfort would be gone.

There were tiny rustlings around her. Rats. Several pairs of red eyes glinted at her, feral and questing in the dimness. She kicked at one nosing her ankle. Oh, God, how she hated such vermin with their scritchy little claws and sharp teeth.

Her arms started to ache. She had no feeling in her fingers. A scream started to build in her throat, but she held it back. No one would hear her in this hell. The walls were a couple feet thick, and the cacophony of a working dock would drown out any cries for help.

All she could do was pray.

"God be praised," she murmured when she heard the door creak open. Torchlight blazed down the stairwell, cutting a wide swath across the chamber. "Who's there? I'm Olivia Warrington. Whoever you are, please help me."

Dr. Pinkerton came into view carrying a smoking torch.

Olivia sagged against her bonds. "Why are you doing this to me?"

"So your father will suffer as I have suffered," Dr. Pinkerton said, his pale eyes darkening in the flickering light.

"Father was wrong to say those things to you," Olivia said.

"But he did and, as they say, 'a bell cannot be unrung.'"

"I'm sure he had no idea your wife would so take his words to heart that she'd die of a broken heart."

Dr. Pinkerton snorted. "She didn't."

"But—"

"That is simply the tale I told Amanda. Gita never knew what Horatio had said to me. But I knew immediately that your father was right. My beautiful little daughter would have no chance in England if Gita came back with us."

Olivia's jaw sagged.

"I loved Gita and I loved my daughter, but it became evident that I would have to choose between them. After several weeks of torment, I hit upon a plan. Like you, my Gita loved flowers and she was obsessive about her English roses. She wouldn't let anyone else tend them. I could never have borne for her to know I had chosen Amanda's future happiness over her, so I painted the thorns with a tincture of curare."

That explained Dr. Pinkerton's use of thorns in his previous attempts on her life. "Your wife died like poor Mr. Weinschmidt."

"Yes, just like your unfortunate lackey. I must say, my lady, you have proven difficult to kill." He met her gaze, and she saw both regret and resentment simmering in his pale eyes. "Nevertheless, I believe I shall succeed this time."

"Why must you do this?" Olivia's question echoed on the stone walls. "Father wouldn't have breathed a word about Amanda's true parentage. He's not that sort."

"No, he's the sort who has success dropped into his lap at every turn," Dr. Pinkerton said. "You can't know how frustrating it's been for me to know how much I've sacrificed for my child while Horatio's girls are coddled and rewarded."

Pinkerton's face hardened. "And now, my dear Olivia, it's time for you to make your peace with the Almighty. If it's any comfort to you, I expect to feel guilt for your death. But know that your passing will mean my wife's death is avenged on the man who drove me to kill her."

He edged toward the stairway.

"You can't mean to leave me here."

"Of course not. That would be unspeakably cruel. It could take you weeks to die of natural causes." He pulled a lever on the wall and the sound of metal grated on stone. A sluice gate opened, allowing a steady trickle of murky water to spread across the fetid floor.

"In ages past, when this *souterraine* grew too dirty to bear, this gate was opened and the floor flooded with Thames water," Dr. Pinkerton explained as dispassionately as if he were giving a lecture on the subject. He pointed to a similar portal on the opposite side of the room. "Normally, the companion gate over there was opened at the same time so the water and filth could be swept out. But I don't intend on opening the other gate just yet."

The brown water swirled toward her toes.

"You don't have to do this." She forced herself to keep an even tone.

"Yes, I do." He cast her a sad smile. "Once a plan is set in motion, it is important to see it to the end.

I didn't spare my own dear wife for Amanda's sake. What makes you think I'd pity my enemy's daughter? My course is determined and I dare not look back." He mounted the first step to avoid the water lapping at his heels. "Don't fight it, Olivia. I'm told drowning is quite painless if one doesn't resist."

"Dr. Pinkerton, no!" she yelled after him.

"God save you," he said softly as he took the manacle key from the hook and placed it in his pocket. The torchlight disappeared as the door closed behind him. "For I won't."

This time, Olivia wasn't able to hold it in. She knew it was useless, but as the water crept up her ankles, she screamed.

Chapter 34

RHYS REINED IN HIS MOUNT AS HE NEARED WAPPING. Somewhere on the docks, the man whose testimony could clear him was wandering free, about to take ship for parts unknown. He dismissed it as trivial. If anything happened to Olivia, it wouldn't matter if he was suddenly named king of all England.

"Why are we stopping?" Babette came alongside him. The horse beneath her danced sideways, spooked by the noise of the maritime gangs hauling away to rhythmic chants.

"Scouting things a bit." Rhys pointed toward the gray stone house with its listing tower. "There's the hired coach. That means Olivia is still there. You saw Amanda Pinkerton with her. How did she seem? Might she harm Olivia?"

"Mademoiselle Pinkerton seemed like any other silly debutant, but looks can be deceiving." Babette grimaced. "Contrary to what you might think, monsieur, the female, she can be more deadly than the male."

"I'll bear that in mind." He surveyed the stone house with a general's eye. "Divide and conquer, I'm thinking. Nip around and down the back alley. See if you can gain entrance through the kitchen. I'll take the front door and meet you inside." Rhys stroked his horse's quivering neck, wishing he had Lord Nathaniel Colton or Sir Jonah Sharp at his side. His friends could be counted on in a pinch, but what could a courtesan's maid, even one who was an accomplished double agent, do? "Be careful, Babette."

The maid tossed him a jaundiced glance. "Do not make to worry for me, my lord. Worry for my lady."

❦

Olivia screamed herself hoarse, but no one came. The retreating dab of sunlight reflected off the rising tide and threw macabre flashes throughout the room. Water was up to her waist now, sending her skirt billowing in the cold murk.

She tried to collapse her hands so she could yank them free. The rough iron tore the thin skin of her wrists, sending shrieking pain along with tiny ribbons of red tickling down her arms. She turned and braced her feet against the gray stone, using her body's weight to try to free herself. Olivia folded her left thumb against her palm tight as she could, concentrating on freeing just one hand. She strained and tugged, worrying her lip against the bite of iron and finally scraped her hand out of the manacle.

Hope surged in her breast, then withered as the water continued to rise. Try as she might, her right hand was stuck fast.

"God help me," she chanted, terror locking her muscles in near rigor. She'd heard that wild animals caught in traps sometimes gnawed off their own limbs in order to win free. She understood that kind of panic now.

∾

"Good afternoon, Miss Pinkerton. You're looking lovely," Rhys lied with ease, his hat in hand. "City life agrees with you."

"Lord Rhys, we weren't expecting you." She gripped the door so tightly, her knuckles went white.

"I understand my wandering wife enjoyed a carriage ride with you today." He leaned as if looking around her. "Might I come in?"

"No. I mean, yes, of course." She waved him in, clearly flustered. "Lady Rhys isn't here."

"Oh? Do you know where she went?" He strode past her into the parlor. "I do like what you've done with the parlor. Your taste is impeccable."

Amanda opened her mouth a couple of times like a carp on a riverbank. "If you wish to find your wife, my lord, I suggest you make a search of the docks. She was looking for someone who was about to take ship. I'm afraid I don't remember the gentleman's name."

"That's not my concern right now," Rhys said. "My concern is Olivia, and I believe you know where she is."

"Even if she did, she wouldn't tell you," a voice came from behind him.

Dr. Pinkerton stood in the parlor doorway with a pistol leveled at Rhys's midsection.

"Amanda's a good girl," Pinkerton said. "She knows how to follow directions—a quality I suspect your wife is sadly lacking. Otherwise she'd be safe at Warrington House."

"Father," Amanda said softly. "Perhaps we should let her go."

"Don't be ridiculous," Pinkerton snapped. "Have you forgotten your mother? Symon's daughter deserves her fate." Amanda turned away from them, head bent.

Good God, what have they done to her? Rhys's gut lurched.

"Let her rot down there," Pinkerton said with vehemence.

Down there. Surely not in the underbelly of this ancient keep. The sick feeling in his belly told Rhys that was exactly where Olivia was.

"Don't worry, Warrington," Dr. Pinkerton said. "You'll be joining her before you know it."

"I think not, *monsieur le doctor.*"

Babette came barreling down the hall and bashed Pinkerton on the back of the head with a very fashionable vase patterned after a Grecian urn. The doctor crumpled to the floor and Rhys dove for his pistol. Amanda leaped upon Rhys's back to defend her father, but Babette yanked her off.

"Did I not tell you I could help?" Babette said.

Rhys rose with the pistol in his hand. "I'll never doubt you again."

"And well you should not. Can you shoot a woman, my lord?"

Rhys glanced at Amanda, whose face went suddenly ashen. "No."

"I can," Babette said as she eased the gun from his grip. "Tell Lord Rhys where to find my mistress."

Words spewed out of Amanda's mouth so quickly,

Rhys could barely follow her garbled directions to the *souterraine* beneath the keep.

"And you, mademoiselle," Babette pointed the barrel at Miss Pinkerton, "if you would be so kind as to truss up your papa with the drapery ties, I will not need to shoot you, *non*?"

❧

When Rhys reached the heavy oak door leading off the kitchen, he heard a sound coming from the *souterraine* beneath him, a keening wail, muffled but unmistakable. Terror-filled, the screams sounded as if they came from a cornered animal instead of a person.

"Olivia!"

Rhys felt as if an anvil had been dropped on his chest. He flew down the stairs two and three at a time, a killing rage roaring in his veins. Pinkerton was going to pay, and pay dearly.

"I'm coming," he bellowed.

The keening stopped and she began shrieking his name.

A second door at the first landing was locked, but he put a shoulder to it and heaved. It gave a little, but still held. He took a run at it and the door splintered open. He tumbled down a few steps.

The bottom of the stairs disappeared into brown water. "Rhys, I'm here," she yelped, sounding more human now.

He plunged into the murk calling her name. It was so dim Rhys couldn't see her at first, but there she was, chained to the wall with water swirling over her breasts.

"Quick! The sluice gate," she said. "It's just in that corner."

Rhys found the lever and heaved against it. "I can't budge it. The pressure of the water's too great."

"Try the other gate." She flailed her free hand at the submerged portal on the other side of the room. "It'll drain out."

The second lever broke off when he tried to force it to move. Panic gripped his heart in an icy hand and squeezed.

He slogged through the water to her, catching her in his arms. Her skin was pebbled with cold, and her teeth chattered near his ear.

"I can't get free," she stammered.

He grabbed up a length of the chain and pulled with every ounce of strength in him. He'd hoped the metal had lost its grip on the stone over the years, but it held fast.

"Olivia—" He couldn't go on. He couldn't lose her like this.

Calm seemed to descend on her like a shroud and she stopped trembling. "Go, Rhys; there's nothing you can do. You can't stop the water."

"I won't leave you."

A tear slid down her cheek. "Only the key will free me and Dr. Pinkerton took it."

Rhys wanted to tear Pinkerton apart with his bare hands. Every moment, the water inched higher up her body. If he left her, she might be gone by the time he returned. If he didn't leave, she'd drown before his eyes.

He hugged her fiercely.

"I'll come back for you. I promise," he said. "Hold on."

He knifed his way through the water to the staircase, then ran up it without looking back. If he allowed himself even one more glimpse of her, he knew he wouldn't be able to leave.

Rhys bolted up the stairs and back to the parlor. Babette had Dr. Pinkerton trussed up like pork loin, and Amanda was sniveling in the corner.

"The key," he panted. "We need the key now and Pinkerton has it."

The doctor was still insensible, and a sizeable lump bulged on the back of his skull. Rhys knelt and rifled through the man's pockets, praying that he still had the key on him. If he'd squirreled it away somewhere, Rhys would never find it in time.

The sound of stone grating on stone made Olivia stop tugging at her wrist. On the wall above the gate, tiny fissures appeared, more water spurting through them.

A hard knot at the back of her throat threatened to choke her. Olivia forced herself to breath slowly. Water lapped at her chin.

She grasped the chain with her free hand and pulled herself up it. Panic clawed her insides.

"Don't fight, Olivia…drowning is quite painless if one doesn't resist." Dr. Pinkerton's words swirled seductively in her brain.

Eventually the water would meet the mold-darkened ceiling. When the time came, would she stop struggling and let the water take her? The doorway to eternity was a dark portal. Though she trusted her soul to God in the next world, her body wanted to go on living in this one. Rhys promised to come back. She'd do everything she could to still be here when he did. She hitched herself up the chain another half a foot.

Odd sounds, a popping and creaking noise, pricked

her ears. Hundreds of tiny pieces of stone spewed out of cracks where more water rushed in. The heavy timber that ran the length of the ceiling bowed and slipped out of its iron casing on one end. It fell drunkenly into the water with a monumental splash.

Olivia's grip on the wet chain failed, and she slipped beneath the surface. The old tower groaned like a wounded boar, the sound amplified and distorted by the rising flood.

The ancient keep had been designed to allow water to pass in and out, but after standing for centuries, it was not built to withstand being filled with water. Olivia realized with a start that she might not have time to drown. The keep threatened to tumble down on top of her. She clawed her way up the chain again but couldn't get a firm enough grip to reach the surface.

She thrashed about, fighting against the urge to inhale, tugging frantically at her heavy iron tether. Her chest screamed for air. Just as she was ready to give up, she felt a pair of arms around her.

Rhys! His lips covered her mouth, forcing a blast of air into her. Then he disappeared, kicking to the surface to catch another breath for both of them.

He was back again in a blink with another gulp of air. Then he went to work on the manacle. She felt a pinch and then the iron fell from her wrist. She flailed upward.

When she broke the surface, she gasped for air. Then she felt herself being borne along by Rhys's strong arms. The ceiling was so close she could reach up and run her fingertips over the blackened wood. Had other tortured souls died gazing at that soot-covered sky?

Rhys carried her dripping up to the top few stairs that weren't covered by water. She let her head loll onto his chest, comforted by the hammering of his heart.

"We've got to get out of here now," he shouted as they sped through the ancient keep back to the parlor. As they neared the front door, Babette and Amanda were dragging Dr. Pinkerton through the exit.

"I can walk," Olivia said, realizing they'd go quicker if Rhys wasn't forced to carry her. He merely gripped her tighter and began to run. Behind them, she heard the growl of grating stone as water pummeled the keep's foundation.

They shot into the late afternoon sunshine, putting as much distance between them and the Pinkertons' home as they could.

Rhys stopped when they reached the edge of the docks, and turned back. He lowered Olivia to stand on her own feet but kept his arms circled round her. As they watched, the tower canted forward. Then with a roar of tumbling stones, the keep crumpled slowly, like an old man falling first to his knees then forward on his face.

"I hope to God no one was in there," she whispered.

"There wasn't," Rhys said. "Thanks to a quick-thinking lady's maid who definitely needs an elevation of station."

Babette had already commandeered the man responsible for Wapping security and was ordering him to summon the magistrate for Dr. Pinkerton's arrest.

Rhys hugged Olivia tighter. "It's over, love," he whispered in her ear. "I won't let anyone harm you ever again."

"Even you? Mr. Alcock told me you intended to be my ruin."

"Even me." He brought her hands to his lips. "My motives were execrable, but instead of me ruining you, you were the making of me. The rake is dead. Only the man is left, if you'll still have him."

She joined her hands behind his neck and smiled up at him. "I wouldn't know how to say no to you."

"And I don't intend to give you a chance to start."

The dock was an upset beehive of men running and shouting and clamoring over the rubble of the tower. But everything around them faded when Rhys bent to claim her mouth with a kiss.

"But I don't want you to change completely, Rhys. I fell in love with the rake, you know," she said, hugging him tightly. "And I want to wake up with him every day for the rest of my life."

"You may live to regret that."

She grinned up at him. "Want to bet?"

Epilogue

Six months later

RHYS WANTED OLIVIA TO THINK HE WAS READING, but actually, he was merely turning pages from time to time. She was so lovely by firelight and the soft glow of his reading lamp, how could he not ignore *Ivanhoe* so he could ogle his very pregnant wife?

When they set up their own household on a quiet but respectable street, Rhys knew they weren't destined to become the most fashionable couple in London. They only attended parties thrown by people whose good opinion they truly admired. They refused to restrict their guest lists to members of the ton. He and Olivia wouldn't win any prizes for social correctness, but they were undoubtedly the happiest couple of his acquaintance.

"*Pardonnez-moi.*" Babette breezed into the comfortable parlor. Now that she was Olivia's companion instead of her maid, Babette was free to wear whatever she liked. Her link to the courtesan in her past showed in the exquisite line of her gown.

"This note, it is just arrived for you, Lord Rhys. Good evening, my lady."

He accepted the missive and broke the seal as Babette glided from the room. Rhys scanned the bottom of the note and frowned at the name of the sender. His gut churned.

"What is it?" Olivia asked.

"A note from Lieutenant Duffy's widow." He refolded it and stuffed it into his pocket.

"Oh. What does it say?"

Nothing he wanted to think about, he was certain. Duffy's fate hadn't crossed his mind in months, and he was happy that way. The last thing he needed was a reminder of Maubeuge. In the confusion of rescuing Olivia from Dr. Pinkerton, Rhys had missed the chance to find Sergeant Leatherby and secure the testimony that would have cleared him in the eyes of the world.

The following months were filled with seeing the doctor tried and convicted of murdering Mr. Weinschmidt. Olivia hadn't wanted to implicate Miss Pinkerton in her abduction and attempted murder, since Amanda didn't have the whole truth of what had happened to her mother. Instead, Miss Pinkerton retired to Kent to live with her father's elderly aunt.

Clearing his name in public didn't seem as important to Rhys now that he was privately reconciled to his family. As long as he had Olivia, he didn't want for anything else.

But he didn't need a reminder of the failure at Maubeuge for which Sergeant Leatherby couldn't exonerate him—Lieutenant Duffy's lingering death.

"I'm sure the note is of no import," he lied.

"Of course it is." Olivia rose from her cushiony wing chair and held out a hand in silent demand.

With a snort, he pulled the letter from his pocket and laid it across her palm. She unfolded the note and read it. Then a hand lifted to her heart, and she sank back into her chair.

"I must read this to you," she said, and went ahead without waiting for his assent.

> My Lord,
>
> I apologize for the tardiness of this note of thanks, but even now, words fail me in expressing my gratitude to you. You see, my husband was Lieutenant Morris Duffy. I understand you were responsible for carrying him from the field of battle and making sure he received medical care, though his wounds were too grievous to be overcome.
>
> While my dear Morris suffered, he dictated a letter to me with the help of the chaplain. Unfortunately, the chaplain died in a skirmish shortly after that as well and his effects were not examined until his unit was sent home. Due to this series of events, the letter from my husband didn't reach me until last month.
>
> You must understand that my husband was never one for expressing his feelings. But in that letter, he opened his heart and revealed depths of love for me for which I previously had only hoped.
>
> I would never have known how my husband loved me, if not for you, my lord. For that incredible gift, I am left with only words, but believe me when I tell you they are heartfelt. Thanks seem so small,

but I can offer nothing more. I shall mourn my loss until I'm dust myself, but the letter from my husband, which your quick action made possible, has healed my heart.

> *With undying gratitude,*
> *Lucille Duffy*

Her heart shining in her eyes, Olivia handed him the letter. "Oh, Rhys. Don't you see? You did the right thing."

He crossed to her chair and knelt beside it. The lump in his throat was so tight, he couldn't speak. He wrapped his arms around her waist and laid his head in her shrinking lap. He'd borne guilt for prolonging Duffy's suffering for so long, he'd grown accustomed to its prodigious weight. Now it lifted from him, leaving him feeling so light, he might float away.

He laid his cheek against Olivia's round belly, and the child inside her gave him a little kick. He laughed and pressed a kiss to her abdomen. "And here's another thing I did right."

Then he kissed his way up her body to the exposed skin at her neckline. "And another thing I did right."

She palmed his cheeks. "Careful. You'll ruin your reputation as a rake with all this right living."

"No fear of that. There's still more than enough wickedness in me to balance it out."

"That," his glowing wife said with a lascivious smile, "is something I'm counting on."

Authors' Note

In November of 1817, Princess Charlotte died after giving birth to a stillborn boy. She was the sole legitimate grandchild of King George III, the only daughter of the Prince Regent and his estranged wife. It didn't take a leap of genius for the younger unmarried sons of King George to realize that they had an opportunity to beget a future monarch. And so the "Hymen Race Terrific," as the London tabloids called it, began.

Three royal dukes were in contention—the Duke of Cambridge, the Duke of Kent, and the Duke of Clarence, who features in *Waking Up with a Rake*. Clarence sired ten illegitimate children upon an actress with whom he lived for twenty years. He was perpetually in debt and tried to woo a great heiress earlier in his life, but the match was forbidden by an Act of Parliament because the lady was a commoner.

In July 1818, the Duke of Clarence married Princess Adelaide of Saxe-Meiningen, a woman half his age. Clarence set aside his mistress, and his new wife welcomed his nine surviving children into their home. By all reports, the marriage was a happy one, and since his frugal German wife took his finances in hand, Clarence's debts began to shrink.

In June 1830, at the age of sixty-four, the Duke of Clarence ascended to the British throne to become King William IV. But he and his queen were never blessed with children of their own, so though he eventually wore the crown, the Duke of Clarence did not win the "Hymen Race Terrific."

That is a tale for another duke.

Acknowledgments

No book comes into being through the efforts of only one person. We have many people to thank. First our editor, Leah Hultenschmidt and our agent, Natasha Kern. Without both of these talented women, our collaboration would never have happened. Then there are all the people at Sourcebooks who prep the manuscript and shape it into its final form—Aubrey Poole, Rachel Edwards, Pamela Guerrieri, and Aimee Algas Alker. We owe a huge debt of thanks to Dawn Adams, who is responsible for the beautiful cover art. You all have our heartfelt thanks!

Outside the bounds of Sourcebooks, we'd be remiss if we didn't thank Ashlyn Chase, our critique partner. Her patient ear and unbounded encouragement are so appreciated. And hugs to Marcy Weinbeck, our beta-reader. Her sharp eye and exquisite taste keep us from running off the rails!

And last, but not least, you, dear reader. Thank you for taking our stories into your hearts.

About the Authors

Connie Mason, who started her romance-writing career after she became a grandmother, once told *48 Hours* that she does her best work in bed. That work being writing, of course! For her newest releases, Connie has teamed up with Mia Marlowe, a rising star of steamy historical romance. Mia learned about story-telling while singing professional opera. A classically trained soprano, she knows what it's like to wear a corset and has had to sing high C's in one, so she empathizes with the trials of her historical heroines.

Connie lives near Tampa, Florida, and Mia lives in Boston, Massachusetts. Credit for putting these two authors together goes to their editor, Leah Hultenschmidt, and their agent, Natasha Kern, who saw the creative potential in this pairing. Both Connie and Mia write sexy, adventurous stories with alpha heroes to love. They hope you'll enjoy the melding of their styles as much as they enjoyed collaborating to bring their new stories to life.

We love to hear from you. You can find Connie at www.conniemason.com and can catch Mia at

www.miamarlowe.com,   www.twitter.com/Mia_ Marlowe, and www.facebook.com/MiaMarloweFanPage.
  Happy reading!
  Connie & Mia